CAROLINA CARPENTER *Brides*

Four Couples Find Tools for Building Romance
in a Home Improvement Store

JANET BENREY · RON BENREY
LENA NELSON DOOLEY · YVONNE LEHMAN

BARBOUR
PUBLISHING

© 2007 *How to Refurbish an Old Romance* by Janet Benrey
© 2007 *Once upon a Shopping Cart* by Ron Benrey
© 2007 *Can You Help Me?* by Lena Nelson Dooley
© 2007 *Caught Red-Handed* by Yvonne Lehman

ISBN 978-1-59789-581-1

Scripture taken from the HOLY BIBLE, NEW INTERNATIONAL VERSION®. NIV®. Copyright © 1973, 1978, 1984 by International Bible Society. Used by permission of Zondervan. All rights reserved.

Scripture quotations marked NLT are taken from the *Holy Bible*, New Living Translation, copyright © 1996. Used by permission of Tyndale House Publishers, Inc., Wheaton, Illinois 60189, U.S.A. All rights reserved.

This book is a work of fiction. Names, characters, places, and incidents are either products of the author's imagination or used fictitiously. Any similarity to actual people, organizations, and/or events is purely coincidental.

Published by Barbour Publishing, Inc., P.O. Box 719, Uhrichsville, OH 44683, www.barbourbooks.com

Our mission is to publish and distribute inspirational products offering exceptional value and biblical encouragement to the masses.

ecpa Member of the
Evangelical Christian
Publishers Association

Printed in the United States of America.

INTRODUCTION

How to Refurbish an Old Romance by Janet Benrey
Brianna Griffith needed to deal with ugly wallpaper in her new
office, so she signed up for "How to Repair Bad Decisions Made
Years Ago," a course at her local Home & Hearth Superstore in
Oak Ridge, North Carolina. Brianna never expected to run into
Zach Wilson, an old flame from her college days. And neither she
nor Zach expected Andrea Lewis—the store's how-to expert—to
help them repair the "bad decision" they made twelve years earlier
when they broke up.

Once Upon a Shopping Cart by Ron Benrey
Kaitlyn Ferrer, an investigative reporter for the *Blue Ridge Sun*, is
furious when her editor orders her to write an undercover story
on the dating scene at the Home & Hearth Superstore. Her half-
hearted efforts accelerate when she meets dashing Chris Taylor
pushing a shopping cart through the aisles. Alas, Kaitlyn doesn't
realize that Chris is also working undercover. It will take more
than good words for these two clandestine overachievers to build
an honest relationship.

Can You Help Me? by Lena Nelson Dooley
When Valerie Bradford asks a Home & Hearth employee for assis-
tance, she doesn't guess that she will get more than she bargained
for. Austin Hodges can't believe what the feisty blond woman plans
to accomplish all by herself. Because of his profession, he knows
how much help she needs, but for right now, his advice will have
to do. Can God lead them through the misunderstandings they
encounter toward a bright future together?

Caught Red-Handed by Yvonne Lehman
Marc Goodson is the chief security officer at the Home & Hearth
Superstore when Laurel Jones begins working in the store's Garden
Shop. His random surveillance of employees and customers is a plea-
surable part of his job until Laurel's activities become suspect. He
can have her arrested or try to save her from a life of crime. Laurel
resents Marc's attentions, believing them a ploy to learn whether
she's honest. Personal feelings and moral responsibility become
entangled when someone is about to be "caught red-handed."

HOW TO REFURBISH AN OLD ROMANCE

by Janet Benrey

Dedication

To Ron.

When I was a child, I talked like a child,
I thought like a child, I reasoned like a child.
When I became a man, I put childish ways behind me.
1 CORINTHIANS 13:11

Chapter 1

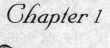

Brianna Griffith heard a swooshing sound and looked up in time to see a newspaper catapulting through the air toward her. She watched it land on her desk with a thud and slither to a stop inches from the edge. "What in the world?"

She heard a giggle and looked up. Sophie Edwards stood in the doorway, a lopsided grin adorning her face. "Sometimes I forget my own strength." She marched into the room and planted herself in front of Brianna's desk. "But now that I have your attention, you absolutely, positively need to take the class advertised on page 2 of today's newspaper."

"You know I have no time for a class." Brianna picked up the newspaper and attempted to hand it back to her assistant.

Sophie recoiled and clasped her fingers. "I'm serious. Please take a look at the advertisement. This is for your own good."

Brianna emitted a long and purposeful sigh of annoyance. Doing things for one's own good usually spelled disaster—at least it did for her. "All the same, I think I'll pass."

Sophie pasted a smile on her face. "Not in your best interest to pass."

Brianna knew it was a waste of time to argue with Sophie. Perhaps if she pretended to go along, Sophie would leave her alone, or at the very least get back to her job. "Very well," Brianna said. "What class do you think I need to take?"

"The one at the Home & Hearth Superstore in Oak Ridge that begins tonight."

Tonight? Not a chance. "This evening I'd planned to make at least twenty cold calls."

Sophie's smile morphed into a pout. "You can just as easily make them tomorrow."

Brianna glanced at her watch. It was almost six. The last thing she needed was to burden herself with a new activity, especially one that wouldn't contribute one penny to her company's bottom line. "But I have a week's worth of laundry waiting for me," Brianna said, knowing that Sophie wouldn't be easily dissuaded.

"Nonsense. You have tons of clothes. I'm the one who has laundry to do. I only have three maternity dresses that fit, and one of them is getting awfully tight." Sophie patted her belly. "Lately I seem to be spilling stuff onto my tummy. So don't give me that old excuse. Next thing you'll be telling me is that you have to wash your hair."

"You took the words right out of my mouth."

"I hate to nag, but. . ."

"Okay, so what is it exactly that I'm agreeing to do?"

Sophie's grin reconstituted itself. She grabbed Brianna's visitor chair and gently lowered herself into it. "You know and I know that you need to redecorate this entire office. You've said so yourself a thousand times." She *tsk*ed. "I mean, take a look at the place."

Brianna glanced at the battalion of teddy bears marching

across her wall and tried not to shudder. The cute, cuddly creatures had been fine for Dr. Anderson, the pediatrician who'd previously owned the condo office. His young patients undoubtedly hadn't complained, but the bears were difficult to explain to the eagle-eyed customers who showed up to talk about travel arrangements. "True enough."

"The folks at Home & Hearth will teach you how to make over this office by yourself. Just think of all the money you'll save."

Sophie had said the one thing that might get Brianna to change her mind. "Saving money is important. My cash flow isn't healthy. And I certainly can't afford to hire a handyman."

Sophie waved a hand in the air. "Which is why you need to take 'How to Repair Bad Decisions Made Years Ago.'" She shifted in her seat. "Isn't that a great name for a class? I wish life were like that. Imagine if you could undo your past mistakes with a fresh coat of paint."

"That's a lovely fantasy you're having while sitting in my chair."

Brianna recalled the decision she'd made seven months ago to move to Asheville and set up Affinity Travel of Asheville in an office condo she'd purchased on Hillside Avenue. She wouldn't call her move a mistake, exactly, but it had certainly stretched her financially. She'd expected it would, but then there'd been a teensy downturn in travel that had caught her by surprise.

"And besides," Sophie rushed on, "I'm told that men go there to meet women."

Brianna laughed. She hadn't expected that bit of news from Sophie. "Tell me you're joking."

"Well, as a happily married woman, I'm kinda disconnected from the singles' grapevine, but my younger sister, Joan, stays up to date on these things. She's my information source. She tells me, 'Bars are out and stores are in. If you want to meet a hunk, go shopping for hardware.'"

"Home & Hearth has got to be the least romantic setting in the whole wide world."

Sophie shrugged. "I'm only telling you what Joan told me."

"I'll file the information in the 'useless facts' corner of my brain. I can assure you I'm not interested in meeting a *hunk* or any other kind of man tonight. I just want to get rid of these ridiculous teddy bears."

"So you'll go?"

"It seems you won't let me *not* go."

Sophie heaved herself out of the chair. "Good. And while we're on the topic of hunks, it wouldn't do you any harm to go on a date once in a while." She circled Brianna's desk. "You're a very attractive woman—slim, strong, athletic. You've got great eyes and fabulous skin. When you dress up, you're a knockout."

"Thanks, but I don't think dating is for me. As the owner of a new business, I'm just too busy to think about men."

Sophie held up her hands in a gesture of surrender. "I won't say another word on the subject. I guess because I have a great marriage, I want every woman I know to be as happily married as I am."

Brianna had heard that comment from Sophie before. It still made her wince. Brianna had been in love once, but she'd encouraged the man of her dreams to slip through her fingers. *Another decision I'll have to live with.*

"Marriage is right for you, Sophie, but I believe God has

other plans for me. Even if He hasn't sent me someone to marry, I can't complain, because so many other things in my life are going well." She regretted the prideful tenor in her voice the moment she spoke the words.

Sophie picked up on her tone. Her expression turned somber. "Maybe it's God's doing you're still single, but maybe it's your own. You're a strong-willed woman, Brianna. Do you really take the time to listen to God's voice speaking to you?"

"Go home, Mrs. Edwards!"

Sophie headed for the door. "You can toss me out, but you can't stop me from telling you to have fun tonight. And to keep your mind open for the unexpected."

Brianna watched her leave. Sophie was twenty-four and had recently graduated from UNCA, the University of North Carolina in Asheville. During her sophomore year, she met the man she eventually married. She was pretty and outgoing, with bright blue eyes that always seemed to twinkle. People seemed drawn to her. Sophie's vivacious personality was good for business. Anyone could see that.

Brianna knew her own personality was vastly different. She was an introvert who didn't enjoy meeting new people. She invariably felt uncomfortable in a room full of strangers. It was also why she hated the singles' scene so much and generally kept her distance.

But she had the skills to manage a successful travel agency— her previous successes in Atlanta proved the point. Her staff liked and trusted her; she frequently received accolades as an effective supervisor. She also had the confidence to make deci- sions quickly, without shilly-shallying.

She switched off her computer and shrugged into her

jacket. *Face it, no one's life ever changed learning how to remove old wallpaper.*

She found the traffic on Route 25 North lighter than she had expected. The trip to Oak Ridge, which usually took at least fifteen minutes, took less than ten. Brianna found a parking spot near the front of Home & Hearth's huge lot. *Good. I have a few minutes before the class begins to browse the wallpaper department.*

She walked through the self-opening doors and scanned the overhead signs. For months she'd dreamed about eliminating the teddy bears, but she hadn't given any thought to an appropriate replacement. "What wallpaper says 'Affinity Travel Agency'?" she murmured when she found the dozen or so oversized scrapbooks that held different wallpaper samples. She would have to select a pattern and color scheme—without the expert help of an interior decorator—and her decision had to be right the first time. *Choose wrong and you'll start having fond memories of teddy bears.*

She opened a sample book titled "Office Adventures" and cringed at the first pattern, a beige-colored plaid that would make her office look like the inside of a designer raincoat.

"Are you shopping for wallpaper?" The masculine voice came from behind Brianna.

She caught her breath and spun around. "Did you say something?"

"I asked if you were shopping for wallpaper."

Brianna found herself looking up into the eyes of a man who'd seemingly sprung out of nowhere. "Uh. . .I'm only browsing for wallpaper tonight," she replied. "I'll buy eventually, I guess."

"Same here. I came to the store to. . .browse." He smiled,

exposing a row of nicotine-stained teeth.

Brianna searched his shirt front for a badge that would reveal his name but found none. *Why did he start a conversation with me?*

"My name is Peter. I'm a high school teacher."

"Are you teaching the class 'How to Repair Bad Decisions Made Years Ago'?"

"You have a great sense of humor—and a touch of extrasensory perception. I teach history."

Brianna felt her brow knit. "Really? I'm here to learn how to replace old wallpaper."

"Ah." The man's smile vanished like a wisp of smoke. "I think I just made a silly mistake." He took a step back as his face turned an odd shade of red. "I'm sorry to bother you. Enjoy your class."

Brianna watched him hurry to the end of the aisle and disappear around the shelving. Then it dawned on her what had happened. *I've just been hit on.* "Well, I'll be," she said softly. "Sophie was right about this place after all."

Brianna looked around, wondering if other shoppers were fending off unwanted advances from men with nicotine-stained teeth. Everything looked normal to her. The store seemed busy, but it might be that way every night there was a class. She glanced at her watch. Only ten minutes remained until her class began. She could see the chairs set up at the far end of the wallpaper department, away from the flow of traffic. In a few minutes she'd stroll over and find a seat in the front row, where she always preferred to sit. And if she could, she'd pretend she'd never heard Sophie's admonition to "keep your mind open for the unexpected."

Zachary Wilson imagined a lot of things, but he never imagined he would take a class on redecorating at the Home & Hearth Superstore in Oak Ridge, North Carolina. Not in a million years.

The name of the class had attracted his attention the moment he'd seen the advertisement. The wallpaper in his new home was a disaster that had to go, and taking this class seemed like the perfect solution to his problem. He'd quickly signed up, but as he climbed out of his truck, he found himself having serious second thoughts.

"I'm too busy to be doing this," he muttered as he locked his door. "I have a travel business to run, and this will eat up hours and hours of my time. Besides, Sami will wonder where I am."

His footsteps faltered as he thought about returning to his truck, but a small inner voice urged him forward. *Take the class, Zachary. It's for your own good.*

He nodded, although there was no one to nod to. "Okay," he quietly reasoned, "I'll take the class. No turning back." His pace quickened as he entered the store.

He made note of the coffee machine near the door, then asked a salesperson where the class was to be held. "Wallpaper aisle," the man replied. "You can't miss it. I'll walk you there if you like."

He didn't. "I'll find it myself. Thanks."

The huge store was brightly lit, and Zachary felt tempted to browse. The class didn't start for several minutes, and he saw no reason to get there ahead of time.

He headed for the kitchen section. The home he'd bought, while not new, offered a great view of the mountains. But certain features needed to be changed, and he knew when he purchased it that he would be the one to do the changing. The kitchen in his house was dated. The countertops were laminate, and he wanted to replace them with granite or stone, although almost anything else would be an improvement. His dishwasher was noisy, and while it did a good job, it lacked a lot of features. He wished his sister were with him; a woman's touch was what he really needed tonight. Next time she and her husband visited, he'd ask her advice. He opened a few cabinets and looked at different woods and wood stains. So many choices.

Out of the corner of his eye, he spied a woman wearing an apron with the store's logo on it approaching him. "May I help you?"

"I'm admiring the cabinets."

She nodded. "There's a lot to choose from, isn't there?"

"It's a little overwhelming, I agree."

"Are you looking for yourself?"

For a second he wondered at the question, then he realized that she was really asking, *Is there a woman in your life who will have to live with your choice?*

"I recently bought a house. The kitchen's okay, but it's. . ."

"Outdated," she said as she reached for a brochure. "This may help you decide. The brochure highlights all of our cabinet styles."

"Thanks." He jammed the brochure into his leather briefcase. "I'll look through it later." He glanced at his watch. "I have a class in a few minutes."

15

The woman smiled. "That will be Andrea's. She's a wonderful teacher. You'll be in good hands with her."

Zachary thanked the woman and made a beeline for the wallpaper aisle. When he arrived, he saw that most of the seats were already taken. He settled into a chair at the back and quickly removed a notebook from his briefcase. He was, he suddenly realized, mostly surrounded by women. Young women. A few turned his way and gave him what he considered to be a good going over. He struggled to suppress a grin. *Well, well. This class offers more than a few possibilities. What a blast!*

Chapter 2

Brianna left the wallpaper samples unexamined and walked slowly along the aisle toward the chairs, her gaze taking in the variety of paints, sponges, and glazes that made up that particular section of the store. She realized she had a lot to learn about paint.

Brianna's instructor turned out to be a middle-aged woman who looked to be a motherly type. Brianna felt a surge of hope. If this motherly type could hang wallpaper well enough to teach her how to do it, then certainly Brianna was capable of learning the right techniques.

Brianna heard chairs shuffling and watched as her classmates took their places.

An expectant hush fell over the crowd when the instructor began to speak. "My name is Andrea Lewis," the woman said as she ran her gaze over her students. "And for the next two weeks, on Tuesday and Thursday evenings, I'll be teaching the course 'How to Repair Bad Decisions Made Years Ago.' In it you'll be learning about paints and how to choose them. You'll be taught about texturing and what *gloss* and *semigloss* mean.

I'll show you how to remove wallpaper and how to prepare the wall to accept new wallpaper. You won't be sitting in these seats for the entire course. We'll soon be hands-on so that you'll get a feel for the materials you'll be working with. We'll also discuss which tools to use. Choosing your tools is almost as important as choosing the right paint for the job or the correct wallpaper for your room."

Brianna liked what she was hearing. "Hands-on" was definitely the kind of teaching she needed. Theory was fine, but even she knew nothing could compare to actually doing the task. She'd painted things before, but she'd never ever removed wallpaper from a wall. Especially not in an office where her customers could view the results.

She glanced at her fellow students. About a dozen or so people, as far as she could see, had signed up for the course. Most were women like her.

"And what's your bad decision?" Andrea asked, suddenly turning her gaze on Brianna. "And before you answer, could you please tell us your name?"

"My name is Brianna Griffith. And my problem is wallpaper," she replied. "I own Affinity Travel of Asheville on Hillside. The former owner of the office was a pediatrician who was partial to teddy bears."

Andrea's eyes twinkled. "I get it. He made a good decision from his point of view but a bad decision from yours."

Brianna laughed. "Totally bad."

"Thank you, Brianna." Andrea raised her hand to silence the tittering. "We'll cover wallpaper removal and installation during our next class. The topic this evening will be paint."

A heavyset man across the impromptu classroom said,

"Painting is good. Why don't you cover up the teddy bears with semigloss latex enamel?"

Andrea took control with a quick smile. "This course is about *undoing* things done wrong. Our goal is not to simply cover over past mistakes but to set them right. The very last thing we will encourage Brianna to do is apply enamel atop her problem teddy bears. But please, tell us who you are and what past mistake you're attempting to remedy."

"My name's Michael Covington. I'd like to turn my family room into a home theater. The paint is important, I'm told. It has to be dark, but I don't want the room looking like a fantasy fun house, if you catch my drift. I want the room to be classy."

Andrea smiled. "I believe I do." She shifted her gaze. "You," she said, pointing to a young woman seated near Brianna. "What is your name and your problem?"

"I'm Jenny Dougherty. I'm here because I want to turn an ordinary bedroom into a nursery." She laughed. "Too bad I can't take Brianna's teddy bears home with me, but the bedroom I want for my baby is a disaster. The former owner of the house added texture to the paint. That's not something I can easily cover up with a second coat." She patted her belly. "And I don't see myself sanding, either."

Andrea shook her head. "I'll have a remedy for that." Her gaze landed firmly on another woman. "And what's the problem you came here to fix?"

"I'd like to paint the trim in my living room, then apply wallpaper. Right now the trim has about four layers of paint on it. Like Jenny, I don't want to just add another layer. Oh, and my name is Marsha Gooding, and I'm allergic to dust."

Andrea went around the room, calling on everyone. Brianna

began to doodle in the notebook she'd brought with her, her way of tuning out the litany of past mistakes others had made. Just dealing with hers was going to take all of her surplus energy.

"My name is Zachary Wilson," a voice boomed behind her. "My problem is wallpaper. I'd like to remove flocked wallpaper from the hallway of the home I recently bought."

Brianna's pencil stopped writing. Zachary Wilson, or Zach Wilson, was the name of the man she had almost married years earlier.

She swiveled in her chair and searched for the familiar face. She found it two rows back.

He hadn't aged much from what she could see. He still had the same dark hair she used to run her fingers through. And the clear blue eyes she loved to stare into were as clear as she remembered them.

Her tongue felt suddenly cottony. All she could do was mouth his name as her emotions threatened to overwhelm her. Zach. . . She was the one who had ended their relationship. Although it had felt like the right thing to do at the time, as the years ticked by she wondered if her decision had been a good one. But she'd been young and inexperienced when she'd tossed Zachary aside.

Regrets? She shrugged. Maybe. But she was never a second-guesser. Seeing him now, and so close, forced her to recall why they'd parted. Careers, hers and his, plus her inability to commit had all worked against them.

Her tongue began to move. "Zachary?" she whispered.

"Ah," she heard Andrea say. "I see two of our students know one another. How lovely. Why don't we take a quick break and return in ten minutes."

Chairs scraped and people moved, but Brianna knew her legs wouldn't hold her, so she sat still, glued to her seat.

She watched as Zachary Wilson made his way toward her, his hand outstretched.

"How are you, Brianna? It's been a long time, hasn't it?"

Twelve long years. And what, Zachary Wilson, have you been doing with yourself all that time? She squeaked a hello as two new questions formed in her mind: *What are you doing in Oak Ridge, North Carolina? And why are you bothering to talk to me after what I did to you?*

It had taken Zach all of two seconds to connect the dots. Brianna Griffith. Here in Oak Ridge. He thought about leaving the store, but he'd have to squeeze past several other class members, and the shuffling would draw attention to him. She'd surely see him then. But another thought pushed itself forward. Why should he leave? She was the one who had broken their engagement. *Impetuously so,* he thought.

Andrea was moving quickly through the class, cutting people off if they went on too long about their past decorating mistakes. Suddenly it was his turn to speak.

"My name is Zachary Wilson," he said as he struggled to keep his voice from breaking. "My problem is wallpaper. I'd like to remove the flocked wallpaper from the hallway of the home I recently bought."

He'd tried to keep his eyes on Andrea, but out of the corner of his eye, he saw Brianna swivel in her chair, her eyes finding him. She whispered his name, and he felt himself nod. He'd been discovered.

Andrea didn't miss the recognition that must have registered on his face. "Ah," she said. "I see two of our students know one another. How lovely. Why don't we take a quick break and return in ten minutes."

Zachary got to his feet. It wasn't in his nature to be rude, and besides, he was curious to find out what Brianna was doing in Oak Ridge. He wondered if she'd changed. He hurried toward her, his hand outstretched. "How are you, Brianna? It's been a long time, hasn't it?"

Zach felt her fingers lightly grasping his own as she gazed into his eyes. He noticed that her voice cracked when she said hello, and he wondered if she felt uncomfortable seeing him. He guessed she did. She had every reason to be nervous. He would have been, too, in her shoes.

Then she did something that caused his breath to catch in his throat. In one fluid motion, she rose from the chair and gave him a hug. He hadn't expected that, but then, she'd always done things he hadn't expected.

Granted, it was a quick hug, lasting only a few seconds. But in that brief flash of time, he smelled her perfume—Angel, just as before—and felt the silkiness of her hair as it bushed against his face. Their twelve years of separation melted away instantly.

Brianna suddenly pulled away from him. "You look good, Zach," she said as she studied him at a distance.

So do you. Way too good. He noticed that the years had made her even more beautiful. Her skin was soft and her face was still unlined, except for tiny crow's feet around her eyes. He remembered the small birthmark on her left cheek and noticed that it was still there. But what could he say to her now? That he had missed her? That he had never found a woman he wanted to be with more than her, although he had certainly given it a try in college? And in a way, he was still trying. Although he had to admit, the game was getting a little wearisome. "I'm doing well," he finally said.

She nodded and smiled at him. "I'm glad, Zach."

Glad what? That I look good, or that we're standing together talking like nothing ever happened? He shrugged, suddenly feeling self-conscious. He was thirty-five years old for crying out loud. Way too old for the cat to get his tongue. *Get a grip, Zach. Focus.*

He glanced around and found Andrea's stare. She smiled at him, and he thought she nodded her approval.

Suddenly, Zach knew exactly what he would do with the time. "Would you care to join me for coffee, Brianna? I take it you're still a coffee drinker." He tipped his head toward the store's entrance. "I noticed a coffee machine when I came in."

Brianna was startled by the invitation. She felt tempted to decline, but something about seeing him after all these years made her accept his offer. Besides, what harm could a cup of coffee do? "C–coffee would be nice," she stammered.

She felt his hand on her arm as he steered her toward the coffee machine. "You took it plain, if I remember."

"I still do."

"I don't think you can ever forget those little details about someone you were close to, do you?"

For the second time that evening, Brianna felt as if her knees would buckle. "Zach," she said, turning to face him, "why would you even speak to me again after what I did to you?"

"I don't bear you any ill will, Brianna. For all I know, you were right to break off our relationship."

"Well, you have every reason to dislike me."

That was true. But he didn't dislike her. Never had, truth be told.

They reached the coffee machine, and she watched as he fumbled through the briefcase he carried. "My treat," he said, retrieving his wallet. "I invited you."

She considered arguing with him but decided to let it drop. "Thank you, Zach."

She watched him feed money into the machine and hand her a coffee before buying a cup for himself.

"So tell me," he said when he was done, "what have you been doing with yourself all this time? What brought you to Oak Ridge?"

"That's two questions."

"We only have ten minutes."

"I own Affinity Travel of Asheville. Perhaps you heard me say that when I introduced myself to the class. One summer, I took a part-time job at a leading travel agency in Atlanta. I discovered I liked the business and decided to stay with it." She extended an arm. "And. . .here I am."

"Did you ever get your master's degree in journalism like you wanted to?"

Brianna felt herself flinch. Her wanting to go to journalism school had been one of the reasons for their breakup. She had never bought into the idea that they could both continue their education and be married at the same time. "I never did go, Zach. What about you? I seem to remember you wanted an MBA."

She watched him take a quick sip of his coffee and wondered what he would make of her answer. She hoped the years had softened the blow. It certainly seemed that way to her.

"Like you, I became a travel agent after graduating," he replied. "I'm currently working with corporations to set up in-house travel desks."

She laughed. "And I discovered affinity groups."

"And you're in Oak Ridge because. . ."

"It's a growing community with a nice climate. What about yourself?"

"Same as you, I guess. I moved in last year because Asheville is a fast-growing city that's attracting start-up tech companies."

Brianna felt amazed at the way they'd lived parallel lives. "Like you, I'm relatively new to Asheville."

"That would explain why we haven't bumped into each other before now. This isn't that big of a town."

"So what's your bad decision?" she asked, anxious to get off the topic of their breakup.

"It's wallpaper. I got a great deal on a house with a spectacular view of a mountain, but the previous owner put up a lot of weird wallpaper that I have to remove. I'm not sure what I'll replace it with. Paint, most likely. I don't think you can go wrong with cream-colored paint, do you?"

"You own a house?"

He nodded. "I live there with Sami."

Brianna felt her back stiffen, although she wasn't sure why. He owed her no explanation. "Sami?"

"My dog."

"Ah, a dog. What kind of a dog?"

"Sami's a Labrador mix. Very friendly. Very sweet."

Brianna finished her coffee and tossed her cup into the nearest bin. "I think our ten minutes is up," she said. "We'd better get back to the class."

"I'll walk with you."

Zach returned Brianna to her seat, his mind easily recalling the details of their past. When they'd met, they'd both been students at the University of North Carolina in Charlotte. They both had ambitious plans. But he never thought she would just walk away. It had been Brianna's decision to earn a master's degree in journalism that had put a strain on their relationship, which resulted in her leaving.

As he walked, he found himself sneaking a glance at her fingers. To his relief, he didn't see a wedding band. Perhaps he should have thought of that before he invited her for coffee. Another thought came: *Why do I still care?*

When they reached her seat, she sat down and crossed her legs, and a new thought raced through his mind. *Don't let her get away again, Zach.* Without thinking, he leaned down so his face was close to hers. "I'd like to see you again, Brianna. May I call you sometime?"

For a moment she said nothing. He sensed the seconds ticking by. *Say yes.*

She suddenly reached into her purse and handed him her business card. "I'm sorry, I wasn't thinking. I figured you'd know where to find me when I said where I worked." She jabbed the card at him. "Please, take it."

He slipped her business card into his pocket. "Enjoy the rest of the class, Brianna."

He returned to his seat and worked at paying attention to Andrea as she discussed how to prepare a wall for paint.

"You'll need to work on a clean surface," she said. "This may require that you wipe down your walls to remove any grease. Don't paint over wallpaper. We'll discuss removing wallpaper in our next class. If the surface has never been painted, then plan on using three coats of paint—one primer plus two coats of finish."

In front of him, he watched as Brianna took copious notes. Removing Brianna from his thoughts wasn't going to be as easy as painting a wall. He wondered if he should simply leave the store and spare his heart from further pain. What would chasing after Brianna do to it after all these years?

Zach tried not to think about Brianna and began to scribble furiously as Andrea explained how to apply paint with a roller. But his thoughts kept returning to her in spite of his best efforts. Would he call her after this class was over? Should he call her? And if he did, what then? He had girlfriends, a job he loved—a good life. Inviting Brianna back into that life could reopen old wounds. But here she was—seated two rows in front of him— apparently unconcerned enough about his being there to be able to concentrate on what Andrea was saying.

He felt himself smile. If he didn't pay attention to Andrea, he was going to have to hire someone to redecorate his house, which would defeat his reason for taking the class.

He forced himself to concentrate. Andrea talked about how to paint the trim and ceiling molding. "This is basic stuff," she said, waving a small paintbrush in the air. "Using the appropriate-sized brush, make sure you paint in one direction—right to left or left to right. Don't apply too much paint, or it will dry unevenly. It's much easier to add a second coat of trim if you need to when the paint has dried properly. Which brings up my next point—never paint in a closed room. Always make sure you have plenty of ventilation. Paint fumes can give you a terrific headache, so if you feel one coming on, stop and get some air. Don't wait until you feel sick." She looked up. "Any questions?"

Zachary leaned back in his seat as people began to ask questions. Brianna fidgeted in her chair and rotated her shoulders. Zach glanced at his watch. They'd been at the store for nearly two hours. The class would end in fifteen minutes. His mind began to wander again. Should he walk Brianna to her car? Would she expect him to? No, probably not, he decided.

"As for cleanup," Andrea went on, "latex paint can be washed off with warm, soapy water. Oil-based paint requires turpentine. Soak your brushes in turpentine—in a glass container is best—until the bristles are soft and flexible."

Zach began to think about all the work he needed to do to his home and how the work would cut into his social life. Being a bachelor had its perks. Rarely did a weekend go by that he wasn't invited somewhere by friends. Then there was Sami. He liked taking long walks in the mountains with Sami at his side.

Andrea's voice broke through his thoughts. "Next time you come," she was saying, "we'll be breaking into groups and tackling a new problem head-on. So dress accordingly. If you come to the store directly from work, think about bringing a change of clothes. So," she said, holding up an index card, "take one of these home with you for your files. If you have questions, our paint department staff can help you. Good night."

He got up slowly, nodded to Andrea, and hurried to the door. He would see Brianna on Thursday, and maybe he'd invite her for coffee after class. Maybe.

Chapter 3

Brianna fidgeted in her chair until Andrea dismissed the class. At the first opportunity, Brianna turned to see if Zach was still in his seat. From the second she heard his voice, her mind had raced at the opportunities facing her. Old feelings fought their way to the surface, as did a few of her old fears. How should she respond to him after all this time? She had nothing against him. In fact, over the years, she'd felt guilty about treating him so badly. But Zachary had shown her great kindness tonight. That should tell her something about his feelings toward her. Shouldn't it?

She felt an unexpected stab of disappointment when she saw Zach's chair sitting empty. He'd left the class without saying another word to her. But what else was there for him to say? Still. . .

Brianna slowly gathered her things and walked out of the store behind her chattering classmates. She nodded good night to them and began the lonely trek to her car.

She thought about calling Sophie to tell her that the unexpected had actually happened—Zachary Wilson, a man

Sophie had only heard Brianna talk briefly about, was back in her life. . .sort of. She quickly nixed the idea. Sophie needed her rest, and besides, she really didn't know the full story. Tomorrow would be soon enough to tell her what had happened.

But she still felt the need to tell someone what had occurred. She dialed her sister's number on her cell phone and listened impatiently as it rang somewhere in Texas. Finally, her sister said, "Hello."

"Brandi, you'll never guess who I ran into tonight."

"Where are you?"

"At the Home & Hearth in Oak Ridge. I'm taking a class on redecorating."

"That's interesting. I never considered you a do-it-your-selfer. More of a 'let's hire someone else to do the job' kind of person."

"Well, money's a little tight right now. But that's not why I called. I saw Zach tonight. He's here in Oak Ridge. I mean, what were the chances. . ."

"Zach? The name doesn't ring a bell." A sniff. "Oh—yes, it does. Zachary Wilson. *Your* Zachary Wilson." A laugh. "No kidding, sis. Wow! I mean"—she paused—"well, I suppose it's always possible to run into an old flame at some time or another, but he was in your life a long, long time ago."

"Yes, well, he's now in my redecorating class. We had coffee together during the break."

"So is he married? Silly question—he has to be. Probably has a ton of kids, too."

"I don't know. I didn't ask."

"Oh, now that should have been your second question, as in 'Hello, Zachary. How are you? By the way, are you *married*?' "

Brianna sighed. Her sister was right. Why hadn't she asked? Had she been afraid of the answer? "To be honest, the subject never came up."

"I'm not buying. You met your old flame tonight."

"He's not that old."

"We'll argue that point later. You have coffee with him and it bothers you enough that you call to tell me about it, yet you didn't ask if he was married?"

"Well, I know he lives with his dog."

Brandi laughed. "A dog—you hate dogs."

"Do not. I hate cats."

"I'll forgive you. My cats will forgive you. What else did you learn about him?"

"Zach works in the travel business. We seem to share careers."

"That's handy."

"He's bought a house he's redecorating. That's why he's taking the class. He asked if he could call me again."

"And you said. . ."

"That it was fine by me."

"I'd probably do the same in your shoes. So *if* he calls you later—and I do mean *if*—what will you do?"

Brianna reached her car and, with her free hand, fumbled in her purse for her key fob. "I don't know, sis. I think I'd at least talk to him. Couldn't hurt to do that."

"Be careful, Brianna."

"I will. Good night."

Brianna climbed into her car and started the engine. "Lord," she said as she released the brake, "I don't know what plans you have for me, but I have to admit, I'm curious about why you sent

Zachary back into my life. And to be honest, I rather like the idea. At least I think I do."

But a little voice inside her signaled a warning. *Of course, this isn't exactly a good time for you right now, not with all you have to do to get your business on its feet.*

Once outside the store, Zachary felt the cool air on his face as he sucked in a deep, calming breath. Meeting Brianna again had knocked the wind out of him. Perhaps he should have ignored her, slipped from the class, and bolted, but he stayed. He even promised he'd call her. How odd was that?

He climbed into his truck and began the journey to his mountain home. He tried to concentrate on driving, but Brianna's face permeated his thoughts.

It was almost ten when he pulled into his gravel driveway. He could hear Sami barking in her run. He unlocked the gate, and Sami bounded out and nuzzled him. "There," he said, fondling Sami's ears. "Let's go for a walk, shall we?"

Sami took off down the driveway toward Route 251, which joined Zach's property to the outside world. One day he'd pave it, but not until he finished working on the inside of the house. Home ownership, he decided, was expensive and depleting him of his savings. The rate of burn was starting to scare him. He realized that if he wasn't careful, he'd have to cut back on dating. He laughed out loud at the idea. "Nothing really wrong with that as far as I can see," he said to Sami, who knew better than to run out onto the road. The dog disappeared into the brush for a while, and Zach waited patiently for her to return.

Back at the house, Zachary fed Sami her dinner and then

made a sandwich for himself, which he ate while sitting at his kitchen table staring at his reflection in the uncurtained window. Zach loved his house, but even he had to admit there were times when he felt lonely in it. If it wasn't for Sami, he knew he might not have chosen such an isolated spot. His thoughts flew again to Brianna, and he suddenly knew that, more than anything, he wanted to restart what she had destroyed all those years ago. Fool that he was.

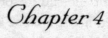

Chapter 4

Brianna sat in her car outside her townhouse and stared up at the darkened windows. Her two-story home looked almost abandoned, mute testimony to the hours she'd been spending at Affinity Travel of Asheville. *How depressing,* she thought as she turned off her car's ignition, which plunged her into even deeper darkness. *Even my carriage light has burned out.*

Disgusted at herself for forgetting to purchase lightbulbs at Asheville's largest home improvement store, she climbed out of her car and pressed the LOCK button on her key fob.

It took ten steps to reach her front door, and Brianna hurried forward, key in hand, just like she did every night. Ten steps to safety inside the world she'd created for herself in the nineteen-hundred-square-foot townhouse she rented from a distant landlord. The neighborhood she'd chosen to live in was a safe one, but the darkness made her feel vulnerable. She reached her front door, inserted her key, and stepped into gloomy silence.

At times like this she wished she owned a pet. Even a goldfish in a bowl would be something to talk to. "Something live should live here other than me and the bugs," she said as she flipped on her hall light and slid the deadbolt in place.

She shot a glance at her telephone answering machine and noticed the blinking red light. She pressed the PLAY button and kicked off her shoes.

Beep. "Hi, Brianna. It's Philip. I was thinking that maybe you'd like to take in a movie with us this weekend. We'll be meeting up at the Palace at seven on Saturday. After the movie we'll head to Giorgio's for pizza. Give me a call if you're interested. Oh, the 'we' is George, Sandi, Jolene, me, and hopefully you. If you would like to bring someone, go right ahead."

Beep. "Brianna? It's your mother. Haven't heard from you in a while. Give me a call. Bye."

Beep. "Brianna, it's your mother again. Sorry, but don't call. We won't be here. We'll be visiting Aunt Kate this weekend. You have her number, don't you? Bye, sweetie. Catch up with you later."

Beep. "Miss Griffith, this is Harrington's Department Store. The dress you had altered has come back. You can pick it up anytime at your convenience. Thank you."

Brianna padded into the kitchen. She really wasn't hungry, but she poured herself a bowl of cereal and ate it over the sink. Before shuffling upstairs to bed, she poured the leftover milk into a bowl and set it outside her back door where the poor feral cat that lived nearby would find it. She'd been placing bowls of milk outside her door for two weeks; they were always licked clean by morning. The cat, when she saw it last, was looking plumper, its ribs no longer evident.

Brianna showered and dressed for bed in a pair of worn flannel pajamas. She pulled back the coverlet and climbed into her bed, then flipped through the television channels hoping to find something to watch. Nothing appealed to her, so she reached for her Bible and read her way through Romans until the words blurred and her eyelids closed.

"How was the class last night?" Sophie asked as Brianna carefully maneuvered her way into her office—a cup of coffee in one hand, her briefcase in the other.

Brianna looked up to find Sophie sitting at her desk attacking the morning's mail with a metal letter opener. "So?" she said, waving the opener in the air like a baton.

Brianna placed her briefcase on top of Sophie's desk and peeled off the lid to her coffee. "I should tell you I stayed home and made telephone calls, but I knew I'd have to face you in the morning, so I went to the class as I promised I would and learned a little about paint."

Sophie crossed her arms over her belly and leaned back in her chair. "Did you meet anyone? Joan insists Home & Hearth is *the* hot spot in town."

Brianna took a gulp of coffee. "And if I did?"

"I'd say you should listen to me more often and that God has a great sense of humor."

"You don't know the half of it."

"I'm listening."

"Well, you've heard me speak of Zachary Wilson. How we were once engaged many moons ago—that is, until I broke it off."

"I do recall your sad tale of lost love. But that was back in the dark ages."

Brianna watched as Sophie's eyebrows suddenly rose. "Oh, no way," Sophie said as she propelled herself forward in her chair.

Brianna took another gulp from the cup. "He was there."

"Yes, and. . ." Sophie lightly jabbed the opener at Brianna. "Don't keep me in suspense and cause me to deliver my baby this morning."

"And he said he'd call me."

"That's it?"

"You want more?"

"I want you to go out on a date with him," Sophie said, nodding vigorously.

"We're not there yet."

"According to you, you were way past there when you booted him out of your life."

Brianna felt herself stiffen at the reprimand. "Ouch. You sure know how to hurt a girl."

Sophie shrugged. "So you gave him your telephone number in hopes he'll call you."

"That about sums it up."

"What's he doing in town, aside from taking a class with you?"

Brianna pulled a chair over to Sophie's desk. "He's in the travel business. Isn't that something?"

"You mean he's your competition?"

"I didn't think about that when he told me what he did for a living."

"Hmm. Well, this certainly makes your life more interesting than it was this time yesterday—which you were due for, by the way."

Brianna finished her coffee and gestured at the mail. "Anything in there that I should see?"

"I was just getting started when you came in. But you do have a phone message. Oak Ridge Bicycle Touring Club's Linda Barnett just telephoned. She didn't sound happy. I left her number on your desk."

Brianna felt her stomach grab. She'd spent a lot of hours working with Linda. Two bicycle touring clubs—one in Oak Ridge and the other in Asheville—were going to California for a one-week bicycle tour of Sonoma County, California. They were flying out in seven days. It had been a challenge to coordinate the thousands of details involved, including booking them into bed-and-breakfasts along their route. Did a call from Linda at this late date mean trouble? "I'd better find out what she wants."

Alone in her office, Brianna quickly dialed Linda's number. "Linda, Sophie tells me you called."

"Bad news, I'm afraid. The Asheville group may have to pull out of the trip."

The Asheville touring club had fifteen members signed on for the trip. Were all of them canceling? "You mean no one is going?"

"Five are backing out. I know the rates you quoted us required a minimum number of participants, and now we can't meet that number."

Brianna felt nauseated. If five members of the Asheville group canceled, then some in the Oak Ridge group might also feel compelled to cancel. That would mean her agency would have to refund the bicyclists' deposits. If that happened, she stood to lose several thousand dollars in revenue—money she couldn't spare. There had to be a way to save the trip from falling apart. "Before we do anything drastic, let me telephone the Oak Ridge group and see if we can't make up the numbers with some of their members."

She sighed. The Asheville club hadn't left her much time. But there were other touring groups whose members might be interested in taking such a trip. Perhaps she could persuade one of them to make up the difference. She imagined a morning of telephoning stretching out before her. If only she had more time. "You can still guarantee ten, is that right?"

"Correct."

"Can you contact those members who initially declined the tour and see if they'd be willing to reconsider?"

"I'll call you back."

"Thanks."

"Five cyclists," she said to herself when she hung up. "Somewhere in the state of North Carolina there must be five cyclists who would love to go to California and tour Sonoma County. Now, where are you folks?"

Brianna switched on her computer and began to search through the various databases she'd created. It took her less than fifteen minutes to identify several bicycling clubs and another ten to track down the telephone number of an officer of the Blue Ridge Bicycle Club in Asheville. By noon she had acquired two names. By twelve thirty she had two commitments.

Linda called at 1:00 p.m. "I've got good news and bad news. The good news is I found you another cyclist. Bad news is you're still down by four."

"Nope. I have two from Blue Ridge. We're only down two." Brianna laughed. "If I wasn't so busy, I'd sign myself up."

Linda laughed. "I didn't know you were a cyclist."

"I'm not. But I'm thinking of taking it up."

"A tour like this wouldn't be a good place to begin this sport."

"I was only kidding."

"I'm sure we can find two people from somewhere."

"I'll keep looking." Brianna rang off and rested her head in her hands. What a waste of a morning.

"Are you taking a lunch break today?" Sophie asked.

Brianna looked up and shook her head. How could she eat with this problem hanging over her head? "I guess I didn't realized how late it is. But you go ahead. I'll grab a bite later."

Sophie stepped into the room. "Did you-know-who call?"

"No, and to tell you the truth, unless Zach rides a bike and wants to go to California with a gang of strangers, I'm not particularly interested."

Sophie sighed as she retreated behind the door. "Oh, Brianna, what a romantic you are."

"I'm too busy to be a romantic," Brianna called out as the door clicked shut. "I need to find two cyclists or this tour will be toast."

Chapter 5

Zachary settled in behind his desk, switched on his computer, and watched as his morning e-mail messages began to download. He stared, bleary-eyed, as the e-mails beeped in, each subject line screaming for his personal attention. The relentless stream of messages caused his eyes to blur, and he blinked to ease the strain. Fifteen out of seventy-five. Sixteen. Seventeen. Some came with little red tags attached. He supposed he should read those first, but all he could think about was Brianna and the phone call he planned to make to her later in the day. He felt eager to reconnect, but he also felt wary. How would she behave away from the superstore? And why did he still care?

He struggled to get his mind on his work. His task was to book sixteen rooms, arrange sixteen airline flights, and prepare sixteen personal itineraries for a small group of company employees who planned to travel to a convention in Los Angeles in less than a month. They'd made the decision to go only the day before, which meant he'd have to scramble to find them suitable accommodations. Just his bad luck if the group was forced to split up because they'd waited until the last minute to book. This wasn't usually what he did. But the company he was working with hadn't yet hired an in-house travel agent, so the task fell to him in the meantime. Zach sighed, stretched his arms in front of him, and imagined them staying in sixteen different hotels. Well, serve them right for waiting until the last minute.

Then his phone began to ring, and any thoughts he still had of Brianna vanished like the morning mist on his mountain. *Face it, Zach, this day's already off to a rotten start.*

It was almost three in the afternoon when he realized he still hadn't called her. He would hardly be, in her eyes, the ardent suitor. He dug her telephone number out of his wallet and dialed.

"Affinity Travel of Asheville," announced a cheery voice. "How may I direct your call?"

"Brianna Griffith."

"May I ask who is calling?"

"Zachary Wilson."

"Ah. . .one moment, please."

He grimaced. So his name had been recognized by the woman who answered Brianna's telephone. Girl talk usually amused him, but now that he'd become its focus, he suddenly felt less amused.

"Brianna speaking."

Her voice sounded clipped. Was she annoyed that he'd called? Perhaps a smarter man than he would have hung up, never to call again, but rudeness wasn't his style. He took a deep breath. "It's Zachary. How are you?"

"Busy," came her terse reply.

He could do terse, too. "Then I won't keep you."

"I'm sorry, Zach. I didn't mean to be impolite, but I've had several cancellations this morning, and I'm trying to find two people to go on a bike tour in California before the whole trip falls apart." She laughed, but it was a hollow laugh, filled with tension she couldn't disguise.

"The trip sounds wonderful."

"It will be." Her voice turned suddenly pleading. "Hey, you wouldn't like to go, would you?"

He chuckled. He knew exactly what she was experiencing. A canceled trip meant that her earnings would plummet and all of her work on it would be for nothing. "Unfortunately, I don't own a bicycle."

She sighed. "Me, either. But don't think I haven't considered buying one."

"Have you called around to other bicycling clubs?"

"I was doing that when you phoned." She paused. "But I'm sure you didn't call to talk about how busy I am or how disastrous my day has been."

"I'd like to know if you'd care to grab a snack with me before our class tomorrow. I recall you used to like pizza."

"And I still do."

"We could meet at the pizza place across from the H&H Superstore."

She paused. It was just for a moment, not even a second really, but he wondered if her hesitation was because she couldn't think of a nice way to tell him no. He had decided on his way to work that if she wasn't interested in getting reacquainted, then he wouldn't pursue her and would probably even drop the course in order to avoid seeing her again.

He hadn't, in his heart of hearts, really thought about what he wanted from her. All he knew was that he had once loved her and could probably do so again without a whole lot of effort on his part.

"What time?"

His fears subsided. "Is six okay?"

"See you at the pizza place."

"You're on. Good luck finding your cyclists."

This time her laugh seemed genuine. "It's just a matter of time, I'm sure. Thanks for calling."

He hung up and pushed himself away from his desk. *I have a date.* He paused. *Is it a date? Yes,* he finally decided, *it really is.* With his ex-fiancée, no less. Who would have believed it? Tomorrow they'd catch up, and after that, well, who knew what would happen.

His phone rang again, and he snatched it up without looking at the caller ID bar.

"It's Brianna," a voice said.

Was she canceling? "Yes," he answered, his voice sounding timorous, even to his own ears.

"Six is a little too early for me, Zach. Can we meet at six fifteen?"

"That will be fine."

"See you then."

He replaced the receiver and slapped the top of his desk. "Okay," he said to no one. "I'll be there with bells on."

No sooner had Brianna hung up than Sophie appeared in front of her. "You scared me," Brianna said. "And you're starting to make a habit of it."

"That was him, wasn't it?" Sophie asked as she leaned on Brianna's desk and massaged her lower back.

Brianna nodded. "I've agreed to meet Zachary for pizza tomorrow night."

"You're skipping your decorating class?"

"I'm not skipping it. We're getting together before our class. Tomorrow we'll learn how to remove wallpaper." Brianna looked around the room. "It can't be soon enough for me."

Sophie straightened up, her gaze mirroring Brianna's. "Me, either."

Brianna nodded. "And before you get too excited about my meeting Zach, remember that we're only having pizza."

"Pizza is promising."

"I'm not sure what you mean by that."

"Pizza can lead to fancy dinners in more upscale restaurants. These things have a way of taking on a life of their own."

"Now you're dreaming. Deep down, you believe everyone in the world should live like you. I'm not sure God intends for me to ever marry."

"I guess time will tell on that one."

There was no point in arguing the matter further. "Don't you have work to do?"

Sophie swung on her heels. "I do have filing, now that you mention it."

"Hop to it, then." Brianna reached for the telephone. "I'm still short a person or two for the bicycle tour, and I need to get things wrapped up before too long and return a couple of phone calls."

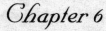

Chapter 6

*D*inner at a local pizzeria followed by a wallpapering *class with Brianna—how do I dress for that?* Zachary wondered as he stared at his image in the tiny bathroom mirror in the tiny bathroom a few doors down a narrow hallway from his office.

He removed his sweater with care, folded it, and placed it in his briefcase, then dug out a worn cotton shirt that he'd brought to work with him that morning. He slipped it over his head and took another look at himself. Better.

Satisfied, he glanced at his watch. It was time to leave. The drive to the pizzeria would take ten minutes, if traffic wasn't heavy. Ten minutes until he was with Brianna again. The thought almost blew him away.

He arrived at the strip mall across from the Home & Hearth Superstore and walked briskly toward the pizzeria. He didn't know what kind of a car Brianna drove, so there was no point in trying to figure out if she was already inside the restaurant. He'd find out soon enough anyway.

He entered and looked around. It wasn't a large restaurant.

There were maybe ten tables in the place, each with a red Formica top. Posters of Italy hung on the wall, and all but two of the tables were occupied. He chose one and sat down facing the door.

She swooped in two minutes later, casting her gaze about the room until she found him. She was wearing a red sweater—her favorite color, he seemed to recall—and dark brown slacks. Her curly hair was cut short. She used to wear it longer, but he liked the way she looked. "Have you been waiting long?" she asked, pulling out her chair and dropping into it.

He shook his head. "I just got here myself."

A waitress appeared and looked expectantly at Zach. "Have you guys decided?"

Zachary shook his head and turned to Brianna. "Vegetable, right? Thin crust, extra cheese."

"You remember after all these years. That's almost scary."

Zachary found himself laughing. "I have almost total recall. Always have."

She nodded. "And I don't. Veggie pizza, extra cheese it is. And iced tea."

"Sweetened," Zachary said to the waitress.

He ordered a drink for himself and clasped his hands on the table, fighting the temptation to reach across and take her hand in his. "Did you find your bicyclists?"

"I located one late this afternoon." She smiled at him. "I think I'm going to be able to salvage this trip." She leaned back. "But I forgot—you're in the same business I am. You should know all about these things."

He nodded. "To be honest, I was stunned when you announced you were the owner of Affinity Travel of Asheville.

I thought you'd be a famous journalist by now."

"I fell into the business, Zachary. It wasn't what I planned to do with my life, but I discovered that I like it." She leaned forward. "How about yourself? I thought you'd be a famous businessman by now, on the cover of *Forbes* magazine or something."

"I fell into the travel business, too. But I do more consulting than actual booking of tours, although today was the exception, not the rule."

"You help companies set up in-house travel departments, as I recall."

"Your memory isn't so bad after all."

"For some reason that stuck with me."

"Which doesn't surprise me. If I were in your shoes, I'd wonder if I was your competition."

"That thought crossed Sophie's mind, too."

"Your assistant?"

"My very pregnant full-time assistant."

He nodded. "You must be doing well to have a full-time employee."

The pizza and drinks arrived, and Zach gave thanks to God for the food. Brianna reached for a slice and slipped it onto her plate. "I'm doing okay, Zach, but I'm finding that business has slowed a little lately."

"I'm a little less out there than you since I just teach companies how to set up internal travel bureaus." He grinned. "When they have to go, they have to go. I'm a little more protected from swings in the economy than you. If times get hard or if interest rates go up or there's a layoff in town, then people tend to cancel their holidays. Sometimes, like today, I do the bookings, but my aim is to let those I train do them."

"It does sound less risky."

He dug into his pizza. "And then, of course, you're dealing with teddy bears."

Brianna laughed. "Oh, those dreadful bears. You remembered. It's like a childish fantasy becoming a nightmare. Sometimes I dream about them running amok with machine guns and chain saws. Pretty awful."

"Well, maybe not for much longer."

"That would be nice." She took a bite of pizza. "And you're dealing with flocked wallpaper in the hallway."

"It has to go."

"That sounds like an awful job."

"It will be." He felt his shoulders sag. "I'm not looking forward to it. But that's just one of the things that needs doing. My whole house could use a makeover. It's well built but miserably outdated."

"Where is your house?"

"North of Oak Ridge, on Route 251."

"You make my teddy bear problem seem insignificant." She sipped her drink. "What do you think of Andrea?"

"Competent."

"I thought so, too. I figure if she can learn to wallpaper and paint, then I can learn, too."

"You always were confident of your abilities. I've always liked that about you."

He watched her gaze settle on his face. "Thank you, Zach."

He shrugged. "How's the pizza?"

"Good."

She looked at him again, then seemed to reach a decision.

"I'm meeting a few friends on Saturday at seven, at the Palace Theater here in Oak Ridge. Would you care to join us?"

"Are you sure?"

She nodded. "I wouldn't have asked if I wasn't."

"That would be great. I'll pick you up."

She nodded. "I live in a townhouse on Evelyn Place." She wrote the address on a business card and handed it to him. "Come by at six thirty. That will give us plenty of time to get to the movies."

The waitress appeared. "How're you folks doing? Can I get you anything?"

"I'd like the bill, please," Zach said.

Brianna dove into her purse. "Let me pay my way," she said. "I insist."

"I asked you to join me."

"I'd prefer that I do," she said as she slapped ten dollars onto the table. "Another time, perhaps."

Her voice sounded determined, and Zach decided not to argue with her. Her stubborn streak hadn't left her even after all these years.

Chapter 7

Brianna, with Zachary at her side, walked briskly to the section of the store set aside for the class. Several students had already claimed the front-row seats. Brianna scanned the cozy space and spotted two empty chairs in the middle of the third row. "Over there," she said. "Two free ones together."

She and Zachary squeezed past several classmates and sat down. Brianna retrieved her notebook from her purse and placed it on her lap. When she finally looked up, she realized that at least three female students were staring at her, their facial expressions bearing testimony to their shared disappointment at seeing her and Zachary together.

Brianna suppressed a smile. They were, she reasoned, probably wondering how she and Zach were able to connect so quickly after only one class. How could they know she'd once been engaged to him? She decided to ignore their glances and focused her gaze on the long table loaded with tools that someone had put up in front of the first row of chairs.

Brianna's heart sank as she mentally calculated the cost of

the equipment she'd need for the job. She nudged Zachary. "I think we're expected to buy all that stuff."

Before he could respond, Andrea appeared and greeted her class with what Brianna thought was an encouraging smile. She was wearing a paint-splattered shirt beneath a pair of well-worn denim overalls.

"I see I didn't scare many of you away," she said. "However, don't get too comfortable in your seats. We're going to break into groups tonight. My goal is for you to get a feel for the tools you'll be using. And when we return following our break, we'll work on the walls that I've prepared for us in a room at the far end of the hardware aisle."

Brianna leaned toward Zach. "I guess we get to play with the toys."

"I want you to break into three groups," Andrea went on. "I'll call you group one, group two, and group three. There should be four or five of you in each group. When you've decided which group you're a part of, I want you to choose a leader."

"Make sure we're in the same group," Zachary said, grabbing her hand as the students stood up and began to form themselves into groups.

Brianna rose along with them as two women, both in their midtwenties, wearing plastered-on smiles and looking way too dressed up for wallpaper removal, suddenly appeared at Zach's side.

"I'm Leeza," one of them said as she gave Brianna a nudge that loosened her grip on Zachary's hand. "I live in Oak Ridge, not far from the store."

Leeza's gaze locked with Brianna's long enough for Brianna to realize that a gauntlet had been tossed at her feet.

"Now, isn't that convenient," Leeza said, her attention returning to Zach. "I can't wait to get started on my project."

It was all Brianna could do not to roll her eyes. *I'm sure you can't.* She was curious to see how Zachary would respond. To her amazement, he seemed to grow taller before her eyes.

"Pleased to meet you, Leeza. I'm Zachary Wilson."

"Yes, I know," she said, shooting him a smile that would have melted butter. "You don't mind me joining you, do you?"

"I'd be delighted," he said as he reached for her hand.

"And I'm Marsha Gooding," a second woman announced as she pushed her way forward. "I'm a little overwhelmed by all I have to learn, but I have to start somewhere, I suppose."

Brianna nodded. Marsha, she recalled, was the lady allergic to dust. "I hope this class doesn't make you sneeze."

Marsha drew a cotton handkerchief from her sleeve. "So do I," she said, dabbing at her nose. "When I get started, I sometimes can't stop until. . . Oh, well, never mind. I'm pleased to meet you, Brianna."

Marsha turned to Zachary. "I vote we make you our leader."

Leeza all but drooled. "I second that."

Andrea's voice rose above the chatter. "Are we all attached to a group? If one of you doesn't belong to a group, I recommend that you join one now. Good. Will the group leaders please raise their hands?" Three people, including Zach, raised their hands. "I see we have three groups. Zachary Wilson, group one. Angela Larson, group two. Letisha Redmond, group three. Group one to this end of the table," she said, slapping it hard with her hand. "Group two to the middle and group three to this end. In front of you are the tools and ingredients we'll be using to remove our wallpaper—a steamer, various scrapers, sponges, commercial wallpaper remover, baking soda, vinegar, and fabric softener. More about those ingredients later. When you're all familiar with the tools, please come up and introduce yourselves to them. We'll take a ten-minute break right now, then meet me at the very end of the housewares aisle. There you'll find a door. Open it and go on into the room. All of the walls in the room are wallpapered in different kinds of wallpaper. Our goal tonight is to strip the walls down to the original wallboard using the tools and ingredients on the table. Please bring these with you when you come. See you in ten minutes."

"Ladies," Zachary said, "I propose we avail ourselves of refreshments while we can." He gestured to the front of the store. "There's a coffee machine by the door."

Brianna felt a stab of annoyance that he'd invited the two women to join them and that he also seemed to get a kick out of being the focus of their adoring attention.

"Oh, please don't include me," Marsha announced after a little consideration. "Coffee will keep me up all night. I'll meet you all later."

"Are you coming, Brianna?" he asked as he extended his arm to her.

She was tempted to tell him no but changed her mind. After all, who was she to feel annoyed if he didn't want to leave anyone out? She took his arm and allowed him to lead her toward the coffee machine, Leeza following closely on their heels. Behind them she heard Marsha Gooding begin to wheeze.

Chapter 8

Zach could hear Brianna grunting as she worked beside him on a small section of wall. She seemed to be attacking the paper with a vengeance, her lips pursed, her entire body in motion. Never in his life had he seen so much determination directed at an inanimate object. Leeza was working beside him, too, on his other side. He tried to ignore her as she kept brushing his arm with hers.

"You might want to use the steamer again, Brianna, if the wallpaper isn't coming off," Zachary said as he continued to work.

"I already used it twice, and whoever put this on must have used superglue." She snorted a laugh. "But perhaps this is the H&H's concept of a brilliant marketing strategy. I mean, if the wallpaper doesn't come off as easily as we think it should, then maybe we'll be tempted to buy the expensive wallpaper remover that's conveniently on sale next to the cash register."

"I doubt that's the store's motivation, although you might be right. Did you score the wallpaper?"

"I most certainly did."

"Then the wallpaper should come off."

In his peripheral vision, he could see Brianna stand up, rub her back, and stare contemplatively at the wall. "Tell that to the wall, why don't you?"

"Are you having a problem, Brianna?" Andrea had been working her way around the room, encouraging her students. Brianna, she must have decided, was in dire need of an extra dose of encouragement.

Brianna turned to face Andrea. "It won't budge. I've scored and I've steamed until the sweat's pouring off my face, but the wallpaper isn't coming off."

Andrea nodded. "Try giving it a little more time. Apply the steamer, then wait and apply the steamer again. And when the paper's good and wet, give it a good old-fashioned pull. And remember what I said about working in small sections. Don't try to attack the entire wall at once."

Brianna nodded and sighed. "I didn't think it would be this hard, Andrea. I seem to be the only one in your class having a problem."

Zachary couldn't help but notice how dejected Brianna seemed, but he reasoned that she probably didn't need advice from him right now. She'd figure things out eventually. She always did.

To his surprise, Brianna lobbed a kick at the wall, making it shudder. "Come off, why don't you?"

He could see heads turning her way. Brianna noticed them, too. "Sorry, everyone," she said. "Y'all don't let me stop you from working." Beneath her breath he heard her mutter, "I'm never going to be able to do my office by myself. It's hopeless. I'm going to have to live with those ugly teddy bears forever."

"I have an idea about that," Zach said. "That is, if you'd care to listen."

"I'd care."

"Throw a wallpaper party—invite your friends over for pizza, put on some lively music, and get to work."

She turned to face him, the scraper in her hand. "And is that what you're going to do to solve your problem? Are you going to invite me to help you improve your house? It'll take more than pizza to get me to agree to that."

He laughed. "I think I can manage my hallway. And stairs."

He watched as her shoulders sagged. "I can't do my office by myself, Zach. I realize that now. What was I thinking?"

"I gave you a solution. Get help."

"My friends are great, but"—she shook her head—"no way would they show up to redecorate my office. My house maybe, but not my office. They'd expect me to hire someone for that."

"Well, this friend would help you."

She shook her head once more. "Thanks, but I can't impose."

There it was again, that stubborn streak. He'd hoped she'd outgrown it, but maybe it was something she would never outgrow. This was how she was. Take it or leave it. And, he reminded himself, it was her stubbornness that had driven her to open her own business. It would be her stubbornness that would make her succeed.

He watched her turn back to the wall and begin to work. This time, he noticed that she made some progress. The grunting stopped as the wallpaper gave way under her scraper. After a while, she'd cleared off a four-foot-square section. Finally, she stood back to admire her accomplishment.

"There," she said at last. "Andrea's advice worked. I guess I needed to slow down."

Zachary leaned over. "It's looking good."

She cast a glance at his section of the wall. Most of the paper was lying at his feet on the floor. "You're almost done," she exclaimed, the annoyance in her voice barely disguised.

Zachary shrugged. "Sorry."

"And so you should be."

He watched her expression change from pleased to disappointed. He could imagine what she was thinking. It had taken her almost an hour to remove four square feet of wallpaper, while he had managed to clear almost double that amount. He felt the urge to put his arm around her, but this wasn't the time—or the place—for a public display of affection. He tried to think of something encouraging to tell her. "Maybe the wallpaper in your office will come off more easily than this."

"Nice try."

Then Andrea began to talk. "Time's up," she announced to her class. "Any questions before you leave?"

Zachary watched as Brianna raised her hand, then quickly put it down. Perhaps she'd decided he was right. Or maybe she'd decided to call it quits.

"I'm ready to go," she said. "How about you?"

"I'll walk you to your car."

"You don't need to. In two minutes the parking lot will be full of sweaty people heading home."

He took her arm. "Come on."

They exited together. Before climbing into her car, she turned and smiled at him. "I'm sorry I was such a grouch tonight."

"I would have been one, too, in your shoes."

"I'm concerned I may have bitten off more than I can chew."

"You'll come up with something."

Her shoulders slumped. Clearly, she didn't seem convinced.

"Good night, Zach. See you on Saturday."

Chapter 9

Brianna pulled away from the Home & Hearth Superstore determined not to look back at Zach, who was standing, she imagined, exactly where she'd left him in the parking lot.

As she entered the highway, she began to wonder if her decision to have him pick her up at her townhouse had been a sensible one. What was this new relationship with Zachary anyway? How far did she want to take it? Did she really want him to know where she lived at this stage of their relationship? And what if he decided it would be so much more pleasant if they spent the evening together, just the two of them, getting to know each other all over again? She remembered how persuasive he used to be and how she used to dig in her heels, causing conflict between them.

The car behind her honked, and she increased her speed to match the speed of the traffic. If she wasn't careful, she'd cause an accident. She clenched the steering wheel tightly and tried to focus on the road. But she couldn't shake Zachary from her mind. She was a different woman now. More mature. Sensible.

In better control of her emotions. Most of the problems they'd had in the past were a result of her insecurities. She could see that now.

She shrugged and moved into the slower lane that would carry her west toward her empty townhouse on Evelyn Place.

A few minutes later, her cell phone began to bleat, and Brianna slid her right hand into her purse, feeling for her cell phone. She retrieved it and recognized Brandi's number.

"Hi, sis. What's up?"

"Was he there tonight?"

No hello? No "How are you?" She hated it when Brandi just started talking.

"Hello, sister. I'm fine, and you? Good. Glad to hear it. Yes, he was there."

"Don't be a princess. You know I like to get right to the meat of the matter." She laughed, no doubt enjoying her own private joke. "So tell me. Did anything happen that I should know about?"

"Tonight we removed wallpaper together. His came off faster than mine."

"Very funny." The line fell silent for a minute. Brandi was obviously probing the dark corners of her mind. "You're holding out on me, Brianna. I know you are." She laughed. "You're going to see him again, aren't you?"

Brianna rolled her eyes and wondered at her sister's uncanny ability to figure things out long distance. "Saturday night. We're meeting up with some friends of mine and going to a movie. It'll be an intimate evening—just the six of us. It would have been five, with me being the fifth wheel, but this time I have a date."

"Bad, bad decision to have Zachary meet your friends so soon in your relationship."

Brianna didn't feel like arguing. And while it had been years since she'd seen Zachary, was this really a new relationship or just an extension of the old one? "Who made you the expert on dating former fiancés?"

"Your friends won't like him, you mark my words."

"That's ridiculous."

"Tell me if I'm still ridiculous on Sunday. You see if I'm not right."

Brianna shuddered. She hadn't thought about her friends not liking Zachary. But what if they didn't? What then? No, that wouldn't happen. Zachary was a decent human being, a nice guy. It would be fine. They'd probably welcome him into their circle. Her sister was just being plain annoying. It was time to get off the phone.

"I have to go," Brianna said. "I'm driving and you're distracting me from the road."

"Call me when you get home."

"No, I'm tired. I want to go straight to bed."

"Spoilsport."

"Love you."

"Love you, too."

Brianna turned off her phone and dropped it back into her purse. Her sister was wrong. Everything would be fine. She was almost sure of it.

Saturday came quickly. Brianna was ready for her date with Zachary well before six thirty. She'd dressed with care in a pair of black slacks and a bright red shirt. After putting them on, she twisted and turned in front of her long mirror, then checked her makeup for the umpteenth time. "You're acting weird," she said to her image, then turned and quickly walked away. Preening was a waste of time.

She remembered her sister's advice about introducing Zachary to her friends, but she still didn't understand why that would be a bad idea. If she continued to see him, they would eventually meet anyway. And come to think of it, what did her sister really know about dating? She'd been married for ten years, for crying out loud.

Finally, her doorbell rang. Zach had arrived. Brianna opened the door. "Would you care to come in?"

He gestured to his car. "I'd better not. I left the engine running."

She nodded. Good. He wasn't about to tempt her to change her plans.

The outside air felt warm, but Brianna knew the movie theater would be chilly. "I think I'll get my sweater. You going to be all right out there?"

Zachary nodded. "I prefer to keep an eye on my truck."

She partially shut her front door, then bounded up the stairs to her bedroom and grabbed her sweater. When she met Zachary at his truck, he was holding the passenger door open for her. She climbed in and watched him march around to the driver's side. "Everything okay?" she asked. "You seem awfully serious this evening."

"I guess I'm a little nervous about meeting your friends."

She nodded. "I suppose that could be intimidating, now that you mention it."

"I know you haven't been in Asheville very long. Where did you find them?"

"I met Philip and Jolene at a singles' get-together at their church. George and Sandi Harmon are married and members of the same church as Philip and Jolene. I went there because I heard about the singles' ministry."

"What church would that be?"

"Oak Ridge Community Church. Where do you go?"

"There's a small nondenominational church near my house that meets in a school. About sixty people show up every Sunday. The pastor's young, and we have a good praise team." He shrugged. "We're friendly folks. I like it."

She nodded. She'd been blessed to meet Philip and Jolene. They helped fill an empty void. Sometimes being a single woman in a couples' world wasn't easy. On arriving in town, she'd joined the local Chamber of Commerce, which added to the busyness of her life. Her work fulfilled her, yet she still longed for more. She supposed that was a natural enough feeling for a woman like herself—a woman who might never marry. Yet here she was again, in an odd twist of fate, going out on a date with Zachary Wilson.

They arrived at the movie theater, a large complex of theaters and shops teeming with teenagers who had no place else to go. The noise and chatter made it difficult to speak. She found herself yelling to Zachary, "Over there. I see them."

She grabbed his hand and pulled him toward her friends. "Philip, George, Sandi," she said, "I'd like to introduce you to Zachary Wilson. Zach and I are old friends from college. He's recently moved to Asheville. We ran into each other at the Home & Hearth Superstore in Oak Ridge. What a coincidence!" She saw no point in going into the details of their past relationship. Not yet, anyway.

Hands were extended. "I know that place well," Sandi said. "I shop there all the time. I understand it has a reputation as a place where gals go to meet guys and vice versa." She laughed. "I guess it's living up to its reputation. Also, people sometimes get married there." She shrugged. "Why not, I say?"

Zach took Sandi's hand. "Pleased to meet you."

He turned to George. "You, too, George. And Philip. Hello."

"We're still waiting for Jolene," Sandi offered. "She's usually late."

"Am not."

Jolene suddenly appeared at Philip's side and planted a kiss on his cheek. "Well, who is this?" she asked, eyeing Zachary.

"Zach," Brianna said, "meet Jolene." Brianna gestured. "We're college friends who bumped into each other at a class we're taking at H&H."

"Did I ever tell you that I took a class there once?" Sandi asked. "I learned how to install a garden fountain."

"Really? That sounds nice."

"It would have been," George said, "if she ever would have installed it."

"You haven't?"

"Not yet. But I will one day."

George rolled his eyes. "When she does, I'll throw a party. Everything she bought is still sitting in a box in our garage. The course was free, but the fountain cost a pretty penny as I recall."

"What movie are we going to see?" Brianna asked, her

fears of her friends not liking Zachary suddenly vanishing. She cast a quick sideways glance at Zachary, who, much to her relief, actually seemed to be enjoying himself.

"I think we should let the women decide," Philip chimed in. "We guys picked last week's movie."

Jolene clapped her hands together. "I vote for the chick flick."

Brianna smiled. "Me, too. I love Keira Knightly."

Philip groaned. "Very well, ladies. Let's get tickets. There's a huge line forming. And if we want to sit together, we'd better get on it."

Chapter 10

Philip managed to find four empty seats together, but there weren't enough seats for all of them to sit together. Zachary wondered how the group would split up, but suddenly, Philip was pointing his way.

"Zach," Philip said, gesturing to the next row back, "why don't you and Brianna grab those two free seats."

He'd imagined them all sitting together, but the idea that he'd be alone with Brianna was enticing. He grabbed her hand and maneuvered her through the dimly lit theater. "There," he said. "This will be fine. Don't you agree?"

"Perfect," she said, taking her place behind Jolene.

After she was seated, he wondered if he should have offered to buy popcorn. Usually he tried to stay away from it, but he seemed to remember she enjoyed it. "Shall I get us a bucket of popcorn?"

A quick shake of her head told him she wasn't interested. "I try to stay away from junk food, Zach. But you go ahead and get some if you want."

He nodded. "I was thinking the same thing myself. But

I thought I'd offer."

The movie theater began to darken, and Brianna drew her sweater around her shoulders and sank deeper into her seat as the movie title came up. He wasn't exactly in the mood to sit through two straight hours of thwarted love—his own romantic life, spare as it was, had to be one hundred times more interesting than anything he was about to watch—but he would endure it for Brianna's sake. In front of him he could see Jolene dive into her purse and retrieve a handkerchief. "I'm ready," she said, waving it in the air. "Roll the film."

Brianna laughed and sank even deeper into her seat. "Cold?" he asked as he reached for her hand and folded her fingers into his.

"Not anymore," she said, flashing him a smile.

Her smile caused his heart to miss a beat. How could he be so fortunate as to find her again after all these years? And to be sitting next to her, holding her hand? Of one thing he was suddenly sure—he wouldn't walk away so quickly this time. He would fight to keep her. He squeezed her fingers and offered up a silent prayer to his Savior. *Thank You, Jesus, for making this possible.*

He tried to concentrate on the film that Brianna was so clearly enjoying as she laughed and sighed beside him. But after a while his eyelids felt heavy and he felt himself drift off, the actors' voices fading into nothingness. . .

An elbow in his side made him jump. "What?"

"Wake up, Prince Charming. The movie's over."

He shook his head to clear it. "I know."

"I don't see how you could sleep through a movie. Why bother coming?"

"I didn't sleep—not really. And I *was* listening."

"You were snoring." Brianna stood up and prepared to leave.

"I'm sorry. I'll be honest—chick flicks bore me."

"That's too bad. Men would learn a lot about women if they watched chick flicks more often. Like the way Mr. Darcy behaved toward Elizabeth. Wasn't that just the most gallant thing you've ever seen?"

"I suppose."

She laughed. "You don't have a clue what I'm talking about, do you?"

He shrugged. "I guess not."

She tugged on his arm. "I won't hold it against you, Zach. I recall you liked Westerns, war films, and thrillers. I suppose some things never change. Anyway, I hope you brought your appetite with you. Giorgio's makes good pizza, and it doesn't like its patrons nodding off at its tables."

He allowed Brianna to steer him toward the lobby, where Philip was standing, his arm around Jolene's shoulder. "I'm sorry," Jolene wailed as she dabbed her nose with a soggy handkerchief. "I always cry at the movies, especially when it looks like the couple might not get together." She sniffed. "I mean, I knew they would, but still, I just had to see them married."

Zachary drew Brianna close to him. "They're a little like us, don't you think?"

"In what way?"

"Oh, I don't know. They had a chance to get together, yet they didn't because of misunderstandings. We had our chance, too, but we broke up all the same."

He realized the moment he spoke that he was walking on dangerous ground. He didn't want to antagonize Brianna just as she was beginning to get used to his being around.

"Well, never mind," he quickly said. He rubbed his hands together. "I'm famished. I understand we're all heading off for pizza."

Brianna's cell phone began to beep. She retrieved it quickly. "It's Sophie," she announced to the group. "You don't suppose. . ."

He watched as Brianna talked. Then she turned to face them.

"Listen, folks," she said, grinning from ear to ear, "Sophie's about to have her baby. She's on the way to the hospital right this minute."

"And she remembered to call you?" Sandi said. "That woman is amazing." She turned to Brianna. "Doesn't this leave you shorthanded around the office?"

"Sophie's arranged for a woman to come in and help me until she returns."

"Oooh, a baby," cooed Jolene, more tears flowing. "I just love babies."

Zachary wasn't sure what Brianna's plans would be. "Do you need me to drive you to the hospital?"

"Oh, heavens no. The last person they need with them now is me. Sophie's with her husband, who's her birthing coach, and her mother. She'll be fine. I'd only get in the way." She twirled on her heels. "Sophie's good news has made me hungry. Onward to Giorgio's."

Zachary again reached for her hand, and together they tumbled out into the parking lot. In that split second of time, Zachary realized what he wanted—he wanted Brianna and he wanted a family. And if God had steered him back to Brianna, then he was going to pursue her with every ounce of his being and not be so willing to take no for an answer.

Chapter 11

For the second time in as many days, Brianna found herself preening in front of her full-length bedroom mirror. This time she chose a black skirt and a green top as her Sunday-go-to-church-and-meet-Zachary outfit, and as she applied her makeup, she thought about Zachary and wondered why the idea of seeing him again excited her.

It was as obvious as the freshly powdered nose on her face that her feelings for him were becoming more and more powerful with every new meeting, but the question she kept asking during those odd moments when she found herself alone was, *Am I falling in love with him all over again?* Or could it be that she simply enjoyed the comfort of discovering an old friend in a new town? Eventually, she supposed, she would sort it all out in her mind.

On the drive home the previous evening, Zachary had invited her to attend his church. "You'll like it, Brianna," he'd added, perhaps sensing her hesitancy about accepting his invitation. "And as an extra incentive, I'll throw in a tour of my home. Of course, I'll also introduce you to Sami."

Brianna wondered how many other of Zach's girlfriends had been introduced to Sami and whether approval by Sami was essential to a continuing relationship with Zach. She wasn't sure she could face a discerning Lab mix first thing on a Sunday morning.

"I seem to remember you were always partial to dogs," Zach continued.

"That's an offer a self-respecting girl like me can't refuse," she said. "What time should I arrive?" *For Sami's inspection,* she almost added.

"Come at nine. Don't bother eating breakfast. I'll have muffins and juice, if that's agreeable."

He'd given her clear directions to his home, which she placed on the passenger seat. The distance to his house wasn't as great as she'd imagined. She easily found his driveway on Route 251 and pulled into it.

It was long and winding, and she drove carefully, trying to keep her wheels from getting caught in the deeper of the ruts carved into the dirt and gravel. She wondered how Zach managed to maneuver through the ruts in bad weather, then she remembered he drove a truck.

She exited her car and shut the door gently, hoping no one would notice her arrival until she had a chance to scope out the place. A dog barked in the distance, and a stern male voice called out, "She's here, Sami. Remember what I told you about not jumping up."

Zach emerged from behind the large two-story brick house with a yellow-haired dog bounding beside him.

"Sami," he said as he approached Brianna, "this is a friend I'd like you to meet. Say hello to Brianna."

Brianna watched as Sami promptly sat down and lifted her left front paw. Brianna eyed Zachary, who was beaming. "Very cute, Zach. You've even trained your dog to be a babe magnet."

Sami began to wobble.

"I know." He tipped his head at his dog. "She's waiting."

Brianna knelt down and took Sami's paw in her hand. "Hello, Sami. Good girl."

The dog's tail began to wag as Sami sprung to her feet and placed a slobbering lick onto Brianna's carefully made-up cheek. Brianna scrambled to her feet and wiped the slobber off with the back of her hand. "That's quite a routine you've developed. Does Sami kiss all of your visitors?"

Zach laughed. "Only the female ones. You'll probably want to wash your face." He turned to retrace his steps. "I'll show you the way. And when you're ready, I have coffee and hot, freshly baked muffins waiting in the breakfast nook."

She followed him into a large rear garden that contained a vegetable patch, several large trees, a patio with furniture, and a huge grill. He took her hand. "Welcome to my world, Brianna." He gestured. "And over there is Zach's mountain. At least that's what I call it."

Brianna wouldn't have called it a mountain—more of a hill. But the trees on it were beginning to put on their fall colors of red, yellow, and orange. "I can see why you love this view, Zach. It's beautiful."

"Not everything around here is beautiful. Wait until you see the wallpaper I want to remove. Your teddy bears can't be as bad as green flocked paper."

He directed her to the washroom along a hallway decorated in what looked to be Christmas wrapping paper. "See," he said, waving his hand at it. "Now you know why I'm taking Andrea's course. There's a lot to remove, which is why I can't afford to pay someone to do it."

"You have my sympathy." She peered up the stairs. "Does it go all the way up?"

" 'Fraid so—all the way to the bedrooms." He gestured to the kitchen. "I need to take the muffins out of the oven. I'll meet you back in the kitchen."

She splashed water on her face and reapplied her makeup, then returned to the kitchen to find Zachary placing assorted muffins onto a platter. "I made the corn muffins from scratch," he announced, "but I bought the others at a bakery in town." He gestured to a built-in banquette. "Make yourself at home."

She slid in. She could see Zach's mountain through the window. She imagined him having breakfast here every morning. "How long have you lived in this house?"

"Several months. I was tired of paying rent. But you can see there's plenty that needs to be done."

Brianna looked around. The kitchen was clean. It was clear that Zachary had recently tidied it up. But that was the best that could be said for it. Brianna figured the appliances and countertops were years out of date. "You have your work cut out."

"After you eat, I'll give you the five-cent tour. In fact, I'm glad you're here. I need a woman's opinion. I need to update everything. The master bath has only a shower—that will be easy enough to do. The second bath is wallpapered with girlie wallpaper." He wrinkled his nose. "Vintage 1979, looks like. I know I got a good deal on the house, but I sometimes have second thoughts. How am I going to get everything done? I'm starting to think that by the time I finish, I'll need to start over again."

"And I thought my office was difficult. Well, it will be."
She shrugged. "Extremely difficult. But I'll manage somehow,"
she said more to herself than to Zach. "I'll just have to."

She finished her muffin, then Zachary walked her around,
asking what she would do and what she would like if she were
the person making the decisions. "I'm not the one who's going
to live here, Zach," she found herself telling him again and
again. "You are."

Finally, he took her fingers and kissed them gently. "I know,"
he replied. "I know."

Brianna enjoyed attending the service and meeting Zach's
church family. She allowed him to introduce her as "his very
good friend from college," which in a way she was. Following
the service, she said good-bye to him and took off for the
Home & Hearth Superstore in Oak Ridge.

Watching Zach's enthusiasm about working on his house
had lifted her spirits, giving her hope she could accomplish
something on her own. She was taking a course that was
teaching her how to fix her decorating problems. Instead of
complaining about the work, she decided to purchase the tools
necessary to remove the marching teddy bears. If Andrea could
do it, so could she. She hadn't come this far to be frustrated by
a few rolls of paper. Hard work had never bothered her.

After purchasing what she needed at H&H, she stopped
to buy a gift for Sophie's baby. She would deliver it tomorrow,
if Sophie felt up to visitors. Then she'd start working on her
office when she had the time.

Chapter 12

It was eight thirty when Brianna slipped her key into the lock of her office suite door as she did almost every workday morning. The door swung wide, causing Brianna to take a step back until curiosity overcame fear long enough for her to allow her presence to be known. "Hello," she called. "Is anyone there?"

"Me is," a female voice answered.

The temp? At this hour? Brianna stuck her head around her door to find a young woman with highly gelled blonde hair, dressed in a black sweater and a long black skirt, sitting at Sophie's desk filing her purple fingernails, both feet propped on the desk.

"Oh," she said as her ankle-high boots clomped to the floor. "I didn't think I'd left the door unlocked. I'm Sophie's friend, Margaret Ann Bronson. I'm here to help you. But you can call me Spike. My friends all do."

Brianna kicked the door closed with her foot, not sure if this arrangement was going to work. Spike didn't look much like office assistant material to her.

Brianna fought to keep the disappointment from her voice. "I didn't realize Sophie had given anyone a key."

"I went by last night and picked it up. Sophie said I should get in early this morning, that you'd probably have a lot to show me."

Brianna nodded. "Good thinking."

Margaret smiled. "And I got to see the baby while I was there." She sighed. "She was sleeping, of course, but she's so cute. Well, all babies are, aren't they? But Sophie's has got to be the cutest."

"I'll stop by this evening," Brianna said.

Margaret grinned, then gestured to the packages that Brianna had forgotten she was holding.

"Can I give you a hand with those?"

Brianna let the packages slide to the floor and stuck out her hand. She guessed she might have to find a new assistant, but for now, Spike would have to do. "I'm glad to meet you, Spike," Brianna said, remembering her manners. "But I think I'll call you Margaret, if you don't mind."

Margaret came around her desk and clasped Brianna's hand firmly. "Hi back at ya, boss lady." Her gaze settled on the packages at Brianna's feet. "Oh, I see you shop at Home & Hearth. I go there all the time. I met Harry at Home & Hearth. We've been seeing each other for about a month now. He was in the music department buying CDs. We discovered we both liked Retarded Fish." She twisted one of the diamonds in her left earlobe. "How cool is that? So what's in the bags?"

"These are the tools I'll be using to remove my office wall-paper," Brianna said, tipping her head toward her door. "I suppose I should give you a tour of the place. It's not very big."

"No need for that. I already took one." Margaret grinned. "I know what you mean about the wallpaper, though. If that was *my* space, I'd want it removed right away. It's good to see you're not wasting any time." She gestured to the small storage room. "Sophie told me to make coffee every morning. I made a pot. There should be plenty left." She shrugged. "I hope it's all right. I drink green tea. Coffee's like poison to me."

"Thank you. But if you don't drink coffee, why wouldn't there be a full pot?"

Margaret tugged on her ear. "He must have had two whole cups already. If he keeps drinking it this fast, I'm going to have to make another pot."

"Who is the 'he' you're referring to?"

"Him."

"Him who?"

Margaret's voice rose an octave. "Why, the man inside your office."

"You let someone I don't know into my office?"

"He said he was your friend."

Brianna almost tripped over her packages as she rushed to her door and flung it open.

Zach had pushed her furniture to the middle of the room and was steaming one wall with the same steamer she'd just purchased. He spun around when she entered. "I wanted to surprise you," he said, grinning.

"You have."

"I could have this room done by the end of the day."

Brianna felt a rush of anger. She'd just talked herself into doing the work herself. She didn't need Zachary's help. She felt annoyed at his assumption that he could just march into her office and do what he wanted with her wall.

Then she remembered that he'd always been that way. Taking charge, he called it. Being a man. She called it being pushy. Memories flooded back as she recalled the fights they'd had over his insistence on doing things his way. She'd rebelled and pushed back. But that was years ago. Hadn't he changed in all this time? Did he still want to ride roughshod over her feelings? Was she being foolish? She didn't think so.

"Zach," she said, "I don't want you to do this."

He turned off the steamer, the smile on his face vanishing. "I thought you'd be pleased."

She shook her head. "You have your house to decorate. I have my office."

"Yes, and. . ."

"And I want to do my office myself."

"But yesterday you seemed so unsure of yourself."

"That was yesterday. Today I'm brimming with confidence. Can't you tell?"

"But wouldn't it be easier if I helped?"

"It might be. Then again, it might not." She stepped farther into the room. "What I'm saying, Zach, is that you need to stop what you're doing and leave."

He placed the steamer on the floor. His face showed his disappointment. "I'm sorry," he said. "I just thought you'd want my help."

"No, I don't."

"No, never?"

She shook her head. "Don't put words in my mouth."

Brianna looked in horror as a large section of wallpaper began to peel away from the wall. "Now look what you've done."

She wagged a finger at the wall.

Zachary beamed. "Isn't that great? It's almost coming off by itself."

"No, Zach. I wasn't going to do this now. Later, but not now. I have to work first. I have calls to make, and I can hardly make them with pieces of wallpaper falling on my head."

His eyebrows rose. "You want me to reglue it?"

Before she could answer, she saw Margaret enter the room.

"See what he's done?" Brianna croaked.

Margaret eyed the wall. "Awesome. Good-bye, ugly wall-paper."

Brianna fought exasperation. "But *I* want to be the one to take the wallpaper down."

Margaret leaned against the doorjamb. "Why?"

"Because it's mine."

Margaret shot her an odd look and spun on her heels. "I think I hear the phone ringing. Brring, brring."

Brianna knew it wasn't. She also knew she was behaving foolishly—and in front of Spike, too—but something inside her seemed to take over.

"Zach," she said, her voice strained, "please take your stuff and go."

He didn't hesitate. "I'm on my way."

She watched him gather his belongings and stuff them into his canvas bag.

"You haven't changed a bit, Brianna," he said as he headed for the door. "You're as stubborn and childish as you ever were."

She watched the door slam shut. "And you don't know when to stop pushing, Zachary Wilson. You never have and you never will."

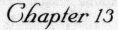

Chapter 13

Zachary stood beside his truck and fumed. He would have kicked the tires, but that would have only hurt his foot—and made him look foolish to the few people crossing the parking lot.

Of all the unthinking things she's said to me over the years, this latest takes the cake. He should have known better than to offer Brianna his help. She'd always fought him when he did that. Always. Some people were just plain ungrateful, he reckoned. And she was one of the most ungrateful ones he'd ever met. He wished he'd never bumped into her.

But even as the thoughts entered his head, he knew he didn't mean them. Perhaps he should have asked her permission. Surely even Brianna would have realized that he only wanted the best for her.

He tossed the canvas bag into the truck bed and took off for his own office. He did have work to do—she was right about that. And he would do it and not think about her—if that was possible.

When he arrived at his office, he changed his clothes in the tiny bathroom in the hallway. By ten he'd almost forgotten about her. By eleven he was thinking about her again. At noon he ate lunch at his desk. It was well past five before he thought of her again, and that was when he reached his house. Then she filled his mind just as he knew she would. Bummer.

Sami greeted him with yelps of joy. "There," he said as he released her from her pen. "You'd let me help you, wouldn't you, girl?"

Sami wagged her tail and took off into the bushes. Zachary waited until she returned, then sat for a while on his patio looking at his mountain as the sun sank behind it. He continued to sit, Sami at his side, until the cold began to seep into his bones. Then he went inside and retrieved his phone messages.

"Hi, Zach. It's Suze. Where have you been? I haven't seen you in a while. How about a movie this weekend? There's a chick flick playing at the Oak Ridge theater. Care to take me? You know where to find me. I'll be waiting."

He pressed the DELETE button and fed Sami. Then he microwaved leftover meatloaf and ate it sitting in the banquette staring at his wall.

Brianna watched Zach stomp out of her office. She heard the front door slam shut. The building seemed to shudder from the force, and the wallpaper strip that had freed itself began to come off, exposing a huge oblong patch of bare wall. "Oh, ugh."

Brianna found a roll of clear tape and taped the wallpaper to the wall, smoothing out the rough edges. "There," she said as she examined her work. "You'll do until I can get to you when *I'm good and ready.*" She maneuvered behind her desk and began to make telephone calls. By lunchtime she'd calmed down enough to call Sophie. "How are you doing?" she asked.

"Great. I'm exhausted, but fine."

"I can't wait to see the baby."

"When are you coming by?"

"When's a good time?"

"How about this afternoon?"

"What time?"

"Three would be good. I'll be through feeding by then, I think."

"Can't wait."

"How's Spike working out?"

"Too early to tell. I've kind of left her on her own today."

"She'll do anything you tell her to. She's good that way."

"I'm sure we'll get along like a house on fire."

"See you later."

Brianna hung up. It was unfair of her not to train Margaret. She got up from her desk and entered the reception area, where Margaret was reading a novel. "Let me show you around properly," Brianna said.

"I was wondering when you would tell me where you kept things."

"Sorry about that."

"How's it going with you and Zach?" Sophie asked after Brianna had returned her baby to her.

"Not good. We had a fight."

"Hmm. Over what?"

"He came to my office this morning and began to remove the teddy bears."

Sophie started to laugh. "Oh, what a prince among men he must be."

Brianna made a face. "Actually, I told him off and asked him to leave."

"I hope he's coming back."

Brianna shook her head. "I don't think he will. I wasn't very nice."

Sophie *tsk*ed. "You'll make it up with him tomorrow."

"Tomorrow?"

"The class. Surely you're not going drop out of 'How to Repair Bad Decisions Made Years Ago'?"

"But he'll be there."

"Let's hope he is and you can tell him how sorry you are you behaved badly."

"But I'm not sorry. He shouldn't have done what he did."

"Which was what exactly? Offer to help you remove your silly wallpaper?"

"He should have asked me first."

"Probably. But there are worse things, Brianna."

"But he always did that to me. He always took over. He's pushy."

"He was trying to help."

"Pushy."

"Okay, pushy. Tell him you're sorry."

Brianna felt herself begin to pout. "I can't."

"Then there's nothing more to be said. Perhaps you really are meant to remain single. If you behave this way over wallpaper, imagine how you'll behave when it's over something really serious, like a sick child."

"You don't understand."

"I think I do."

"I have to go."

"Thank you for the gift."

Brianna hugged Sophie. "I'll think about what you said."

"This time, don't take twelve years."

Brianna laughed. "You're a very lucky woman."

"Luck has nothing to do with it." Sophie released Brianna and pushed her toward the door. "Take care of Margaret for me. She's had a rough time of it. But she has a great heart."

"Doesn't everyone?"

"You have one, too, Brianna. You just sometimes forget you do."

Chapter 14

Zach arrived for the class with no time to spare. He'd made the decision to complete Andrea's course in spite of his fight with Brianna. If she was there, he would apologize. He'd made that decision, too. He had no illusions about her accepting his apology. He knew she could be stubborn—childish sometimes. It was the way she was. He would love her anyway.

He entered the room and looked for Brianna. He found her waiting with the rest of the students for Andrea's instructions.

Andrea glanced at her watch, then clapped her hands. Her students fell silent.

"Class," she said, "it's time to begin. The wallpaper has been removed." She gestured. "The wall surface needs to be prepared for paint, and for this you'll need your putty knives, which I hope you've purchased.

"You'll notice I've placed buckets of soapy water and sponges around the room. Our job this evening is to clean and prepare the wall for paint. We've already discussed this, so consider this a reminder."

Zach watched Brianna locate a section of wall and stand in front of it. He joined her. "Hi," he said.

She nodded. "Zach."

"I'd like to apologize for my behavior the other day. I shouldn't have marched into your personal space like I owned it. I hope you were able to repair the damage."

Brianna dipped a sponge into a bucket of water and squeezed out the excess water. "I was. I accept your apology, Zach."

"Thank you. I appreciate that."

"You should really thank Sophie. She told me to forgive you."

"She's wise beyond her years."

That drew a smile. "I realize, Zach, that half of our problems come from me. I can be stubborn at times. Childish, too."

"And successful."

She laughed. "I suppose. But I also need to apologize. I completely overreacted to your help. I'm trying to learn that a relationship is two people working together. I shouldn't always try to do everything on my own. I also need to work on depending on God more."

"I forgive you, too." He dunked his sponge into the bucket of water and began to work alongside Brianna. "So where do we go from here?"

Andrea's voice interrupted Brianna's response. "Good paint performance depends on good paint adhesion," Andrea boomed. "It's important to make sure the surface you intend to paint is clean. Remove dirt, grime, and dust by washing well. Always start with a clean surface."

Zachary tipped his head at Andrea. "She could be talking about us."

"Allow the surface to dry completely before you spackle and fill holes and cracks in your wall. Use your putty knife to apply the spackle."

Brianna nodded. "She's telling us that we can start over with a clean wall." She turned to face him. "I think I'd like that, Zach."

"Caulk should be feathered as soon as it's applied," Andrea went on. "If stains still show, use a latex or oil-based stain-blocking primer so the stain doesn't bleed through. Always use a top-quality paint."

Zachary reached for Brianna's hand and pulled her close. "I'd be happy to paint walls with you for the rest of my life." He could hardly believe he was saying this to her, but it seemed so right. He wanted to settle down—with Brianna. If he let her go now, ignored what she'd just said, it would be over. He'd never have the chance again. "Do you want that, Brianna?"

He felt her squeeze his fingers. "I'd be happy and honored to remove wallpaper with you for the rest of my life."

Zachary felt a hand on his shoulder. He spun around to find Andrea at his side. "Did I hear a proposal of marriage in this room?"

Zachary looked beyond Andrea's shoulder. The students had stopped working and were looking at him, their expressions curious. Most were smiling. Then he realized he was smiling, too. Perhaps he shouldn't have made this such a public proposal. But he had. He felt warmth spread across his face.

He dropped to one knee. "Brianna," he said, "will you do me the honor of becoming my wife?"

"Stop," someone yelled before Brianna could give him answer. "He needs a ring. Does anyone have one he can use?"

"We have wallpaper. And scissors," Marsha Gooding called out. "Let's make the man a ring."

Brianna grinned and dried her hands on her pants, seemingly oblivious to what was going on around her. "I will be your wife, Zach."

Someone handed him a paper ring, and he slipped it onto her finger. "I guess this makes it official."

"Kiss her," someone yelled.

Zachary rose and took Brianna in his arms. He kissed her gently, then released her to the sound of generous applause.

Andrea wrapped her arms around them. "Would you like to get married in the store? It's becoming quite fashionable. And you can invite the class to your wedding."

JANET BENREY

Janet brings a diverse business background—including experience as editorial director of a small press, a professional photographer, an executive recruiter—to writing and literary representation. With her husband, Ron, she has written seven Christian romantic suspense novels for Barbour Publishing and other publishing houses. Janet operates her own literary agency—Benrey Literary—that represents well-known writers of general and genre fiction and nonfiction books. Over the years, Janet has also been a writing coach and a marketing communications writer. She earned her degree in Communication (magna cum laude) from the University of Pittsburgh. She also is a graduate of York House College in Kent, England, where she studied commerce and languages.

ONCE UPON A SHOPPING CART

by Ron Benrey

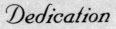

Dedication

To Janet.

*"Forgive us our sins, for we also forgive
everyone who sins against us."*
LUKE 11:4

Chapter 1

Kaitlyn Ferrer stared at the yellow pad in her lap and told herself to stop thinking of her new boss as an idiot. She took a deep breath and began to speak as evenly as she could manage.

"Well now, Julia. . .as I understand my first reporting assignment, you want me to find a home-improvement super-store somewhere in the vicinity of Asheville and investigate the, uh. . .*dating scene* that goes on inside."

"Correct. Women meeting men—and vice versa—in hardware and tool departments seems to be a new social phenomenon across the country. I want you to write a feature story about the trend in western North Carolina—a piece based on personal experience."

Julia Quayle ended her statement with a curt nod that made a lustrous wave ripple through her flowing red hair. Kaitlyn felt a stab of jealousy; her own red hair was too unruly to leave long. And while an array of perfect freckles seemed to complement Julia's glowing complexion, the random assortment of spots on her pale cheeks merely reminded the world that Kaitlyn Ferrer had been out in the sun too long.

Julia must attract men by the dozens. Why should she care about dating?

Kaitlyn forced herself to nod back. Julia obviously believed that she'd come up with a fabulous idea, and it would be difficult to convince her otherwise. Pointing out its many obvious flaws might make Julia angry—which would hardly be wise after less than a week on the job. Kaitlyn decided to change tacks and try a practical argument instead.

"I agree that the story is worth publishing, Julia, but am I really the best writer for this assignment? My strength is investigative reporting. I write articles about political corruption, health-care quackery, corporate financial shenanigans, price gouging by oil companies—"

Julia jumped in. "Exactly! The *Blue Ridge Sun* hired you because you're superb at digging out facts."

"*Unpleasant* facts, Julia. I never probe cheerful activities, like dating."

"In this situation, you're the ideal undercover investigator. A single female, age twenty-eight, new to the Asheville region, who hasn't made any local friends yet. Just the kind of woman who might seek out an unusual way to meet men. *No one* will suspect you're working for a newspaper."

Kaitlyn couldn't stop her eyes from rolling. Julia had pegged her wrong. The very last item on her current agenda was meeting a new man. One of the chief reasons she'd left a good reporting job in Colorado Springs was to move a thousand miles away from the treacherous Keith Batson. It would take several months to get his disloyalty out of her heart and head. Perhaps then she would contemplate a new relationship.

One more try. "Julia, as you know, my prose tends toward blunt. Shouldn't you send a reporter who writes good-natured feature articles?"

Julia shook her head. "Blunt may be just what we need. I want a hard-hitting story that tells the truth. For all we know, the whole concept of singles mingling and meeting in the tool aisle is nothing but a cynical marketing ploy to bring more customers into home improvement superstores."

Kaitlyn let herself sigh. *You're stuck, so why not be gracious?*

"Okay, Julia," she said with a smile. "I'll get right on it."

Kaitlyn discovered four amused people smiling at her when she returned to her corner of the bull pen.

Dale Jones, Kaitlyn's nearest neighbor, a heavyset man of thirty with thin sandy hair and an impressive handlebar moustache, leaned back in his swivel chair. "Your new colleagues deduce from your unhappy expression that Madam Managing Editor refused your request to kill the love-in-the-hardware-aisle article."

Kaitlyn felt startled. How on earth had four other members of the *Blue Ridge Sun* editorial staff learned about her assignment? Dale, a longtime sportswriter who hoped to graduate to the crime beat one day, fancied himself an amateur detective, but he wasn't a mind reader. Julia had just told her about the article—behind closed doors.

Sadie Gibson, a lanky brunette, one of the paper's general assignment reporters, chimed in. "You've just learned a valuable lesson—once our Ms. Quayle makes up her mind, she never budges."

Nate McGuire, the gray-haired and leather-faced copy editor, nodded in agreement. " 'Fraid so. Julia is anything but flexible. You're stuck like the proverbial fly."

Kaitlyn was about to ask if the group had bugged Julia's office when she noticed the extra broad smile on Estella Santacruz's pretty face. Stella, as everyone called her, was the *Sun*'s senior photographer.

"I get it!" Kaitlyn said. "Julia assigned you to take pictures for the article. She told you I would be the writer."

Stella's smile became a nod that transmuted into a scowl. "I have to follow you around the store with our handbag camera and make candid shots of you getting hit on." She added a shrug. "I also tried to get out of the silly job. Julia wouldn't let me loose, either."

Kaitlyn dropped into her chair. "Anybody have any thoughts on where we can find a home superstore that's also a singles' meeting place?"

"Hmmm," muttered Sadie Gibson. "Well, there's a lovely Home & Hearth Superstore in Oak Ridge. If I had a reason to look for men among building supplies, that's where I'd go. However"—she held up her left hand so her new engagement ring sparkled—"Kevin and I have shopped there several times to pick out appliances. It really is a phenomenal place. They sell everything—"

Kaitlyn decided to stop Sadie's rambling. "Moving right along. . . Can someone give me directions to Oak Ridge?"

"I know the way," Stella said. "I'll drive."

"Bless you." Kaitlyn scrawled "H&H Superstore" across the top of her yellow pad. "I presume that Home & Hearth is called a superstore because it's as large as a stadium?"

"A *big* stadium," Stella said.

"In that case, where in the vast interior am I likely to find the dating scene?"

Sadie smirked, then said, "Ask where the barbeques are on display. Where else should a lady go looking for a *new flame*?"

"No way!" Nate spoke up. "I'd try the hardware department. That's where all the *nuts* are located."

"Don't be silly," Dale said. "You need to hang out in the tool department. That's the place to acquire a new *main squeeze*."

Kaitlyn groaned. "What did I do to deserve three punsters in the same room?"

"I am *not* looking forward to this assignment." Kaitlyn unsnapped her seat belt and let out a long, slow breath.

Stella giggled as she set the parking brake of her red Pontiac and turned off the ignition. "You sound like a woman about to undergo a root canal."

"That's the way I feel. The very last thing I want to do is pick up a man tonight."

"Don't worry. The miserable look on your face—along with the negative signals you're sending—will keep every eligible man in the store at least a hundred feet away from you."

"Assuming there are any eligible men shopping for building supplies."

"Well, there's a gentleman I consider eligible." Stella pointed through the windshield at a tall man walking across the parking lot. "I wouldn't mind sharing a tool belt with him."

Kaitlyn looked up in time to glimpse an attractive profile and a neatly trimmed goatee as the man passed under a light pole that had just switched on. Stella continued, "I didn't spot a ring on his finger. He looks like fair game."

"He seems. . .preoccupied."

"That's the way guys get when they approach tools and hardware. It's like little boys going into a toy store. Their eyes glaze over and they walk like zombies."

Kaitlyn reached for her door handle but stopped in mid-motion.

"What's wrong now?" Stella asked.

"I'm not sure I'm appropriately dressed to attract men. Maybe I should have worn my red pantsuit."

"This is Home & Hearth, not a singles' party. Most of the female customers are wearing T-shirts and cutoffs. Your blouse is elegant and your khaki slacks fit you perfectly. You look great." Stella added, "If anyone should complain, it's me. I have to carry a stupid old-lady handbag because the clown who built our hidden camera didn't have any fashion sense."

Kaitlyn had to admit that Stella was right. The other women in sight were wearing ultra-casual clothing. Her ecru blouse and tailored slacks were almost too dressy.

"Tell me once more," she said, "what's my strategy once I'm inside?"

"I don't know why you think I'm an expert at picking up men." Stella grimaced. "I'm three years older than you and still single. However"—she took a few seconds to gather her thoughts—"attaching yourself to a man inside Home & Hearth strikes me as a fairly easy process. You simply cruise the aisles looking for unmarried males who are browsing for items that guys like. Tools. Gadgets. Shiny hardware. You pounce when you see one who strikes you as attractive."

"Pouncing is the part that worries me."

"It's a piece of cake." Stella reached across Kaitlyn and opened the passenger door. "Smile prettily, look bewildered, and ask for his help selecting one of the gadgets he's looking at."

"And try not to laugh in his face, right?"

"Act like a damsel in distress. When he talks, hang on his every word. Put the item he suggests in your shopping cart and thank him profusely."

"What if he doesn't ask for my telephone number?"

"He probably won't the first time around. You have to meet him *accidentally* in another aisle and give him a chance to show off again. That's when he'll feel comfortable enough with you to go beyond talking about hardware."

Kaitlyn groaned. "I will truly hate myself tomorrow morning."

"Of course, nothing you do will make any difference unless God wants you to meet an eligible man."

"*What?*" Kaitlyn didn't mean to raise her voice, but Stella's startling mention of God took her by surprise.

"Well, your case is different—you're doing research for a story—but I'm talking about the women who are really looking for men. It's good for a woman to put herself in situations where she will meet other people, as long as she realizes that the timing is in God's hands."

Kaitlyn didn't know how to respond. She believed in God, but she doubted He would take time from His busy schedule to orchestrate—or discourage—the meeting of two people inside a Home & Hearth Superstore.

"One more thing. . ." Stella said.

"What?"

"Don't look for me. I'll be taking pictures from a distance. You won't even know I'm here."

"I wish I wasn't here."

"Nonsense! It's gonna be great fun."

"Yeah!" Kaitlyn said. "I can hardly wait."

Kaitlyn touched the small brooch she'd pinned near her blouse's left lapel and activated the tiny wireless microphone inside. The mike was designed to broadcast to the voice-operated electronic recorder she carried inside her purse. The gizmo had a six-hour recording capacity, so she planned to use it to capture her thoughts as she walked through the store and also to record any interactions with eligible males she met.

She averted her head so none of the other customers in the entranceway could see her talking softly to her brooch. "7:32 p.m. Arrived at the Home & Hearth Superstore in Oak Ridge. Pushing an empty shopping cart. Will begin in the gardening department. Stella is still outside, taking background photos."

Kaitlyn looked around the Garden Shop and quickly realized her mistake. Single men didn't shop for garden chemicals and plants. She tossed a pair of gardening gloves into the shopping cart—who knew when she might need them—and moved to the garden tools aisle.

Bingo! A lone man, fairly presentable, no wedding ring, looking at a gas-powered hedge clipper.

She ambled toward him, pushing her cart. About ten feet away, she smiled at the man. A woman in tight blue jeans and a halter top stepped in front of the cart and gave Kaitlyn a nasty look.

Rats! He's taken. And he has a protective girlfriend.

Kaitlyn steered her shopping cart around the couple and headed for the cleaning products aisle, staring at the vinyl tiled floor, trying hard to ignore the jolt of embarrassment that made her insides feel like jelly. Was she *that* obvious?

"Good evening, ma'am. Can I help you find something?"

Kaitlyn glanced up. . .and found herself looking at a gray-haired woman of perhaps sixty years who wore a friendly expression. Kaitlyn realized that she'd been lost in thought and hadn't registered the woman's words.

"Pardon?" Kaitlyn said.

The woman touched her hand to a Home & Hearth name badge on her shirt that read MY NAME IS ANDREA. "Can I help you find something in the store?"

"No, thank you. I'm just browsing."

"Really?" Andrea smiled. "Customers rarely browse in a building supply store. They come in knowing exactly what they want."

"Well, I'm just looking around."

Andrea's smile deepened. "Good hunting." She leaned toward Kaitlyn and said, "If *browsing* doesn't do the trick, you might want to sign up for one of the how-to classes I teach. I organize my students in small groups, which is an excellent way to meet men." She reinforced her suggestion with a wink.

Kaitlyn felt herself blushing. *No job is worth this much humiliation.*

"Cruising the aisles for men is getting *boring*!"

Kaitlyn leaned against a cardboard display that declared

the virtues of a new robotic vacuum cleaner, hunched her shoulders, and continued to speak into her brooch. "I've made one full loop of Home & Hearth and didn't encounter any unattached eligible males. My shopping cart is getting heavy to push. I'm tired, cranky, and thoroughly fed up. There has to be an easier way than this to meet a mate."

She'd lost sight of Stella Santacruz and wondered if the *Sun*'s photographer was still following her around the superstore.

Kaitlyn turned the corner, leaving the home appliance aisle and entering lighting fixtures and ceiling fans. She couldn't help blinking when she looked up at the large array of brightly lit chandeliers and hanging lamps and consequently failed to notice another shopping cart directly ahead of hers.

The loud *clang* of the collision took her breath away.

"Oh my—I'm so sorry," Kaitlyn murmured. As her eyes reacclimated, she realized that the tall man with the goatee was looking at her with a mixture of amusement and curiosity.

"No need to apologize," he said. "You hit my shopping cart, not me."

Kaitlyn quickly decided that Stella had been right about the man, too; he seemed worth meeting. He stood about six-one, with an athletic build and a confident stance. She guessed his age at just over thirty. She peeked at his hands, verified the absence of a wedding ring, and noted a neat manicure. They were the hands of someone who worked in an office rather than outdoors. His clothing—designer polo shirt and designer jeans—reinforced her impression that he was a professional of some sort. In short, a clean-cut, law-abiding citizen. And handsome, too.

He seemed to be sizing her up as quickly. His big brown

eyes glanced at her hands and finally settled on her face.

Ask him a question about hardware. To Kaitlyn's astonishment, a lighting-related question popped into her mind. "You seem to know your way around lighting fixtures," she said. "Can I ask you a question?"

The man seemed nonplussed for a moment. He recovered quickly. "I'll try."

"There are signs all over the place that read, 'This fixture uses halogen bulbs.' What makes halogen bulbs special?"

The man grinned. "Now that's a question I *can* answer. The halogen gas inside the bulb enables the filament to burn hotter and still last a long time. That makes halogen bulbs brighter and more energy efficient."

"I see." She nodded. "Thank you." He seemed encouraged. Perhaps Stella's strategy was working.

To her surprise, he went on. "The most common halogen gases are argon, xenon, and krypton."

"That's fascinating," Kaitlyn fibbed. *Time to change the topic of conversation.* "Are you also shopping for lamps?"

"Nope. I need a ceiling fan." He frowned. "Except I don't understand how they work."

"They go round and round."

"I figured out the turning part," he said dryly. "But these fans are all reversible. Why do they need to work in two directions?"

Kaitlyn laughed. "Believe it or not, I know the answer. During the summer, you set the fan to blow downward so you feel a cooling breeze. During the winter, you reverse the blades so that the fan circulates warm air upward through the room but doesn't make you feel cool."

"I get it! Up during the winter, down during the summer."

She nodded. "Are you going to buy a fan?"

"I was. . .until I saw there are about fifty different styles. Now I'm not sure which will match my living room." He added, "Are you going to buy a lighting fixture?"

"Uh. . .I have sort of the same problem," she said quickly. "There are so many fixtures on display that I'm not sure which one I want."

He looked at his watch. "It's getting late. I suppose I should head for home."

"Me, too," she replied, wishing Stella had told her what to do in this situation.

Say something. If you don't, he'll walk away. "Do you come here often?" The words flew out of her mouth before she could stop them. *Rats! What a stupid thing to say!*

"Umm. . .not often. Only when I need a fan or something."

The expression on his face abruptly changed. He looked as embarrassed as she felt. He took a deep breath, then said, "My name is. . .ah. . .Jake Sinclair."

Kaitlyn felt on solid ground for the first time since she'd rounded the corner. She was ready with a response. She extended her right hand. "It's a pleasure to meet you, Jake. My name is Dori Johnson."

Stella had come up with the false name during their drive to Oak Ridge. "Anyone you meet is bound to ask for your name and phone number and probably where you live," she had said. "You need a phony name, a false number, and a fake address on the tip of your tongue."

Right again, Stella.

Jake, too, seemed to regain his former confidence. "I find myself in the mood for a caffe latte. The monster bookstore next door has an awesome coffee shop. Would you like to join me?"

Kaitlyn thought about it and couldn't find any reason why she should refuse. "That sounds like a grand idea. I'd love to." Out of the corner of her eye, she caught a glimpse of Stella standing at the head of the aisle, her large, ugly handbag perched in the child seat of her shopping cart.

Kaitlyn decided to risk a surreptitious wave. *Meeting men at Home & Hearth is a lot easier than I thought it was going to be.*

Kaitlyn noticed that her mouth felt dry and quickly figured out why. For the past fifteen minutes, she had done most of the talking while Jake Sinclair smiled, nodded, and occasionally spoke friendly "uh-huhs."

Of course you're long-winded. It's been ages since you've chatted with a man who's a good listener.

Kaitlyn sipped her mega caffe latte. The truly amazing thing, she decided, was not her verbosity this evening but rather her ability to make up Dori Johnson's life on the fly. It had been an exercise in improvising. Her approach had been to mix truth about herself with falsehood.

Dori grew up in Phoenix, Arizona—as had Kaitlyn.

Dori held a degree from the School of Journalism and Mass Communication at the University of Colorado—as did Kaitlyn.

Dori had become a freelance writer who worked for a variety of different clients, mostly nonprofit organizations—much like Kaitlyn's college roommate, Jessica Deale.

Dori had recently moved to the area from Colorado Springs and rented a great apartment in downtown Asheville. Kaitlyn in fact had found a delightful apartment in Black Mountain, an arty town about fifteen miles east of Asheville.

Dori enjoyed skiing and hiking on mountain trails. Kaitlyn would have refused to move to western North Carolina if these activities hadn't been available within reasonable driving distance.

She had talked. . .and talked. . .and talked, yet Jake had seemed captivated by every minor detail and never once yawned or looked away.

Kaitlyn took another sip from her tall Styrofoam cup. "So much for me, Jake. What do you do for a living?"

"Surprisingly, I'm a wordsmith, too. I write advertising copy."

"Does that mean you work for an advertising agency?"

He nodded. "A small one in Asheville named the Lenard Company. We have an office downtown, on O'Henry Drive. Most of our clients are industrial companies, so most of my writing ends up on trade-show exhibits and in technical magazines." He suddenly laughed.

"What's so funny?"

"I just realized that we both write dull copy for specialized audiences. Chances are you'll never read anything I write and I'll never see any of your stuff."

Kaitlyn stared into bits of foam in the bottom of her cup. *You definitely won't want to read my next article.* She drove the thought out of her mind and asked, "Do you live in Asheville?"

"Indeed I do. On Biltmore Park Drive." He peered at her. "Do you know the area?"

"I'm afraid not."

"That's surprising. It's only a few blocks from where you live."

"Really?" Kaitlyn fought to keep her voice from squeaking. "I haven't had a chance to learn much about Asheville. Completing two assignments and furnishing my apartment have kept me busy every minute of the day."

She noticed a flash of motion behind Jake and looked up to see Stella waving at her. Stella tapped her wristwatch, pantomimed a deep yawn, and then pointed toward the parking lot.

Yikes! I forgot that Stella provided the transportation this evening. Kaitlyn glanced at her own watch. Almost nine thirty. Time to bring her impromptu "date" to an end.

"Goodness, Jake! I had no idea it was so late. I'm about to turn into a pumpkin."

An unhappy look crossed his face. "Tomorrow is a workday, isn't it?"

"A busy one for me."

"Same here." He leaned across the table. "I really enjoyed talking to you."

"Even though I didn't let you get a word in edgewise?"

"Tell you what—*next time* I'll bend your ear. I'd like to do this again. Soon."

Kaitlyn started to say, *That would be lovely,* but then she remembered that she wasn't on a real first date. Chatting with Jake Sinclair was merely research for a newspaper article. "Thank you for being such a good listener, Jake."

He unclipped a digital telephone from his belt. "This gadget is also my electronic address book." He murmured, "Dori Johnson," as he tapped the stylus against the screen, then he smiled at her. "We've come to the part where I ask for your telephone number."

Kaitlyn felt an unexpected twinge of regret. She'd also

enjoyed the hour she spent talking with Jake and drinking coffee. Everything about him seemed right. If she'd been in the mood to meet a man, he'd be just the kind of man she'd want to meet. Kaitlyn heaved a quiet sigh and then gave him the false phone number that Stella had invented.

What a pity. I'll never see Jake Sinclair again.

Chapter 2

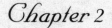

I don't care how much you disagree with me," Estella Santacruz said adamantly. "The goofy look in your eyes *proves* that you fell for the man you met last night."

Kaitlyn ignored the three large photos lying on her desktop, but she couldn't disregard the print that Stella had taped to the front of her computer monitor. *Goofy* was the perfect word to describe the puppy-dog gaze of adoration on her face. *It's too soon for me to feel that way about a man again.*

Kaitlyn yanked the print loose, tore it in quarters, and lobbed the four pieces into her wastebasket.

Stella uttered a mocking, "Ha!" and dropped into Kaitlyn's visitor chair. "My inkjet printer can turn out copies faster than you can tear them up. More to the point, throwing a tantrum doesn't change the simple—and obvious—fact that you like Jake Sinclair."

"You're wrong!" Kaitlyn gave an exaggerated shake of her head. "I was acting last night, playing a role. Of course I had to pretend that I liked him."

"No one is that good an actress. Your expression in these

pictures is the real thing. You care for Jake Sinclair. End of story."

Kaitlyn rolled her chair back from her desk. "Okay, let's assume there's a glimmer of truth in what you say."

"Hooray." Stella raised her hands in a gesture of triumph.

"What difference does it make if I do like him? He's an advertising man—the kind of guy who reads the newspaper every day. He'll see my story, realize that I gave him a false name and number, assume that I took advantage of him, and tell me to buzz off." Kaitlyn let herself frown. "We don't have a future together. End of the *whole* story."

"Not necessarily! Let's say that I retouch the photos I took so that we can't see his face clearly. And let's say that you write glowing things about the man you met at Home & Hearth. Jake might end up liking the finished article."

"I don't think the male brain works that way. He'll feel used—no matter what I write about him." Kaitlyn let her eyes settle on the wall over Stella's shoulder. "And what about the lies I told? I can't retouch those out of his memory."

"Then switch to plan B. Call Jake right now and tell him the truth. Explain that you really had a good time last night but that you also have a job to do. Jake seems smart enough to grasp why an investigative reporter needs to use an alias. He'll understand why you didn't think you could give him your real name until after the article was published."

Kaitlyn shook her head. "Even if he understands my reasons, he'll never forget that I lied to him."

"Now you're being melodramatic."

"Actually, I'm being realistic. It doesn't make any difference what I say today; the fact is that I misled him last night. Our relationship started off with a volley of untruths. Why would he ever trust me again?"

"Maybe because he likes you as much as you like him?" Stella slid one of the photographs closer to Kaitlyn. "Check out the look on Jake's face. My mother would describe it as 'gaga.'"

"Gaga?"

"A perfectly good word that means carried away by love."

"Stop talking crazy! No one said anything about *love*."

Stella tapped the photograph with her index finger. "My mother also says that a picture is worth a thousand words."

"Speaking of words"—Kaitlyn rolled her chair back to her desk—"Julia Quayle expects to see two thousand well-chosen words in forty-eight hours. She wants to run the article in the 'Weekend People' section. I'd better get cracking."

"What about Jake Sinclair and you?"

"Think of us as two shopping carts that passed in the lighting fixture aisle."

Stella spoke a Spanish phrase that Kaitlyn felt happy she didn't understand.

"I love your article!" Julia gushed, loudly enough to make Kaitlyn, who didn't enjoy effusive praise, feel uncomfortable. "Your first story for the *Blue Ridge Sun* will hit a home run. It's comprehensive, compelling, and beautifully written. I especially like the bit about the shopping cart collision." Julia gave a signature toss of her long red hair. "We'll make it the lead article. Give it star billing."

Kaitlyn managed to smile. "I'm glad you like the piece, but

keep in mind that I had lots of help from Sadie Gibson. She located the two men and two women I interviewed about their experiences meeting people in home improvement stores."

"Absolutely. But what makes the article sing is your personal experience at Home & Hearth." Julia peered at Kaitlyn over her reading glasses. "Tell the truth—admit you were wrong for arguing with me the other day."

Kaitlyn returned an easy nod. "I admit that I enjoyed writing an optimistic investigative article. I'd never tackled this kind of story before."

"Pushing the envelope is a good thing."

"And, ignoring a few embarrassing moments, my evening at Home & Hearth was mostly fun."

"Why *mostly*?"

"Well, I've used many false identities in the past, and I've never minded, because I was going after bad guys. But I can't stop feeling guilty about lying to a nice person."

"Ah. The man you call 'Jon' in the article."

"His real name is Jake Sinclair. I think he'll try to find Dori Johnson." She stared down at her hands. "Of course, he'll stop looking when we run the article and he learns who I really am."

"He'll probably send you a thank-you note. You make 'Jon' sound like the most eligible bachelor in Asheville."

Kaitlyn looked up when someone knocked on Julia's closed door. The door opened before Julia had a chance to say, "Come in." Stella strode into the office, a determined look on her face.

"Stop the presses!" she said with a flourish of her left hand. "You know, I've always wanted to say that."

"What's going on?" Julia asked.

Stella held up the folded newspaper she carried in her right hand. "I have here the latest issue of the *Asheville Gazette*, the *other* rag published in our fair community." Much to Kaitlyn's surprise, Stella didn't give the newspaper to Julia. Instead, Stella tossed the *Gazette* into Kaitlyn's lap. "Take a gander at the feature article on page 3."

Kaitlyn opened the *Gazette* to page 3 and immediately saw a large photograph of Jake Sinclair. Except the caption under the picture announced, "Christopher Taylor is the *Asheville Gazette's* senior investigative reporter." Kaitlyn's eyes moved to the top of the page and read the headline: "NEED A DATE FOR SATURDAY NIGHT? TRY HOME & HEARTH."

Kaitlyn heard a long, low moan. It took her a moment to realize that she was producing the sound. She bounded out of her chair. "The stinker lied to me!"

"Look at it this way," Stella said. "You also lied to him."

"That's different. I was on assignment."

"Apparently, so was he."

Julia spoke up. "Will someone please tell me what's going on?"

Kaitlyn slid the open newspaper along Julia's desktop. "We've been scooped by the *Asheville Gazette*."

Julia read the article quickly, then looked up. "Oh well. They scoop us; we scoop them. Scoops happen because great minds think alike. We'll just have to find a different spin for your story." She added, "Now, you said something about the author lying. Lying about what?"

Kaitlyn looked at Stella. "I can't even think about it. You tell her."

"Tell me what?" Julia asked, her voice beginning to rise.

Stella tapped the photo of Christopher Taylor. "That's the eligible bachelor that Kaitlyn met the other night at Home & Hearth."

Julia looked at Kaitlyn. "This is the man you know as Jon—I mean, Jake Sinclair?"

Kaitlyn nodded.

"Oh boy," Julia said. "Let me get this straight. Christopher Taylor, the *Gazette*'s number one investigative reporter, conned my number one investigative reporter into an undercover interview in a coffee shop?"

Another nod.

Julia glared at Kaitlyn. "How can an experienced professional like you get led down the garden path? Can't you tell when another reporter is taking advantage of you?"

Kaitlyn could almost feel a sheepish smile form on her face. "It didn't dawn on me that he might be a reporter. He was. . .a nice guy."

"A nice guy. . .who liked you and intended to call you back?"

"Yep. He seemed enthusiastic when he asked for my phone number."

Julia turned to Stella. "You tell her. I don't have the heart."

"Tell me what?" Kaitlyn asked.

Stella picked up the newspaper and began to read from the end of the article. "As you would expect, many of the singles you meet cruising the aisles of Home & Hearth are losers—unattractive and uninteresting people, generally desperate for companionship. Most of the women I encountered during my investigation fell into that category. I spent an hour chatting with one of them—a lonely woman, new to town, who told me her life history as we sipped mega caffe lattes. She got my attention inside Home & Hearth by almost running me over with her shopping cart."

Kaitlyn moved behind Stella. "Give me that paper!" She quickly found the paragraph in question and read it twice.

"That miserable, arrogant, lying halfwit!" she shouted. "That no-good, two-timing twerp. I should have killed him with my shopping cart when I had the chance."

Chris Taylor slammed the newspaper on Hank Vandergrift's desktop. "I don't care if you are the managing editor of the *Asheville Gazette*. You had no right to distort the words I wrote."

Chris moved to Hank's visitor chair, sat down, and waited for his boss to respond. Hank finished typing a paragraph on his computer before he turned around.

"*Distort* is much too strong a word for the handful of minor changes I made to the text you submitted," Hank said calmly. "I told you up front when I assigned the story to you that the *Asheville Gazette* management isn't happy about singles meeting in home improvement superstores. We certainly don't want to promote the practice; in fact, one purpose of the article is to discourage local singles who want to give Home & Hearth a whirl. All I did was take a little poetic license to make your article fit our corporate position on the subject."

"No! All you did was make Dori Johnson sound like a loser. You described her as unattractive, uninteresting, and desperate for companionship."

"As I recall, you told me that several of the women you encountered in Home & Hearth fit that grim description."

"*One* woman did, but definitely *not* Dori Johnson. Truth be told, she's the best-looking, most intriguing gal I've met since I moved to Asheville last year. When she reads this article, she'll go ballistic. I'll be on her jerk list forever."

"*If* she reads the article. The lady is new to town, and she's busy, so she probably doesn't subscribe to a newspaper yet. And even if she does, she may have chosen the *Blue Ridge Times* instead of the *Gazette*."

"Dori is a freelance writer, the kind of woman who takes an interest in where she lives. She probably buys *both* newspapers to keep up to date."

"Humph! Why speculate when we can easily learn the facts?" Hank abruptly spun his swivel chair around and began typing "Dori Johnson" on his keyboard. After a few seconds, he said, "Aha!"

"Which means?"

"I guessed right. We don't have a Dori Johnson on our subscribers' list." Another pause. "That's strange—"

"What is?"

"I don't find a Dori Johnson listed in any of the Buncombe County databases we routinely access."

"Big surprise! For starters, Dori is probably a nickname. I'll bet her full first name is Doris or Doreen. Second, she recently moved to Asheville. She probably hasn't switched her telephone service or acquired a North Carolina driver's license or registered to vote."

"I suppose you're right," Hank said with a shrug. "In any case, you've gotten upset without knowing how the lady really feels. Give your new friend a call. Find out if she read the article. If she did and if she's mad at you, put the blame on me.

Tell her that our Asheville Interactions Web site generates a bundle of money for the paper's owners and that your evil boss rewrote your article to discourage superstore romances." He smiled. "I'm sure she'll be dazzled to learn that you're a famous, hotshot investigative reporter."

Chris stood up slowly. "When Dori tells me to get lost, I'll hunt you down like the dog you are and beat the living daylights out of you."

Hank's eyebrows rose to a majestic height. "You can't be serious!"

Chris sighed heavily. "Of course I'm not serious. I need this job." He scowled at Hank. "But I may hire a hit man to throw a whopping big pie in your face."

Chris made a snap decision as he walked back to his desk. He would follow Hank's "advice," call Dori Johnson this morning, explain what happened, and apologize profusely. *I'll do whatever it takes not to lose her.*

He had another, related idea. Why not offer to buy her the best dinner to be had in Buncombe County? He'd been told about a small restaurant in Black Mountain that had a world-class chef. The price was high, but the food was supposed to be unbeatable. "I'll put the bill on my expense account," he muttered. "That's the best way to punish Hank Vandergrift."

He punched Dori's telephone number into his cell phone and was surprised to hear, "We're sorry, but the number you dialed is not in service at this time."

Whoops! Maybe I dialed incorrectly.

Chris tried again and heard the same disappointing message.

Uh-oh! I must have made a mistake when I wrote down her number.

He stared at the bad number, not sure what to do next. An answer popped into his mind. *Maybe Cassie will know what to do.*

Chris headed to the other side of the *Gazette*'s bull pen, to an island of eccentricity in the corner of a routine metal and plastic business office. Cassandra Evans had placed a brick-colored Oriental rug under her old mahogany desk. On the wall behind her head she'd hung a cloth banner that had been used in a recent publicity campaign: THE ASHEVILLE GAZETTE: HOME OF NORTH CAROLINA'S GENUINE BRITISH AGONY AUNT. The shelves of her bookcase were filled, not with books, but with framed photographs of Cassie with local and national celebrities.

Chris had had to ask for a definition of "agony aunt" when he first met Cassie. She had frowned at him. "My word, young man! Where on earth did you receive your education? *Everyone* knows that 'agony aunt' is a colorful alternative for 'advice columnist.' It's a term used on both sides of the Atlantic, although one is more likely to hear it across the pond."

The *Gazette* had imported Cassandra Evans from London, England. She had long raven-black hair, a dark complexion, exotic features, and a hearty English accent that occasionally veered into Cockney intonations. No one knew how old Cassie really was, but estimates in the newsroom ranged from fifty years to more than seventy.

"Cassie, I need a favor."

"For you, my dear, *anything*." She added a sly smile.

"I asked a woman for a telephone number the other night—"

"Blimey! I have competition. Say it isn't so!"

Chris ignored her mock distress and pressed on. "I apparently made a foolish mistake when I wrote the digits down. Is there any way you can help me find the lady?" He handed her a slip of paper with Dori Johnson's name and number.

Chris perched on the end of Cassie's desk. She often received outlandish questions from readers who wanted to remain anonymous, so she'd perfected a host of techniques to locate the correspondents and make sure they were real people. Cassie wasn't about to be fooled into answering a silly question concocted as a prank by a group of college sophomores at a frat house.

Her smile faded as she studied the piece of paper. "The area code is correct, but the prefix—the next three digits—is completely out of whack. We have nothing close in Asheville."

"Like I said—I made a mistake when I wrote the number down."

"I don't think you did. The error involves at least two digits. It seems more likely that Dori gave you a false telephone number." She looked up. "What's more, luv, the name she gave you is probably false, too."

"How do you deduce that?"

"Johnson is the most common name in the United States."

"That proves nothing."

"No, but it's highly suggestive. A good way to invent a convincing counterfeit moniker is to tack an unusual first name in front of a common last name. Cassandra Evans is a brilliant example—and so is Dori Johnson. Add that to an obviously false telephone number, and, well, Bob's your uncle—one must conclude that the lady intended to lead you astray."

"Why would she lie to me?"

"Perhaps she feared you were a serial killer."

"Very funny."

"Then perchance she has another boyfriend. Two inamoratas at the same time tend to be highly inconvenient. I know that from personal experience." She placed the slip of paper on her desk.

Chris picked it up. "There has to be a way to find her," he said.

"My goodness, am I hearing the pain in your voice correctly? Can it be that Christopher Taylor is enamored of this Dori Johnson person?"

"Let's just say that I want to see her again."

"Perhaps you should tell me the whole story. From the beginning."

Chris pulled a chair next to Cassie's desk. "Well, a week ago, Hank asked me to write a story about the singles' scene in home improvement stores."

"You poor man," she exclaimed. "The mind boggles."

Chris laughed. "That's exactly how I felt. Anyway. . ."

Kaitlyn sat down at the small conference table, vaguely worried that the next hour would be a complete waste of her time. *Don't be so skeptical. Your new friends are trying to help you.*

"Are we ready to begin the brainstorming session?" Dale Jones asked.

Sadie Gibson, sitting next to Kaitlyn, said, "Yeah, but Stella hasn't shown up yet. Shouldn't we wait for her to get here?"

"She can join us when she arrives. Until then, we'll have to make do without her."

"In that event," Sadie said, "I'm ready to begin."

"Me, too," Kaitlyn said. She muttered under her breath, "The sooner we begin this silly exercise, the sooner we'll finish."

"The question before us," Dale said, "is how can Kaitlyn restructure her feature article about singles in superstores without doing a complete rewrite? Changing the article has become necessary because the *Asheville Gazette* ran a story that readers might see as similar to Kaitlyn's initial effort." He glanced at Kaitlyn. "Do you agree with that summary statement?"

"Yep." Kaitlyn replied. "That's my problem in a nutshell."

"Good," Dale said. "Who has any ideas?"

Sadie raised her hand. "It seems to me that the *Gazette's* article set out to shoot down the superstore dating scene. I think that Kaitlyn should counter their downbeat article with an enthusiastic piece."

"I agree," Dale said. "I must say that I don't understand their negativity. Kaitlyn had a mostly positive experience."

"That's true," Kaitlyn said.

"And you interviewed several happy shoppers who found love among the paint cans. I don't think Chris Taylor talked to anyone before he wrote his story."

Sadie spoke, this time without raising her hand. "You didn't use names in the first draft. Go back to the four interviewees. Ask permission to tell their stories in more detail."

Dale immediately took over. "The *Gazette* used a stock photograph of Chris Taylor, plus a photograph of the exterior of Home & Hearth. Stella took several candid shots of you walking up and down the aisles and also talking to Chris. I suggest that we include as many photos as possible. That way, your piece will seem much more real than the *Gazette's*."

"Those are all great ideas." Kaitlyn realized that she meant it. *Maybe brainstorming is more valuable than I thought.*

"That's the whole story," Chris said.

"And quite a sordid tale it is." Cassandra Evans moved her bulk backward in her chair. "Apparently you lied to this shining example of womanhood whilst drinking coffee, and then two days later we vilified her in print. Do I have that right?"

"Well. . ."

"I'll take that as an affirmative." She inhaled deeply and continued. "However, despite your rotten behavior—and the insults heaped upon her by the recently published article—you blithely assume that she'll be willing to move ahead with your relationship. All you have to do is find her, whisper a few words of apology, and smile charmingly."

"Even though you put it that way, my answer is yes."

"Hmmm."

"What does that mean?"

"It means that I'm pondering the unfairness of it all." Cassandra made a face. "The unhappy truth is that you may be handsome enough to pull it off. I fear that the average woman in Asheville would be sufficiently taken with your manly appearance and craggy good looks to forgive your trespasses, as my pastor would say." She growled softly.

"Was that a growl?"

"Indeed it was. I am frustrated beyond words by the easy forgiveness granted to pretty people such as yourself."

"So you think an apology from me would work?"

"Yes, blast you, I do."

"Great. Then how do I find her?"

"Aye, there's the rub." Cassie giggled. "I love to drop lines written by William Shakespeare into everyday talk."

"Stick to the point."

"The point, luv, is that you don't have enough information on your silly slip of paper to begin looking for the new love of your life. So get used to it! You may never see her again. Or have the opportunity to apologize." She began to chuckle. "God is in His heaven and all is right with the world—not to mention the Home & Hearth Superstore."

"Thanks loads."

"My pleasure."

"You know, you just gave me an idea."

"I don't believe you." She made a face. "What kind of idea?"

"Home & Hearth has a community bulletin board. It may not work, but it's worth a chance."

"Oh, how I hate pretty people who are also clever boots."

"I'm sorry I missed your brainstorming session this morning."

Stella's loud voice caught Kaitlyn's attention. She looked over her shoulder. "Where were you?"

"Believe it or not, I was at the Home & Hearth Superstore in Oak Ridge."

"Why go there?"

Stella hesitated. Kaitlyn thought she took longer than necessary to answer a simple question. "Uh," Stella finally began, "I needed an odd-sized metric bolt to repair one of my tripods. I hoped Home & Hearth would have it, but they didn't." She added, "However, while I was there, I found a fascinating handwritten message pinned to the community bulletin board. I took a picture of it."

Stella placed a freshly made print in front of Kaitlyn. The ink wasn't fully dry, but the image was crisp and clear:

Dori,

I apologize for the article and for not telling you who I am. I want to see you again.

Chris ("Jake")

Stella continued, "There was a telephone number on the bottom of the message. I think it's a local cell phone number. I wrote it on the back of the print."

"Good heavens," Kaitlyn said, "do you know what this means?"

"Sure. The man likes you, he really wants to apologize, but he doesn't know how to find you."

Kaitlyn shook her head. "I'll tell you what this note means. Christopher Taylor doesn't know who I am. Specifically, he doesn't know my real name or that I work for the *Blue Ridge Sun.*"

"And your point is?"

"We can use his ignorance to our advantage."

"What advantage? Have you forgotten that you like this guy? Can't you see he's doing his best to apologize?"

Kaitlyn smiled at Stella. "Oh, I'll let him apologize. . .after I grind his bones into the dust."

Chapter 3

Kaitlyn Ferrer stood to her full height of five feet, eight inches and held her right index finger aloft in a gesture of determination. "This is a matter of principle and journalistic integrity."

"Even if you feel that way"—Stella frowned with obvious displeasure—"I can't see why you intend to throw away your original article and begin from scratch, including a new set of candid photographs."

"My original piece no longer applies, not after Christopher Taylor used his position as an investigative reporter to insult the women of Asheville. If I don't stand up and confront the bozo, who will?"

"Now you're being melodramatic." Stella paused, then added, "In any case, which king appointed you the defender of womanhood in Asheville?"

"What's wrong with Kaitlyn looking after our interests?" Sadie Gibson asked. "I like the idea of having a defender."

Stella gave a disparaging wave. "You don't need a defender. You have a fiancé."

Kaitlyn ignored the detour. "Let's get back to the problem at hand. The *Gazette* article written by this man was an affront to every female in Buncombe County, don't you agree?"

"All I agree is that you're stretching the facts way too much."

"Not at all. Think of the countless women who push shopping carts up and down aisles every day."

"Most of them are taking care of their families," Stella said. "Only a handful are trying to find men." She glanced at Sadie. "Isn't that right?"

"I've never told anyone this"—Sadie promptly flushed beet red—"but I met Kevin on a Wednesday evening in Wal-Mart."

Stella took her head in her hands. "I give up! This newsroom is a haven for dingbats."

"To the contrary," Kaitlyn said jubilantly. "The ladies of the *Blue Ridge Sun* represent a typical cross-section of Asheville women. Moreover, Sadie's experience proves my point. You can't say she's unattractive, uninteresting, or desperate for companionship. Yet she pursued—and found—a mate at Wal-Mart."

"Actually, Kevin pursued me. We were both in the optical department getting new eyeglasses. He came up to me and said, "You look beautiful blurry—like a ballet dancer painted by Degas.""

"A true romantic," Stella said.

"I told him that his face looked as blank as a crash-test dummy to me."

"Good for you!" Kaitlyn said.

"We both began to laugh, we put on our new eyeglasses, and the rest is history."

"Excuse me!" Stella said. "What does Sadie's experience have to do with Chris Taylor?"

Kaitlyn sat on the edge of her desktop. "It's one more chunk of irrefutable evidence that Mr. Taylor's article is pure baloney. Despite his gloomy pronouncements, good-looking, well-adjusted women *can* meet good-looking, well-adjusted men in superstores."

"And the new article you're developing will explain that fact?" Stella asked.

"Precisely. And also point out that Mr. Taylor is both a chauvinist and a fool."

"Aren't you being revengeful?"

"Not at all," Kaitlyn said. "I'm merely reporting the truth." *And if the truth hurts Chris Taylor, so much the better.*

🔨

"I couldn't create a war room," Kaitlyn said, "because I don't have my own office. But I did find the space for a war wall. As you can see, I've made significant progress gathering information during the past two days." She tapped the three photographs that she'd taped to the patch of blank wall next to her desk. "I found three pictures of Chris Taylor in our files. The yellow sticky notes around the photos contain various interesting facts I've discovered. For example, he's been engaged twice but never married. And he was homecoming king during his senior year at college. He attended the University of Kentucky, by the way, and although I'm loath to admit it, he graduated with honors from the Kentucky's School of Journalism and Telecommunications."

"Smart *and* good-looking," Dale said. "I hate him."

"And well you should!" Kaitlyn said firmly. "He is an exceptionally devious person."

"I know I'm going to regret asking," Stella said, "but in what way is he any more devious than you? The other night at Home & Hearth, you wore a hidden microphone and recorded every word he said. Doesn't that count as devious?"

"I'm glad you mentioned my brooch microphone." Kaitlyn slapped a document that was taped below the photographs. "This is a transcription of part of the conversion I had with Chris Taylor, alias Jake Sinclair."

"I don't want to see it," Stella said.

"Okay, I'll read it to you." Kaitlyn yanked the paper off the wall. "Listen closely to how 'Jake Sinclair' spoke with extreme care, never fully answering my questions. His responses were remarkably clever.

"Dori: 'Where did you live before you moved to Asheville?'

"Jake: 'Not too far from Minneapolis. I think you said you moved from Colorado Springs. When I lived in Minnesota, I really missed the mountains. Did you make use of the mountains in Colorado?'

"Dori: 'Absolutely. I love to ski.'

"Jake: 'That's interesting. I've never skied. Tell me why folks like you consider skiing so much fun.' "

"Yikes!" Stella said. "The man ought to be arrested for saying things like that."

"Don't you get it?" Kaitlyn tried not to sound too exasperated. "He seemed responsive at the time, but he didn't tell me anything about himself. Instead, he repeatedly brought the conversation back to 'Dori Johnson.' No wonder my throat felt dry. He kept me talking all evening."

Dale chuckled. "I think that's on page 1 of the *How to Get a Date* manual. Don't monopolize the conversation. Encourage the woman in front of you to talk about herself and her interests."

"Be that as it may," Kaitlyn said airily, "Chris Taylor manipulated our conversation to achieve his disgraceful purposes."

Stella peered at the war wall, then moved past Kaitlyn for a closer look. "I thought this photo looked familiar. I took it about a year and a half ago—at a charity ball out at the Biltmore Estate."

"I know you did," Kaitlyn said. "In fact, I was going to ask you if you remembered anything about the woman."

"Sorry. I just work the camera. It's up to the reporter to keep track of names and biographical details."

"Well, a note on the back says that her name is Jill Lenard and that she was a copywriter at Higgins & Higgins, a small advertising agency in Asheville."

"Lenard and advertising. . .why does that ring a bell?"

"Jake Sinclair supposedly wrote copy for an advertising agency named the Lenard Company."

"Aha!" Dale laughed. "That's the trouble with telling lies. The details you use as building blocks are often close to the truth."

"Why do you care about Jill Lenard?" Stella asked cautiously.

"I think she was Chris Taylor's girlfriend last year. I may call her." She took the photo off the wall. "The note on the photo reads, 'Jill Lenard moved.' The old phone number was scratched out and a new number written in, this one with an 858 area code." Kaitlyn revolved her swivel chair. "Does anyone know what part of the country has an 858 area code?"

"I'm pretty sure it's San Diego," Dale said.

"Excellent. I'll try her this evening."

Stella let loose a stream of Spanish words that reminded Kaitlyn of Ricky Ricardo yelling at Lucy.

Kaitlyn waited until 9:00 p.m.—6:00 p.m. in California—to call Jill Lenard. There was no reason, Kaitlyn decided, not to call her. After all, Chris and Jill weren't an "item" any longer, as her mother might say.

"Hello."

Kaitlyn thought the voice on the other end of the line sounded sleepy. "Good evening. Is this Jill Lenard?"

"Uh-huh."

"This is Dori Johnson. I'm calling from Asheville, North Carolina."

"Asheville? Have we met?"

"No, but we have a common friend. I found a picture of you standing next to Chris Taylor. I understand that you were once his girlfriend?"

"That's a weird statement to make to a stranger over the telephone."

"Well, Chris asked for my name and number the other evening. I gave them to him but then began to wonder if I'd made a bad decision. I'm a bit concerned about getting involved with a newspaperman. I'm not interested in the details of your relationship, but I'm at a vulnerable time in my life, and I don't want to get hurt by a guy who may treat me. . .ah. . .shabbily."

"What did you say your name is?"

"Dori Johnson."

"How did you get my telephone number?"

"I have a friend who works at the *Asheville Gazette*. Your

new number was in the files."

"That makes sense, I guess. I was well known in Asheville."

"Absolutely!" Kaitlyn swallowed a laugh. Jill had been second-string copywriter at a small advertising agency. That hardly gave her celebrity status.

Kaitlyn heard Jill make a soft whistling sound. "I don't suppose there's any reason not to tell you. Chris is a nice guy who has one blind spot. He tends to put investigative reporting ahead of everything else he does. If you date Chris, be prepared to be stood up if he's working on a great story. Trouble is, he considers all of his stories great stories. I finally got tired of being his *second* love—if you know what I mean."

Kaitlyn understood the problem. There were those in Colorado Springs who claimed that she drove Keith Batson into the arms of another woman by caring more about her career than about him. "I know exactly what you mean."

"Don't tell Chris that I talked about him. We parted amicably. He still sends me a card on my birthday."

"Very considerate."

"Like I said, he's a nice guy." Jill hung up without saying good-bye.

Kaitlyn put down her phone. *Nice—as long as being nice doesn't get in the way of a good story.*

"You're obsessing." Stella pointed an accusing finger at Kaitlyn. "You've been working on the so-called war wall for three whole days. What you're doing is nuts. If you don't regain your senses soon, Chris Taylor will be forced to take out a restraining order against you."

Kaitlyn crossed her arms defiantly as Stella took a step closer to her desk. "Don't be silly! It's not obsessive behavior to do thorough research."

"The Bible tells us there's a time for everything," Stella said. "*Now* is the time for you to forgive Chris Taylor. Put your ideas of revenge behind you."

"I am not being revengeful. I'm merely doing my job. The public has a right to know the truth about the *Gazette*'s star investigative reporter."

Stella sighed loudly. "I acknowledge that he insulted you in his article. But no one except a select few in this newsroom knows that he was writing about you. Forgive what he did and move on."

"I assure you that any insult to me has been both forgiven and forgotten. I'm a firm believer in the wisdom of sticks and stones. . ."

"Baloney! Someone in your position knows that words really can hurt you."

"Please believe me. I'm strong enough to slough off a childish slur."

"Yeah? Well, let's take a closer look. Which of the words that Chris used upset you most?"

"This is a stupid game," Kaitlyn said. She swung her swivel chair to the right, but Stella pulled it back.

"You know you're attractive," Stella said, "and you don't seem desperate for companionship. But I'll bet you *hated* being called uninteresting. Am I right?"

Kaitlyn stared straight ahead and said nothing. If Stella wanted to play shrink, she'd do it on her own.

Stella went on. "You're purposely ignoring the fact that

Chris hurt you deeply. Until you recognize that, you won't be ready to forgive him, and you'll become more bitter with each passing day. I know it's not easy to forgive a hurtful insult—it probably pains you to even think about forgiving Chris—but God will help you if you let Him."

Kaitlyn counted to ten silently. "If you're finished talking about God, forgiveness, and me," she finally said, "let's talk about work. I need you and your hidden camera at Home & Hearth this evening."

Stella's face darkened. "Why?"

"Chris Taylor will be in the lighting aisle at seven thirty to meet Dori Johnson."

"And how do you know that?"

"Dori telephoned him at the *Asheville Gazette* twenty minutes ago and suggested a meeting. She told him that she saw his note on the Home & Hearth community bulletin board."

"Loco!" Stella said softly.

"Crazy like a fox, you mean." Kaitlyn sniggered. "I've got Chris Taylor exactly where I want him."

"Rats!" Kaitlyn said to Stella. "We chose a night when Home & Hearth is having a sale."

"A big sale, judging from the condition of this parking lot." Stella killed the engine and set the parking break. "However, *you* arranged this foolishness, not *we*."

Kaitlyn stepped out of Stella's Pontiac and looked around. The only available parking spots had been near the back of the lot, a football field away from the superstore's front entrance. Lines of shoppers walked toward the building, and a big banner high over the glass doors read ANNUAL "DO IT ON THE CHEAP" SALE, EVERYTHING AT LEAST 20% OFF.

"Chances are," Kaitlyn said, "only a few of these people want lighting fixtures."

"You're not that lucky."

Kaitlyn didn't wait for Stella to remind her to go off by herself and not look back. She made for Home & Hearth, half walking, half jogging, enjoying the cool evening air. What, she wondered, could she do to stop Stella's grousing and complaining? She and Stella had every reason to become good friends, but that wouldn't happen if Stella kept finding fault with everything Kaitlyn did.

"Oh boy," Kaitlyn murmured as she entered Home & Hearth. "They must be giving wrenches away." She pirouetted slowly. Every aisle, every checkout lane, seemed to overflow with people. *How are you going to find Chris Taylor tonight?*

"Dori! I'm over here!"

Kaitlyn turned to her left at the sound of Chris's voice. She spotted him standing near a display of fire extinguishers, waving at her, a happy grin on his face.

Showtime! She stood still as he pushed his way past several people to reach her.

"I'm so glad to see you tonight." Kaitlyn could hear genuine excitement in his voice. "I was—well, worried that you'd decide not to come at the last minute."

"Nothing could have kept me away."

"Really?" He peered at her with an expression full of curiosity. "I wasn't sure if you're mad at me for—"

Kaitlyn finished his sentence. "For the way you described me in the article you wrote for the *Asheville Gazette*."

He nodded. Then grinned. Then nodded again. "For that, and also because I fibbed to you about my name. 'Jake Sinclair' was a nom de plume, a pen name."

"Don't forget the fib about your occupation."

"Oh. Right!" His glance darted toward the floor. "I'm obviously not an advertising copywriter." He hesitated a few seconds, then said, "Can we go somewhere a little less noisy? I'd like to apologize properly and explain something about that miserable article."

"Let's go back to the bookstore," Kaitlyn replied. "I'm in the mood for a caffe latte." She hoped Stella, somewhere behind her, had managed to shoot a photo of Chris Taylor. His contrite expression was worth recording for posterity.

Kaitlyn walked close to Chris as he blazed a trail through the crowd in the front of the store. She noted that other women glanced at her with obvious envy in their eyes. Why not? Chris was a handsome man who moved well—with confidence and contained strength. And he seemed to have his attention wholly on her, repeatedly looking over his shoulder to make sure she was still behind.

He has no idea what you're about to do. Kaitlyn caught herself sighing. She didn't have to go ahead with her plan. She could merely accept his apology and see where the evening led. Except. . .

"Except the stakes are bigger than that," she muttered. "This isn't about you spending time with a good-looking guy."

"Did you just say something?" Chris said over the combination of car noise and chatter outside the superstore.

"Not really."

"Well, in that case, let me ask you a question. I made a

mistake when I wrote down your cell phone number in the coffee shop. Can you tell me your number again?"

Kaitlyn scanned her surroundings. She had planned to do her talking at a quiet table rather than a noisy sidewalk that connected Home & Hearth with several other superstores in the shopping center. But Chris's question forced her to respond now.

She moved in front of him and stopped walking. "I'm not going to give you my telephone number. Not now, not ever."

"What?" Chris look stunned. "But I thought. . ."

"Let's be realistic. Christopher Taylor, alias Jake Sinclair, is a snake. I forgive you for your article, but I can never trust you again."

"Wait. You have to hear me out. You don't understand—"

Kaitlyn kept talking. "I don't fault you for using a pen name, as you call it. I'm sure every investigative reporter does the same thing. No, your real sin was lying about me in a way that you knew would cause me pain. I'm a big girl, but I'll tell you, those words you wrote knocked the tar out of me. I don't claim to be the prettiest or most interesting woman in town, but your article hurt, even though I've been pretending to my friends that it hasn't."

"Look, Dori, that's what I want to talk to you about." Chris began to speak quickly and emphatically. "You have to understand the way a newspaper works. I'm a reporter, not the editor. Please let me explain what happened."

Kaitlyn let her jaw jut out. "Trust me, I *know* how a newspaper works. And I'm not the only woman in Asheville who deserves an explanation and an apology. I'll bet that dozens of women have browsed the aisles of Home & Hearth hoping they would meet a man. Imagine how your article made them feel."

"Dori, all I need is two minutes to tell you the full story."

"I don't do stories from Chris Taylor anymore." She took two steps toward the superstore, then spoke over her shoulder. "There's a *real* man at Home & Hearth I have to chat with this evening. Good-bye, Mr. Taylor." She moved into the crowd, feeling an ache in her heart and a chill in her stomach.

It had to be done. I didn't have a choice.

Chris slammed the door to Hank Vandergrift's office with sufficient force to make the wall shudder.

The managing editor of the *Asheville Gazette* looked up at Chris and said wearily, "I assume you want to talk some more about the Home & Hearth article."

Chris moved closer to Hank's desk. "I'm tired of being blamed for your words. My inbox is full of complaints, and last night I. . . Well, never mind what happened last night." He took a deep breath. "You have to fix the problem. The best way to start is to publish a retraction."

"Actually, I plan to label it an apology." Hank added, "Sit down. You can help me write it."

Chris sat down. He took a few moments to digest what his boss had said. "You agree with me? I don't have to threaten you with quitting?"

"I also received a bunch of letters and e-mails complaining about the article. My total is about fifty—at last count." Hank tipped his head toward a stack of papers about an inch high on his desktop. "I seem to have riled up the women of Asheville. I think it's time to eat some crow."

Chris reached for one of the blank yellow notepads stacked on Hank's desk. "I'd be delighted to help you prepare an extra large portion."

Kaitlyn studied the collection of photographs that Stella had spread across her desk. "I like the second one best. You really captured his goofy expression."

"That's heartbreak, not goofiness. Chris Taylor was devastated when you left."

"I really doubt that. However"—Kaitlyn picked up the print—"this will really complement the story I wrote. My working title is REAL MEN OF ASHEVILLE—DON'T OVERLOOK THE HOME & HEARTH DATING SCENE." She smiled at Stella. "But I'm sure Julia will come up with a less controversial headline."

Stella moaned.

"What's wrong?" Kaitlyn asked.

"I know you're going to read the opening to me. I thought I'd start expressing my pain before you begin."

Kaitlyn laughed. "As a matter of fact, here goes." She picked up a sheet of paper and began to read aloud:

> *As anyone who reads Asheville's other newspaper knows, the man in the photo on this page is an investigative reporter for the* Asheville Gazette. *However, the other evening, in Home & Hearth, he introduced himself to me as "Jake Sinclair," and I introduced myself to him as "Dori Johnson."*
>
> *Strange as it may seem, we were both engaged in similar research—looking into the dating scene inside home*

improvement superstores. But at that point, our similar activities become quite dissimilar.

While I had a good experience at Home & Hearth, Mr. Sinclair came away unhappy because the only women he met that evening were "unattractive, desperate for companionship, and uninteresting," to quote the recent story he wrote.

It's difficult to know what kind of woman would survive Jake Sinclair's scrutiny, but I did discover that other men have other opinions. For example, I chatted with Marc Goodson, Home & Hearth's security director. "I walk the store often," he told me, "and see lots of people browsing in our aisles. When I spot a woman who's dressed up, who isn't actively searching for a hardware item, I assume she's come to the store for social reasons. Are these women unattractive? Definitely not. Are they uninteresting? I certainly don't think so. Are they desperate for companionship? No more than me or you. Aren't we all looking for someone to love?"

Marc goes on, "I know it sounds foolish—meeting people next to cans of paint or alongside a power nail driver—but apparently a woman who knows her way around tools and hardware is irresistible to a man. I think it's great that we're helping to make Carolina carpenter brides."

Ladies, that's a real man talking—not some self-absorbed pretty boy who obviously thinks he's God's gift to the women of Asheville and is happy to insult us in print.

Kaitlyn smiled as she dropped the sheet of paper on her desktop.

"Stop grinning like a loon," Stella said. "The opening isn't *that* good."

"I was thinking about Marc Goodson. He's a real hunk. Pity I didn't meet him the other evening."

"Julia actually let you get away with it?" Kaitlyn heard the pitch of Stella's voice rise steadily as she spoke her question.

"Julia knows it's time for me to move on to a real investigative reporting assignment," Kaitlyn replied. "I think she was happy to see a finished article. She plans to run it in tomorrow's edition."

"Even though you made Chris Taylor seem like a dimwit?"

"She had no trouble with anything I wrote about Chris. I think Julia enjoys taking an occasional swipe at the competition." She smiled. "In this case, the man deserved it."

"I wonder. . ."

"What do you wonder?"

"When you'll begin to regret your article."

Kaitlyn made a face. "What's to regret? Every word in my article is the absolute truth."

"I admit it!" Kaitlyn said to Sadie Gibson. "I slept late this morning. That's no reason to give me a strange look."

"Uhhh. . ." Sadie began to say something but ended by shaking her head. "You're absolutely right. Sorry." She stared intently at her computer monitor.

"What's going on?" Kaitlyn asked.

"Nothing. Absolutely nothing." She kept looking at the

glowing screen. "However, I think you can stop defending the women of Asheville, North Carolina. Your work is done."

"Sadie, stop being cryptic. What are you trying to tell me?"

Sadie gave another shake of her head. "I can't do it."

"But I can!" Stella strode into the bull pen. "Sadie doesn't want to tell you that your Home & Hearth article went down the wrong road and that you'll soon feel like a total fool."

"I beg your pardon!"

"I have here today's *Asheville Gazette*. The paper apologized for its gaffe."

"Wonderful!" Kaitlyn swung her right fist victoriously. "My article will have even more impact."

"Not quite." Stella opened the *Gazette* to the editorial page. "The paper published three letters of complaint—two from women, one from a man—expressing annoyance, I quote, at 'Mr. Taylor's chauvinistic and insulting comments.' Let me read you the paper's response."

Stella spread the open paper on Kaitlyn's desk. "The headline is 'WE APOLOGIZE!' The article goes on: 'The *Gazette* acknowledges that the article published beneath Christopher Taylor's byline conveyed the impression that Mr. Taylor was critical of the women he met at Home & Hearth. In fact, the article as published does not convey Mr. Taylor's experience or feelings. During the editing process, significant changes were made to the words Mr. Taylor actually wrote. These changes distorted his observations and caused many readers pain. The editors deeply regret the actions they took and apologize to both Mr. Taylor and to many lovely women of Asheville who shop at the Home & Hearth in Oak Ridge.'"

Kaitlyn felt wobbly. She dropped into the chair behind her

desk. Her heart had begun to thump, and for some reason she had stopped breathing. She managed to croak, "You mean Chris *wasn't* responsible?"

"Nope. I think he tried to tell you that the other night, but you wouldn't let him get a word in edgewise."

"But. . .but. . .it makes no sense. Why would the editor of the *Gazette* change the words Chris wrote so significantly?"

Stella grimaced. "As I understand it, the *Gazette* operates a Web site for singles called Asheville Interactions. Apparently, the managing editor was concerned that male subscribers might leave the site and go to Home & Hearth instead."

"How do you know that?" Kaitlyn asked.

"Uh. . .it's common knowledge," Stella said quickly.

"Well, I sure didn't know it," Sadie said.

"Look, why the editor did it is water under the bridge," Stella said. "What matters is that the *Gazette* has apologized. Case closed."

"Oh boy," Kaitlyn said softly. "I goofed, didn't I?"

"Big-time. It's too late to shout, 'Stop the presses!' The trucks are carting today's edition around town as we speak."

"I feel like a total jerk." Kaitlyn went on before Stella could respond. "Don't say it! Don't even think about saying, 'I told you so.'"

"*Moi?* Say something as tacky as 'I told you so'?" Stella chuckled. "Now that I think about it, I told you so about a thousand times."

Kaitlyn covered her face with her hands. No way did she want anyone to see that she'd begun to cry.

Chapter 4

Kaitlyn tapped on Julia Quayle's open office door and asked, "Did any new comments come in today?"

Julia glanced up from a stack of galley proofs spread across her desk. "I'm afraid not. I'd say that your piece has run its course."

"So the grand total of reader reaction to my article on shopping-cart romance is two measly letters and five e-mails?"

"*Six* e-mails. All of the comments we received during the past week were positive. That's not bad, considering—"

Kaitlyn finished Julia's sentence. "Considering that the *Gazette* published an apology the same day my article ran."

Julia shrugged. "What can I say? Timing is everything in the newspaper biz. You know that."

Kaitlyn sighed. "Yeah, but I still feel foolish getting scooped twice by Christopher Taylor."

"You may have been scooped, but the *Blue Ridge Sun* came out *way* ahead. The scuttlebutt is that the *Gazette* received several dozen complaints about Chris's story, lost two major advertisers, and may have alienated a thousand female readers."

Kaitlyn nodded. Julia was right. Women across Asheville would remember the *Gazette*'s foolish article for years—and think of Chris Taylor as one of the city's leading chauvinist jerks. Her own experience proved the point: Her modest infatuation with Chris Taylor, aka Jake Sinclair, was fading quickly. *Give me another two weeks and he'll be a distant bad memory.*

"Well, if you put it that way. . . ," Kaitlyn said. "Since I seem to have scored a competitive coup, how about giving me a nice, juicy scandal to investigate? I'm getting bored editing other reporters' writings."

"Funny you should ask. I have a new assignment you'll enjoy. Two months ago, our county commissioners appointed a task force to improve homeland security in Buncombe County. I'd like you to prepare an in-depth report. Tell our readers how the task force is doing—and whether we're safer because it exists." Julia added, "You can begin this afternoon. The task force plans to holds a ninety-minute public session at 3:00 p.m. every Wednesday at the Buncombe County Courthouse, in the same meeting room that the county commissioners use. The first one is today."

"Can I give you a hug?"

"I'd rather you write me a great article."

"Consider it done. I may need Stella to take pictures."

"She's yours."

Kaitlyn felt exhilarated as she dropped into the chair behind her desk. *No more fluff. No more silly feature articles. I'm back to solid investigative reporting.*

The elegant panelists' table—a curved affair made of handsome walnut—surprised Kaitlyn. So did the dark gray backdrop that spanned the front wall and the well-padded theater-style seats for the onlookers. She had expected less sumptuous furnishings in a courthouse meeting room.

She took a seat in the back of the large room. Her strategy today would be to listen—to watch the members of the task force in action. She'd ask questions—and have Stella take pictures—at future meetings, once she understood the capabilities and interests of the four men and three women who were chatting together on the dais, waiting for the clock to reach three.

Kaitlyn counted about a dozen other individuals scattered throughout the room. Most of them looked like businesspeople who hoped to sell homeland-security products and services to Asheville. But she recognized a reporter from a local TV station.

Another reporter!

A sudden chill tore through her body. What if the *Asheville Gazette* had sent Chris Taylor to cover the same task force?

You should have thought of that earlier.

Kaitlyn gulped several raspy breaths.

Why are you panicking? You're bound to run into Chris Taylor sooner or later.

She stared at her lap and drove herself to think through the obvious. They were both reporters doing similar jobs in a small city. Of course they would cover the same stories in Asheville from time to time. Of course they would end up at the same news events.

And what of it? He's part of your past, not your future.

"In fact," Kaitlyn murmured softly, "our past is hardly worth recalling. One impromptu 'date' when we spent part of an evening together drinking coffee." *No wonder I've been able to forget him so easily.*

She began to whistle the chorus from "I'm Gonna Wash That Man Right Outta My Hair" and lifted her eyes at the exact moment that Chris Taylor walked into the room. He froze in the side doorway, perhaps twenty feet away, when he saw her, then peered at her intently through a startled expression.

She could almost hear his thoughts as he, too, remembered their identical occupations and a look of understanding washed across his face. He turned away and walked quickly to a seat on the other side of the room.

Kaitlyn felt her cheeks begin to burn. What had just happened? How could she explain her conflicting emotions? On one hand, she was glad Chris had ended a potentially awkward situation by retreating without speaking to her. On the other hand, she was angry at the obvious snub he'd delivered.

Now you're being foolish. How would you have reacted if he'd come over and said something to you?

A gavel tap at the front of the room caught Kaitlyn's ear. The members of the task force had taken their seats; the meeting was beginning. The chairperson, an intense-looking woman, fiftyish, blond, a bit chubby, began to talk, but Kaitlyn couldn't focus on the brief speech. All she could think about was Chris Taylor sitting in the same room.

He looked even more handsome than he had at Home & Hearth. *Of course! This is a workday; he's wearing a blazer and a tie, not the casual clothing he chose for his undercover evening.*

Forget about Chris Taylor. Keep your mind on the job you have to do.

Kaitlyn rummaged in her handbag and found a notepad and pen. She took a few notes as another member of the task force, a thin man in his forties with a bony face and a reedy voice, talked about the challenges of protecting Asheville's infrastructure—its electric power plants, telephone facilities, water system, and bridges—from a terrorist attack.

Kaitlyn found that the act of putting pen to paper helped her concentrate on investigative reporting. Chris Taylor gradually moved to the back of her mind as she listened to the increasingly lively discussion about homeland security.

The chairperson tapped her gavel again. "We'd be delighted to take questions from the members of the general public here today."

Kaitlyn looked around the room, surprised that no one in the audience responded to the invitation. Suddenly, Chris Taylor raised his hand.

The chairperson beamed at him. "The gentleman on the left side of the room."

A bearded man in a plaid sport coat scurried up the side aisle to reach Chris with a handheld microphone.

Chris cleared his throat and said, "Madam Chairperson, how has Buncombe County performed in tests and simulations of terrorist attacks?"

The woman nodded expressively. "An excellent question, sir. We've done quite well, but of course, there's always room for improvement." She launched into a rapid-fire description of technical details that had Kaitlyn scrambling to capture them on her notepad.

She looked up from her scribbling in time to see Chris sit down, a satisfied smile on his face.

If he can do it, so can I. Kaitlyn thrust up her right hand.

"Yes, ma'am," the chairperson said.

Kaitlyn waited for the microphone, then said, "I understand that there are computer programs available that enable governments to model the risks of terrorist attacks. Does Buncombe County make use of such technology?"

"Indeed we do." The chairperson turned to a slender male panelist on her right. "I believe that Dr. Grover would be the best member of the task force to answer your question."

Kaitlyn added three more pages of scribbles to her notepad as Dr. Grover cheerfully described the two large programs that Buncombe County had acquired to simulate terrorist disasters. She glanced sideways at Chris Taylor and noticed that he was writing as fast as she was.

See! I can ask good questions, too.

"We have time for two more questions," the chairperson said.

Kaitlyn looked at the big clock on the wall and decided to leave now. The very last thing she wanted to do was bump into Chris in the hallway or parking lot. She gathered her things, slipped out through the side door, and took the stairway downstairs rather than wait for the elevator—all the while feeling as if she was escaping from an unpleasant experience.

Why are you running away from him? She asked herself this question twice—first when she unlocked her Honda Civic and again when she turned onto Broadway Street—but she couldn't come up with a satisfying answer.

Chris Taylor bugs you when he's around. That's all there is to it.

Kaitlyn checked the dashboard clock. Just past four thirty—too late to go back to the office but too early to go home, especially since she had no plans for tonight. She thought about eating a microwaved frozen dinner, then spending the rest of the evening watching television or reading a novel. She decided she didn't fancy either activity.

The only alternative she could think of was a drive in the Blue Ridge Mountains. She opened the Honda's sunroof, made two right turns, and headed for Town Mountain Road, which would intersect the Blue Ridge Parkway at Craven Gap.

Kaitlyn slowed to let an 18-wheeler pull in front of her on College Street. As the huge rig turned, she read the bold logo painted on the side of the long trailer: HOME & HEARTH SUPERSTORE.

She immediately experienced a pang of. . .what? Loneliness? Trepidation? She wasn't sure how to label the strange sensation, but it was an unpleasant emptiness inside her, a feeling of total hollowness that made her want to go back to her home and hide.

Almost simultaneously, a sense of self-understanding swept through her. *You miss "Jake Sinclair." You know he's gone forever. That's why you find it so hard to be around Chris Taylor.*

She stomped on the accelerator and pointed the Honda toward her apartment.

"I must be crazy!" she said again and again.

"I have another great picture of you," Stella said. "It was taken yesterday."

Kaitlyn studied the print for few seconds and abruptly realized that the shot had been taken inside the county com- missioners' large meeting room. The photographer had stood somewhere in the front and pointed the camera toward the audience. The photo showed Chris Taylor and her on opposite sides of the room, clearly casting furtive sideways glances at each other.

"Where did this come from?" Kaitlyn could hear the bewilderment in her voice. "You didn't attend the task force meeting yesterday."

"That's true, I didn't."

"Well, if you didn't take the picture, who did?"

Stella hesitated, then said, "The task force has its own photographer, the same guy who shoots pictures of county commissioner meetings. I often work with him. He recognized you and e-mailed me the picture."

"Why would a county photographer take a picture of me?"

"Give me a break! What we have here is a classic image of two people who are doing their level best to pretend they don't know each other. It would be a prizewinner in a photo contest." She added, "And before you get all frazzled, no one's going to enter it in anything."

Kaitlyn took a closer look. The photographer had certainly captured the way she felt about Chris Taylor. She had a goofy expression on her face coupled with a definite look of longing for the person across the room. Strangely, Chris had a similar look on his face.

"When are you going to stop pretending that you don't love Chris?" Stella asked. "And that Chris doesn't feel the same way about you?"

"You weren't there yesterday. I was. He had no interest in me. I could tell the instant he walked into the room and saw me. He made a major effort to find a seat as far away from me as possible."

"Very interesting!"

"*What* are you talking about?"

"You didn't even try to deny that you have a thing for Chris Taylor."

"Go to work, Stella. I'm too busy studying the details of Homeland Security to waste time verbally fencing with you."

Stella took three or four steps toward the door, then turned and winked. "Can I be maid of honor at your wedding?"

Kaitlyn threw an empty Styrofoam coffee cup at her. She ripped the photograph into sixteen little pieces and tried to erase the image of Chris from her mind.

Stella, you've become an annoying jerk! I spent half the night thinking about him. Now you've got me doing it during the day.

"Care to tell your friendly agony aunt what's ailing you?" Cassandra Evans plunked down into Chris Taylor's visitor chair with a jolt that shook the surrounding floor.

"I'm in the pink," he replied softly. "Totally happy."

"Pish-tosh! Have you seen your face lately? It's grim as a rainy day on Dartmoor." She fluttered her eyelashes and laughed. "Tell Auntie Cassandra your troubles."

"Well. . .it's none of your business, but I had an unexpected run-in with Kaitlyn Ferrer." Chris abruptly made the time-out signal with his hands. "I mean that I didn't expect her to be at the task force meeting, although it makes perfect sense that she was."

"I have absolutely no idea what you just said. Please start your story at the beginning."

"I didn't sleep very well last night, so bear with me." Chris sighed heavily. "It all began when Hank Vandergrift assigned me to cover Buncombe County's Homeland Security Task Force."

Chris needed almost fifteen minutes to tell the full story of his encounter with Kaitlyn Ferrer. He sensed that Cassandra became bored when he described the stylish outfit Kaitlyn wore and the way her face lit up when she asked a question.

When he was finished, Cassandra said, "Let me summarize in a single sentence your seemingly endless tale of unrequited love. When you stumbled upon Ms. Ferrer yesterday, you realized that in spite of everything that has happened, in spite of stupid things that you and she have done to each other, you want to see her again because you plainly care for her."

Chris took a moment to frame his answer. "Crank up the volume on 'care for her,' and you're right." He added, "Does that sound silly?"

"Not at all. I'm a firm believer in clichés. I think love at first sight happens a lot—too often to people who aren't prepared to act on it."

"Love? Isn't it too early to talk about love?"

"I think not. It's chiefly the look on your face when you talk about the woman—something around your eyes goes all strange and gushy. I'd stake my professional reputation on the fact that you love Kaitlyn Ferrer."

Chris looked down at his feet.

"I'll take your eloquent silence as agreement."

Chris shrugged.

"Crikey! How I enjoy being right." Cassandra frowned. "However, I don't foresee a happy outcome. I also believe that there are star-crossed lovers who never get together. It may be that you and Ms. Ferrer are fated to live separate lives."

"Do you really think so?"

"Most definitely. . .unless you get off your big duff and do something to restore your relationship. You seem inclined to do nothing."

"What should I do?"

"Well, you could simply march up to Ms. Ferrer and tell her how you feel. You might even punctuate your admission with a robust kiss."

"I don't want to get skinned alive again."

"Faint heart never won fair lady."

"Kaitlyn may be fair, but she's also as tough as a steel-belted radial tire."

"You have a touch of the poet, Christopher. I'm sure she appreciates that about you."

Chris felt a tap on the shoulder. He looked up and around into Armando Collins's finely chiseled face.

"I vote with Cassandra," Armando said. "Tell the fair lady you've fallen for her."

"Thank you for butting in on my private conversation."

"Hey! There's *nothing* private about the way you feel for Kaitlyn Ferrer. I've been your photographer for the past two weeks. She's all you've talked about."

"That's not true. We've talked about lots of other things. Sports. Cars. Vacations."

"Oh yeah? Then how come I know the details of everything you saw or thought during your one and only date with her? I think it's absolutely fascinating that 'she has an ethereal look and her eyes twinkle when she laughs.'"

"Well. . ."

"The truth is, I don't mind listening to you talk about her endlessly. What's getting me mad is that you're going to lose her if you don't take action soon. Cassandra is right. Go see Kaitlyn. Tell her how you feel." Armando perched on the edge of Cassandra's desk. "Let me tell you something else, Chris. She *won't* give you a hard time. The fact is, she's pining over you."

"How would you know that?"

He smiled. "A little birdie told me."

"Right!"

"It's the truth. I saw how intently Kaitlyn watched you at the task force meeting. I know how women think. She actually seemed proud when you asked a question."

Cassandra shifted her bulk and grasped Armando's hand. "My dear Mr. Collins, you are tall, dark, and handsome personified. When you walk into a room, ladies swoon. You naturally assume that all men have the same effect on women. Are you confident about your observations?"

Armando nodded. "No doubt about it. The lady is in love with him."

"In that event"—Cassandra turned back to Chris—"you must act at once."

Chris thought about Armando's pronouncement and Cassandra's edict for a few seconds before he responded. "There's nothing I can do to change her mind. She looked annoyed and uncomfortable when she saw me yesterday. And she took off like a frightened rabbit when the meeting was over. That's loathing, not love."

"You are a dunce," Cassandra said.

"A world-class nincompoop," Armando chimed in.

"Perhaps I am, but I'm also a realist. Kaitlyn Ferrer is not interested in me. End of story."

Kaitlyn lobbed a bottle of premium olive oil into her shopping cart, just missing a carton of free-range eggs but denting a fresh loaf of French bread. She grimaced at Stella. "Now see what you made me do."

"Blame the Holy Spirit because you feel convicted, not me. All I did was point out that the Bible advises against revenge for good reasons. As Paul wrote in Romans, 'Do not take revenge, my friends, but leave room for God's wrath.' In other words, don't make vengeance part of your job description."

Kaitlyn pushed the shopping cart faster and enjoyed watching Stella struggle with her own cart to catch up. Maybe it was a bad idea to go shopping with Stella after work, even though her favorite photographer was trying hard to keep their friendship going. Stella had suggested that they pay a joint visit to a newly opened gourmet food store but had prefaced the trip with a lecture on revenge.

"I'm not surprised you still feel awkward," Stella continued, "especially now that your opinion of Chris Taylor has changed. You've discovered what the Bible tries to teach everyone—a vengeful person pays a high price for getting even."

"I agree with you. I've learned my lesson; the price I paid is a ruined relationship with Chris. It's time for me to forget him and move on."

Stella moved forward and positioned her shopping cart in front of Kaitlyn's. "That's a *ridiculous* thing to say. You don't have to walk away from Chris."

"I disagree. I'm not proud of my behavior during the past few days. I've thought the problem through and I really have only two choices. One, I can put my brief relationship with Chris Taylor behind me and think of him solely as a fellow investigative reporter. Two, I can admit defeat and move to another city."

"What about doorway number 3? End this foolish separation and begin over again with Chris."

Kaitlyn heaved a deep sigh. "There is no option 3. The more I thought about how Chris treated me at the task force meeting, the more I realized that he hates me."

"Has he told you that? Or are you just guessing?"

"Actions speak louder than words."

"And a picture is worth at least a dozen actions. You can see the simple truth that he loves you written all over his face. Don't let a good man get away."

"Then why hasn't he made any attempt to tell me? Why is he avoiding me?"

Stella rolled her eyes. "Because the man is afraid of you." She shook her head slowly. "I know that sounds ridiculous, but it's true."

"How could you know a thing like that?"

Stella smiled. "A little birdie told me."

"What little birdie?"

Stella gripped Kaitlyn's arm. "The minor details aren't important. All I ask is that you be sure of how Chris Taylor feels before you make any life-changing decisions."

"Well, I'm not sure how I'll accomplish that, but I'll try." She tried not to cry as Stella gave her a mighty bear hug. She would miss Stella more than anything—or anyone—else in Asheville. *Except Chris Taylor.*

Kaitlyn pushed the shopping cart toward the coffee and tea aisle. There were so many unusual packages to look at that Stella, bless her heart, was bound to lose track of their earlier conversation.

Kaitlyn began browsing through tins of loose tea. She knew herself well enough to recognize that she would never be able to drive Chris out of her mind if she stayed in Asheville. No, her only sensible course of action was to find a new reporting job in a faraway place. Possibly somewhere in New England. Or maybe a city in Texas.

What else could she do? Chris hated her, but she—well, she obviously felt differently about him. Why keep talking about a minor infatuation? The truth was, she loved him.

More than I've loved anyone else in my life.

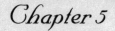

Chapter 5

You look *appalling* this morning."

Kaitlyn responded to Stella's uncomplimentary comment by sticking her tongue out.

"*Truly* appalling—right down to the coating on your tongue."

Kaitlyn swallowed the last sip of coffee in her mug. "How could I not look awful? I was awake half the night thinking—and praying."

"Does that mean you figured out what to do about Chris Taylor? It's been a week since our unhappy trip to the supermarket. I hope you're going to call him today."

Kaitlyn decided not to offer a snappy retort. She merely glared at her friend.

Stella dropped into Kaitlyn's visitor chair. "Okay, I'm game. What did you think and pray about last night?"

"I decided *not* to leave Asheville. I concluded that that would be a foolish thing for me to do. I'm not the kind of woman who runs away from problems and hides. Besides, I like my job, the people I work with, and Asheville."

Stella reached out and touched her shoulder. "That's

wonderful. I applaud your wisdom."

Kaitlyn stared at her desktop and hoped she didn't look too guilty. She'd mostly told the truth. Stella didn't need to know that some of her most fervent prayers had asked God to take charge of her relationship with Chris. "I've muddled everything," she'd prayed. "I need You to work it out. If Chris is the right man for me. . .well, You figure out how to make it happen. I'm clean out of ideas."

Stella went on, "I agree with you. You're not a woman who runs away from a challenge."

"Good. Now get out of here and let me think some more."

"In a minute."

"Leave now."

"Sheesh! You're also in an appalling mood."

"Absolutely true."

"Say *cheese*!"

"What?" Kaitlyn looked up at the same instant a flash of white light erupted from Stella's right hand. "Did you just take my picture?"

"Yep, with the miniature digital camera I carry everywhere." She added, "This time, try to look less grim."

"Don't you dare take any more pic—" Another blast of light interrupted Kaitlyn. "Why do you want photos of my total *appallingness*?"

"I'm planning a surprise for you." Stella rose and hurried off, a big grin on her face.

"What was that all about?" Kaitlyn asked Sadie Gibson, who had just returned to her desk in the editorial bull pen.

"I can guess," Sadie replied, "but I don't want to ruin your surprise."

"Go ahead—ruin it!"

"Stella often has her pictures applied to photo cakes. She gave me one for my first anniversary on the job. I bet she's planning to have one made for you—to cheer you up."

"Great! I can't wait."

"Yeah, it'll take lots more than your picture on sugar icing to cheer you up." She snickered. "Maybe Stella can arrange for Chris Taylor to deliver it."

Kaitlyn couldn't help sighing. "I never thought I'd carry a torch for anyone. I feel positively. . .*teenage*."

"Torches are age-independent. We've all been there, girl." Sadie began to smile. "You know, there is a guaranteed way to make the love-blues depart."

"Tell me."

"Meet someone better-looking and more compatible than Chris."

Kaitlyn returned a sour expression. "On that note, you can depart, too." She turned to her computer and opened a new word-processing document.

Maybe some work will clear my head. Assuming, of course, I can focus on work.

"I want the old Chris Taylor back," Hank Vandergrift said. "Your lousy mood—and all this brooding—is affecting your writing."

Chris forced himself to look up. "Says who?"

"Says me, your managing editor. The last article you wrote was barely worth publishing." Hank alighted on the corner of Chris's desk. "It's time to push Kaitlyn Ferrer to the back of your mind."

Chris rolled his head back against his chair. "The truth is I was awake half the night thinking about her."

"Think about someone else."

A woman's voice burst in. "What sort of cockamamie counsel is *that*? Stick to correcting spelling errors and rearranging split infinitives. Leave the advice-giving to experts."

"I don't believe it," Hank said. "Cassandra Evans makes house calls. You've actually walked clear across the bull pen to visit Chris."

"Desperate times demand desperate acts." She poked at Hank's chest. "But nobody is desperate enough to listen to you. One questions if it is even possible for a sensitive male like Christopher to stop contemplating his inamorata. Poets throughout the ages have waxed poetic about the power of such thoughts. By definition they are overwhelming. And you say, 'Think about someone else.' Pah!"

Chris rocked his chair forward. "I don't need anyone's help."

"*Au contraire*, my lovelorn lad." Cassandra shoved Hank to his feet and leaned close to Chris. "You need the guidance of someone experienced in matters of the heart. Specifically me. You are presently wallowing in doubt and self-pity. I must help restore your self-confidence."

"Let me reiterate. I don't need *anyone's* help." Chris popped ear buds in his ears, switched on his iPod, and turned his attention to the half-finished article on his computer monitor. Through a pause in the score from *Titanic*, he heard Cassandra say to Hank, "I do believe we will have to perform a serious intervention to get our boy-wonder out of his amorous funk."

Chris gritted his teeth. *Why are there so many meddlers in Asheville?*

Kaitlyn had made a habit of checking out rival newspaper dispensers in whatever city she worked. And so, after the monthly luncheon meeting of the Asheville Media Club, she walked back to the *Blue Ridge Sun*'s editorial offices on College Street and glanced without thinking at a bright yellow dispenser at the corner of North Lexington Street.

Her mind needed a moment to catch up with what she saw. Her photograph was on the front page of the latest *Asheville Underground*—right next to a matching picture of Chris Taylor.

"What on earth!" Kaitlyn lunged at the pull-down door and retrieved a copy. The *Underground* was free for the taking, an "alternative" tabloid that covered the strange and unseemly side of Asheville. Hardly the sort of newspaper she aspired to.

She'd never seen this particular photograph of her before. She was sitting at her desk, gloomy faced, her chin resting on her hand.

The pieces fell into place. *It's the candid shot Stella took of me last week.*

Chris appeared equally disheartened in his photo. He sat slouched in his chair, his hands clasped high on his chest, a melancholy frown on his face.

And then Kaitlyn spotted the headline and byline of the article that began under the photograph: TWO INVESTIGATIVE REPORTERS FALL IN LOVE AT A HOME & HEARTH SUPERSTORE, by Estella Santacruz.

"Stella, I'm going to kill you!" she said, loudly enough to earn a panicky look from a nearby pedestrian.

Kaitlyn unfolded the *Underground* and read the lead paragraph:

> *Once upon a shopping cart, two strangers met under*
> *false pretenses and fell deeply in love with people who*
> *don't exist. Kaitlyn Ferrer is an investigative reporter at*
> *the* Blue Ridge Sun *while Chris Taylor holds a similar*
> *position at the* Asheville Gazette. *And therein lies a*
> *fascinating tale.*

"This can't be happening!" She scanned the article quickly, picking out words here and there: *Jake Sinclair. Dori Johnson. Freelance writing. Advertising. Falsehoods. Deception. Phony names. Reality. Sadness. Pride. Stubbornness. Love.* A short sentence caught her eye: *The truth, of course, is that Kaitlyn Ferrer regrets the way she deceived Chris Taylor and longs to see him again.*

"I'll rip her to shreds!" Kaitlyn nearly tore the *Underground* in half as she searched for the end of the article in the back pages. She ignored more photos of Chris and her and read the final paragraph:

> *The strange coincidence that brought Kaitlyn and*
> *Chris together and then wrenched them apart must have*
> *been the work of Providence. Although the pair pretends*
> *to be angry with each other, they make a perfect couple. It's*
> *only a matter of time before they recognize what everyone*
> *else who knows them can see—they are destined for a long,*
> *happy life together.*

Kaitlyn felt light-headed. She looked around, wondering

if the other pedestrians on College Street were staring at her. How many people actually read the *Asheville Underground*? Five thousand? Ten thousand?

More than enough to make me notorious.

She half ran along College Street, charged through the *Sun*'s revolving doors, and climbed the stairs two steps at a time to reach the third floor. Stella and two other photographers shared a small office area carved out of one corner of the graphics department. Kaitlyn found Stella piling papers into a large corrugated cardboard box.

"You. . .you. . .*Jezebel*!" Kaitlyn shouted. "I trusted you." She crumpled her copy of the *Asheville Underground* and hurled the mass of paper into Stella's carton.

"Good!" She smiled. "You've seen my article."

"You wrote that I'm in love with Chris Taylor. That I'm sorry for what I did to him. That I am dying to see him again."

"Yep. Every word is true."

"But I didn't want *him* to know that's the way I feel."

"Why not? He feels the same way about you." She shook her head. "Aren't you fed up with falsehoods and deceptions? The time has come for everyone to tell the truth." Stella stopped smiling. "Anyway, if you really are mad at me, I'll be out of your life soon. I'm leaving the *Blue Ridge Sun*."

"I get it! Julia fired you when she saw your stupid article."

"Boy, are you wrong! Julia helped me write the piece."

"She. . .*what*?"

"Sadie and Dale also made suggestions." Stella dropped a small potted plant into her carton. "No one could stand your miserable expression anymore. We all agreed it would take a shock to get the pair of you off dead center. Of course, I did most of the planning."

"What *are* you talking about?"

Stella reached for the phone. "Hi, Sadie. She's up here in my office with me. You and Dale had better come up—in case she doesn't cooperate."

"Stella, what's happening here?"

"Be patient." She glanced at her watch. "You'll find out in twenty minutes."

"Uh. . .let's go back a notch." Kaitlyn had finally grasped the full impact of Stella's earlier reply. "Did you just tell me that you quit your job at the *Sun*?"

Stella nodded. "Effective today. I decided to go into the photography biz. I'm going to be a full-time professional photographer. That's always been my dream. It'll give me a chance to be more creative. I'll do portraits, fashion photography. . .maybe even some architectural work." She retrieved the balled-up *Underground* from her box and lobbed it back at Kaitlyn. "This article is my going-away present to you. One of Christopher's friends provided his perspective—and of course I knew your side of the story."

"Oh my! If you go, I won't have any friends on the staff."

"You have lots of friends on the paper. Besides, I'm not going far. We plan to set up our studio in downtown Asheville."

"We?"

"All will be clear in twenty minutes—as soon as we get there."

"Get where?"

"Don't ask unnecessary questions."

"I'm not going anyplace with you this afternoon. I have work to do."

"I don't think so," Stella said in a singsongy voice.

Kaitlyn started to object again but was interrupted by the arrival of Sadie, Dale, and—most surprising of all—Julia Quayle. Stella and the newcomers surrounded her like secret service agents guarding the president and propelled her as one into the elevator.

I work with a bunch of nitwits and fools. Kaitlyn let herself be hustled through the basement garage and was astonished when the four helped her climb into the back of a recreational vehicle the size of a small bus. They steered her to a captain's chair that was facing rearward and snapped her seat belt shut. The RV's side and back windows were covered with shut Venetian blinds. When Stella, Sadie, and Julia took seats around her, she realized that Dale must be up front driving.

"Is this your RV, Dale?" she asked.

"Nope, although borrowing it from my cousin was my idea. You can't see out of the windows, so we don't have to make you wear a blindfold."

Kaitlyn found it impossible to be angry about being "kidnapped" from her office. Her workmates had obviously gone to a lot of trouble to plan whatever was about to happen. Even more important, their infectiously happy mood had banished her gloom and annoyance.

Dale started the engine and put the RV in gear. Kaitlyn tried to deduce the route from the turns she felt but soon lost all sense of direction. The combination of speed and smoothness led her to conclude that they were driving along an interstate highway. Given the length of the drive, they were probably five miles or so from downtown Asheville.

The RV slowed to a stop. Julia and Sadie slipped outside,

leaving Kaitlyn alone with Stella.

"What happens now?" she asked.

"You stay put." Stella patted her head. "We need a few moments to get everything else ready."

"I work with a bunch of maniacs."

Kaitlyn had begun to ponder what "everything else" might be when a heavy hand thumped on the RV's side door. Stella flung it open and threw her arms around the tall man standing in the doorway. A long kiss later she smiled at Kaitlyn.

"Stop looking so bewildered. This is Armando Collins. We're engaged and partners in Asheville's latest photography business."

Armando joined in. "We're going to call ourselves Santacruz and Collins. It has a nice ring to it."

"Speaking of nice rings"—Stella slid a diamond engagement ring on her finger—"I can finally show you mine."

Kaitlyn made a feeble gesture of surrender. "Whoa! Start from the beginning. When did you two meet?"

"That first night at Home & Hearth. Armando is Chris Taylor's photographer. He was taking candid pictures for the *Asheville Gazette*. As you can imagine, we both ended up working from the same vantage points. The rest, as they say, is history."

Kaitlyn stood up and hugged Stella. "I admit it—this is a whale of a surprise."

"Don't be silly. *Your* surprise is outside." Stella gestured grandly toward the open door.

Kaitlyn stepped to the doorway and was greeted by applause. Someone grabbed her hand and tugged her down the single step. She blinked as her eyes, acclimated to the darkened

RV, readjusted to the glare of a brightly lit patch of concrete and she saw her destination.

They brought me to the Home & Hearth parking lot!

Kaitlyn scanned her surroundings slowly. To her left stood four smiling people—Julia and Dale from the *Blue Ridge Sun* and two others she knew worked at the *Gazette*, Hank Vandergrift and Cassandra Evans.

Directly in front of her was Andrea Lewis, Home & Hearth's how-to lady, standing next to an empty shopping cart.

And to her right. . . *Oh my! It's him.* Chris Taylor, looking as sheepish as she felt, seemed to be hiding behind another empty shopping cart.

Kaitlyn struggled to keep her composure. In the distance she spotted a *Gazette* delivery van parked alongside Dale's RV. Chris must have been "kidnapped" at work just as she had been.

Andrea broke the awkward silence. "Good afternoon to both of you. Welcome back to Home & Hearth. You have your shopping carts, and the store awaits. Your friends and colleagues believe that another stroll down the aisles will have a beneficial effect."

Stella jumped in. "Actually, we're convinced that a fresh jaunt through Home & Hearth will help you untangle the mess you've gotten yourselves into."

Kaitlyn cautiously gripped the shopping cart's push bar and smiled at Chris. His expression immediately brightened, and he took a few tentative steps toward her.

Both the *Sun* and *Gazette* staffers hooted and cheered.

"Let's get out of here," she murmured, "before I start pushing this cart into editors and photographers."

"You lead," he murmured back. "I'll follow you anywhere."

"Even though I'm not Dori Johnson?"

"As it happens, I'm not Jake Sinclair, either, although we do have a lot in common."

Kaitlyn laughed, which triggered another round of hoots and cheers. She accelerated her cart toward the superstore's automatic front doors. They opened just in time to let her cart pass. She heard Jake's cart clatter through behind her, followed by a fresh barrage of cheers.

Kaitlyn looked up at a crowd of men and women, at least fifty people of different ages, standing in the lobby, all with shopping carts. Several waved copies of the *Asheville Underground* at her.

Andrea appeared at her side as if by magic. "The funny thing is that the original articles you and Chris wrote about finding love at Home & Hearth didn't have much impact. But then the *Underground* published its story. Wow!" She chuckled. "We ran out of shopping carts during lunch hour today."

"Then reclaim our carts," Chris said. "I don't think we need them anymore."

Kaitlyn felt a delicious shiver of delight as he unexpectedly took her hand. She didn't pull away, adding further to her surprise.

Andrea glanced around furtively, as if to make sure no one else was listening. "Very few shoppers browse the carpet aisle this time of afternoon." Her mouth bent into a grin. "Do either of you have a yen for floor coverings?"

"Hmmm. A small Oriental rug might cheer up my apartment," Chris said.

"In that case, take the shortcut through the paint department. The folks with shopping carts won't be able to follow."

Kaitlyn let Chris lead her through the maze of aisles and counters.

"I've been thinking," he said. "We have lots of apologizing to do."

"I've been thinking the same thing. We'll waste *hours* if we go back and forth rehashing the stupid things we've done to each other."

"I suggest we move immediately to the forgiveness thing."

"Right! Along with a promise."

"You mean no more trickery, no more deception?"

"Well, certainly not to each other."

"Good point! We still are investigative reporters."

He stopped short; Kaitlyn bumped into him. "I have to tell you something," he said. "I decided that you were meant for me the instant I first met you. I knew that I loved you before we sat down in the coffee shop."

"It took me a bit longer."

"How much longer?" She could hear the alarm in his voice.

"You might as well know the truth now. *Nothing* gets between me and a mega caffe latte—not even you."

Chris began to laugh, a deep, echoing rumble that made Kaitlyn begin to laugh, too. She leaned back in his arms as he picked her up, spun her around, and then kissed her gently.

She heard a distinct roar in her ears and wondered if they were near Home & Hearth's power tool aisle. What else could cause the trembling she felt down to the soles of her feet?

He lifted his head. She pulled his face forward and kissed him again.

Epilogue

As appeared simultaneously in both the *Blue Ridge Sun* and the *Asheville Gazette* later that year:

Asheville's two leading newspapers are proud and delighted to announce a staff merger of sorts. Kaitlyn Ferrer, the Blue Ridge Sun*'s senior investigative reporter, and Christopher Taylor, her counterpart at the* Asheville Gazette*, were married today in a ceremony at Oak Ridge Community Church.*

In keeping with the finest journalistic traditions, the color scheme was black (for the groom) and white (for the bride). The matron of honor, Estella Santacruz Collins, the bridesmaid, Cassandra Evans, the best man, Hank Vandergrift, and the groomsman, Armando Collins, wore shades of gray.

The happy couple exchanged vows in which they pledged to honor and obey each other and the First Amendment. Following a reception held inside the Home & Hearth Superstore at Oak Ridge Plaza,

Kaitlyn and Christopher told this reporter that they "intend to stop the press of work for a glorious three-week honeymoon in an undisclosed location." Given the sudden shortage of investigative reporters in Asheville, it is likely that the honeymoon site will remain a closely guarded secret.

RON BENREY

Ron is a highly experienced writer who has written more than a thousand bylined magazine articles, seven published nonfiction books, and seven Christian romantic suspense novels (cowritten with his wife, Janet) for Barbour Publishing and other publishing houses. Ron also is an experienced orals coach who helps corporate executives give effective presentations. He holds a bachelor's degree in electrical engineering from the Massachusetts Institute of Technology, a master's degree in management from Rensselaer Polytechnic Institute and a juris doctor from the Duquesne University School of Law. He taught advanced business-writing courses at the University of Pittsburgh, where he was a member of the adjunct faculty.

CAN YOU HELP ME?

by Lena Nelson Dooley

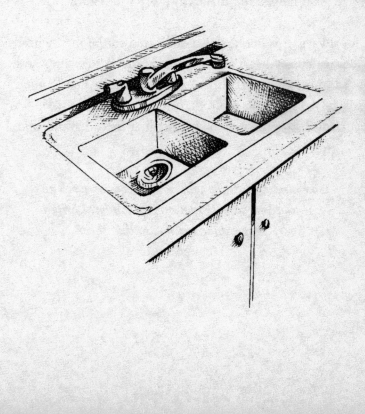

Dedication

This book is dedicated to the members of
American Christian Fiction Writers.
The love you poured out on me at the national conference
in 2006 was above and beyond anything I had ever dreamed.
You are comrades in this writing walk,
and I treasure each one of you.

Special thanks to Rhonda Duke, sales specialist
at my local home improvement store.
You helped me make my story more authentic.

As always, this book is also dedicated to the man who has
warmed my heart and supported me in so many ways
for more than forty-three years—James Allen Dooley.
I love you more than words can express.
And I love my very own Austin, a special grandson.

*God is not unjust; he will not forget your work and
the love you have shown him as you have helped
his people and continue to help them.*
HEBREWS 6:10

Chapter 1

Austin Hodges strode across the vast showroom of the Home & Hearth Superstore in Oak Ridge, North Carolina. He would've rather just ordered the kitchen cabinet knobs from a catalog, but the particular style his best friend Scott and his bride had chosen for their home was a special design and could be obtained only from an H&H store. Some sort of incentive to get people inside, probably so they would buy more than they planned to. If their friendship hadn't been so long-standing, Austin would've suggested that Scott and Lisa choose something else for their first home.

With fisted hands on his hips, Austin surveyed a display wall extending the entire length of one aisle. On the wall, tiny cabinet doors hung one above the other in stacks of at least a dozen, showcasing a different knob on each. There had to be hundreds, or maybe more, on the long expanse. He pulled a folded page torn from a design magazine out of his front jeans pocket and frowned at a photo the size of a picture postcard. How would he ever find the knob on the cabinets in that kitchen? He might be here all afternoon, or longer.

"Sir, can you help me?"

In his distraction, Austin didn't even consider that the question was for him until a finger gave his shoulder a poke. He turned and stared down into eyes that looked like dark pools of melted Hershey bars—his favorite snack. "Yes?"

"Can you help me?" The determined feminine face was surrounded by a cloud of golden blond hair that looked like a hurricane might have styled it. "I really need to decide which cabinets to buy, and everyone else seems to be busy."

Something about this woman intrigued him. Of course, he had never seen a blond with eyes that particular shade of brown, but it was more than that. The aura around her held an alluring magnetism, and she had a feistiness about her.

Without even folding it, Austin shoved the bit of paper back into his pocket. "How can I help you?"

The woman turned and marched toward the end of the display. He watched her quick steps until they disappeared around the wall.

In only an instant, she thrust her head back and peered at him. "Aren't you coming?" Her voice sounded commanding.

What was she—a drill sergeant? "Sure." He quickly joined her, and they headed down the next aisle.

"I'm remodeling my kitchen, and I'm trying to decide which cabinets to use." The words poured from her in a torrent. "And I'm not really sure how these things are attached to the wall. Do you screw them up or glue them?"

From the serious expression on her face, Austin knew she wasn't joking. Surely she didn't think any glue would hold a cabinet full of dishes.

"Well, ma'am"—he eyed the wooden structures they had

stopped in front of—"there are several ways a cabinet can be attached to the wall. It's according to how they're constructed."

The woman stared at him with an intent expression as if she were taking in every word, but something in the depths of her eyes told him he was speaking in a language foreign to her.

"How do I find out about the ones I want?" She didn't blink as she continued to stare at his face.

Austin wasn't used to this kind of scrutiny from a woman, so he glanced back toward the displays of kitchens. "Which of these cabinets are you interested in?"

Her gaze shifted toward them before she answered. "I'm not sure—whichever ones are easiest to install."

After widening his stance and crossing his arms, he cleared his throat. "It won't matter to the guys who do the installation. They just have a basic charge for most of these cabinets."

She touched him lightly on his forearm. "I'm sorry. I must not have explained it right. I want to know which ones would be easiest for *me* to install." Then she glanced at her hand on his arm and jerked it away as if she hadn't realized she'd even touched him.

He straightened to his full height. "You want to do it yourself? Is your husband going to help you?"

The expression in her eyes hardened. "I'm not married." She spat out the words as though they tasted rancid.

Austin ran his hand around the back of his neck. "I'm sorry, ma'am. I just assumed you were, since you weren't using the installation service." After he stuffed his hands into the front pockets of his jeans, he continued, "So who's going to help you?"

"I'm doing it myself, I told you." She raised her voice

slightly as if he hadn't heard her the first time.

Austin stepped back. "Ma'am, let's start this conversation over. Okay?" He stuck his right hand toward her, hoping she wouldn't leave it dangling there. "I'm Austin Hodges." He waited to see if she would respond.

Several long seconds later, she gave his hand one quick, strong shake. "And I'm Valerie Bradford."

"Valerie. . .I like that." He smiled at her. "I'll feel better calling you by your name."

Finally, she laughed. "And all those 'ma'ams' were a little much. I teach at the high school, and I hear enough of them during weekdays. But at least some of the students are still being taught manners."

Austin tucked his fingers back into the front pockets of his jeans, encountering the wad of paper in one of them. Soon he'd have to get back to looking for the knobs for Lisa. "No matter which of the cabinets you choose, Valerie, I'm afraid you're probably gonna need help hanging 'em."

Valerie huffed out a sharp breath. Why did men assume that just because she was a woman, she wouldn't know how to do things? "I'm remodeling the house I inherited from my grandmother, and I've been doing all the work myself, because I can't really pay to have it done. I'm pretty handy."

As if on a mission, the man marched down the row of cabinets away from where they stood. Valerie quickly followed behind him, taking two steps to his one. She hoped the tall, ruggedly handsome stranger wouldn't get into trouble with his boss for spending too much time helping her. She tried not to notice, but his muscles filled out his blue polo shirt in a very pleasing manner. The waves in his deep auburn hair bordered on curly. One lock had fallen over the center of his strong forehead, quickly curving into the signature Superman curl. For a moment she imagined him as an auburn-haired superhero. The thought of him in tights brought a flush to her cheeks. The muscles of his legs almost stretched the dungarees to their limits, much as his shoulders and arms did the shirt. *The man must really work out. Probably has a membership at a gym. Or can people who work at Home & Hearth afford that?* As a schoolteacher, she sure couldn't.

She almost ran into him when he stopped and turned around. "Oops."

He caught her by both shoulders to keep her from crashing into him. "I wanted to show you these." He gestured toward several rows of cabinets, their doors showing through the openings in the front of the cardboard cartons. "Those cabinets you were looking at have to be ordered from the factory, but here are some you can buy and take home with you. They're a little less expensive, too. You might check to see if you like any of them."

Valerie studied the structures with a critical eye until she came to the white ones. "These would brighten up the kitchen." She glanced up at her helper. His name was Austin, wasn't it? Why didn't the man wear his name badge? *Maybe it gets caught on things or something.* She hadn't noticed whether anyone else in the store wore them or not.

Once again, the man crossed his arms. *If he shaved his head and wore a gold earring, he'd look a lot like Mr. Clean.*

"Do you need both upper and lower cabinets?"

She nodded. Did the man really think she'd replace only part of them?

"These cabinets are easier to install than the ones you order from the factory, but I still don't think you can do it by yourself. Do you have anyone who can help you?"

Valerie rubbed her fingers across her forehead where a slight ache was trying to take hold. This was becoming more complicated than she thought it would be. "I could ask a couple of the boys from my high school speech class to help."

He didn't waver. "Have they done anything like this before?"

What is wrong with this guy? You'd think he doesn't want to make a sale. "I doubt it."

Finally, he relaxed some. "Look, I'm not trying to be difficult. If you're handy"—he gestured toward the cabinets that would go on the bottom—"you might be able to do these, but not the top ones. They're a two-man job, and at least one of the people working with them should know what he's doing."

She scowled at him, hoping he would take the hint. Did he realize what he'd said? *Two-man*, emphasis on the *man* and what *he's* doing. For a moment, anger rose within her, but that wouldn't help her, so she decided not to tell him what she thought about his terminology.

"Do you have the measurements, Valerie?"

Austin might look like a hunky movie star, but he didn't have to treat her as if she didn't have a lick of sense, as her grandmother used to say. "Yes." She dug through her shoulder bag until her fingers closed around her notebook. "Here they are."

He took the proffered notes and studied them. "Okay, you want lower cabinets all across this one wall, and two different sections of cabinets above. Is there a window above the sink?"

At least the man could decipher her drawings. "That's right."

After handing back the diagrams, she watched as Austin studied all of the cabinets in front of them. "If you use three of this model on each side of the window, you'll need seven of these other ones. You'll put the sink in the middle one. Are you gonna use the same sink or replace it?"

She stuffed the notebook back into her tote bag without taking her attention off the man standing before her. "Can't I decide later?"

He rubbed his chin with one hand. "You could, but it'll be easier to cut the correct-sized hole in the cabinet before it's installed. After it's attached, you can only get to it from one side."

"Okay." She might as well decide now. "With the new cabinets, I would like a new sink, if it's not too expensive."

Austin looked as if he was about to say something but stopped himself. She wondered what that was all about.

With his hands thrust under the opposite armpits, he rocked back on his heels for a moment. "Look, I know you don't have any reason to trust me, but I could give you references if you want me to. I'd like to come over and help you install these, at least the top ones, but I'd like to help you with the bottom ones, too."

Valerie was surprised by his offer, but maybe he didn't understand what she'd tried to tell him before. "I can't afford to pay you much at all."

He nodded. "I know that, and we'll discuss that later. Since you're a teacher, you have weekends off, don't you?"

Now it was her turn to nod. "Of course."

Austin reached into one pocket and then another one as though searching for something. "I don't have a card with me. Do you have something to write on?"

She started to shake her head before she remembered her notebook. Once more, she pulled it from the bag. "Here."

He fished into one of his pockets and extracted a pen before scribbling something on one of the pages. "Here's my phone number. Think about it, and call me to let me know if I can help you." Austin glanced at a man walking by the end of their aisle. "Wait here. I'll get George to write these up for you and get them loaded in your truck." He loped off, leaving her staring after him.

Truck? Did he say truck? She didn't have one. Then it hit her. How was she going to get these cabinets to her house? Maybe one of the men at church could help her pick them up. She really didn't want to pay a delivery charge or have to rent a truck.

When George came down the aisle after the consultation with Austin, he was alone. For just a moment, Valerie wished the tall man had come back with him. Then a question shot into her thoughts. *Why didn't Austin write up the order himself?*

Chapter 2

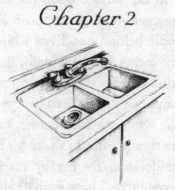

Valerie rushed into the sanctuary just as the congregation stood to sing the first worship song. She didn't like being late, but she'd overslept for the first time in years. Spying a space at the end of a pew, she hurried toward it and slipped in. When she reached to put her purse and Bible down, she noticed the other people sharing the bench with her. A family with several children took up over half the room. With his hands held high and his eyes closed, a tall auburn-haired man standing right next to Valerie seemed lost in the music.

Austin. She didn't know he attended the same church she did. Maybe he usually went to a different service. Should she move into a different pew or stay where she was?

With a slight shrug, she faced the front and found her place in the words of the song on the screen at the front of the room. When she closed her eyes and sang along, she could forget about the man so near her. . .almost. Even without looking at him, she felt an awareness of his presence, which kept intruding on her thoughts. *Lord, I don't need to be distracted.*

This morning is all about You.

At the point in the service when the worship pastor instructed the congregation to greet those around them, she turned to the people behind her. Even while she shook their hands, she couldn't forget Austin. Finally, she faced him.

"Valerie, I didn't know you went to my church." A bright smile lit his face and put a twinkle in his eyes.

"And I haven't seen you here before, either." She didn't know whether she should offer to shake his hand.

He made the decision for her by reaching toward her. When his hand encountered hers, a tingle shot up her arm.

"I usually go to the late service, but I have something to do today."

Not knowing what to say, Valerie settled on the cushioned seat with her face toward the front. When Austin also landed on the pew, he was closer to her than he had been when standing. She tried to ignore him, but by the time the service ended, she couldn't tell anyone what the pastor's main points had been. She quickly gathered her belongings and started looking for a break in the crowd that filled the aisle.

"Did you eat a good breakfast?"

At the question, she glanced up at Austin. "Did you just ask me—"

"Yes, and I sounded like my mother." A sheepish grin gave him the look of a mischievous little boy. "Sorry about that."

Valerie clutched her Bible to her chest, almost as if it were shielding her heart. "Why would you ask about breakfast?"

"Because it's too early for lunch. If you didn't have much breakfast, we could go to brunch together." The dazzling smile he flashed erased all traces of the boy. The man probably drew women like bees to honey.

"Actually, I overslept, so I only grabbed a glass of OJ."

"Good. Will you join me for brunch?"

Did she want to be one of those honeybees swarming around him? Before she could decide, an opening appeared in the crowd. She pushed into it and looked back to decline.

Unfortunately, he'd been able to exit with her, and he placed his hand on the small of her back while he bent close to her ear. "Please."

"Okay." *What could it hurt?* Since he went to the same church, maybe it would be all right to talk to him some more about the cabinets.

Austin pulled up in front of Mother's Kitchen and Pancake House and watched Valerie fit her car into the spot beside his. She must be a good driver, because she didn't have any trouble getting into the tight space. Parking was the main problem with this restaurant, which had been here as long as he could remember. Whoever planned the parking lot hadn't had much foresight. Of course, Austin viewed everything through the eyes of a construction engineer, and he learned early on that parking was a critical issue in the mobile society of today.

By the time he exited his vehicle and pushed the LOCK button on his key fob, Valerie joined him on the sidewalk. He escorted her through the doorway and glanced around. The place didn't look too crowded. "Where would you like to sit?"

When he spoke, Valerie looked at him, and the impact of her dark eyes hit him in the solar plexus. "Anywhere is fine."

"How about over here by the window?" He urged her forward with one hand on the small of her back, noticing she seemed to be the right height for him. He could see over her head just fine, but she wasn't so short that he would have to bend too far down to— Whoa, he didn't want to go there. "The view of Oak Ridge from here is nice." After she chose one side of the booth, he dropped into the other.

A waitress quickly arrived. With a snap of her gum, she asked, "Are ya having the buffet, or do ya want to order from the menu?"

He gave Valerie a questioning glance.

"The buffet is fine." She unwrapped her silverware and arranged the utensils side by side on the napkin before looking back toward the waitress. "And I'll just have water."

"Are you sure?" Austin studied her expression. "They have good coffee. I think they even have lattes." He noticed a spark of interest that quickly vanished.

"No, I often drink water with my meals."

He gave his attention to the waitress, who stood with pad in hand. "Coffee and water for me, and water for the lady. But we'll probably have a latte to top off the meal." Before Valerie could say anything else, he stood. "Let's go see what they have today." When he offered her his hand, she took it, and he realized his mistake too late. Her touch did something to his equilibrium. . .in a way he had never experienced before. *Lord, why is this happening?*

While he loaded up with scrambled eggs, bacon, and biscuits, she put small amounts of fruit on a little plate before placing a waffle on another and topping it with honey and a little granola. She returned to the booth before he did. He arrived about the time the waitress started setting Valerie's drink on the table.

"Thank you," he told the young woman when she set his coffee and water in front of his plate.

Valerie sat with her head slightly bowed and her eyes closed. He had planned to ask her if she minded his saying a blessing, but she had no way of knowing that. This one time he thanked the Lord silently, but not sharing the custom with his companion gave him a feeling of loneliness.

"So did you get the cabinets home okay?" He took a quick bite of the scrambled eggs he'd heaped with shredded cheese. When Valerie didn't answer, he glanced back at her only to find her staring out the window as if fascinated by the budding leaves on the trees.

She slowly turned back toward him. "No, I haven't worked it out yet. George said they would hold them for me until I could pick them up. I'm sure one of the men at church will help me."

Austin laid down his fork and tented his fingers over his plate. "Have you thought any more about letting me help you?"

She took a deep breath. "Are you sure you really want to do that? Don't you work on Saturdays?"

"Not usually. I pretty much have my weekends free."

"But yesterday. . ."

"Yeah, I was at H&H, but that was a special circumstance." He tried to think of a way to get her to agree. He knew she couldn't complete the project alone, and for some reason, he wanted to be the person who helped her. Maybe they could get to know each other better. He didn't realize he was staring into her eyes until she blinked and turned away.

"I could use some help, and you do go to the same church I do." He could tell from her expressive face that she was fighting an internal battle.

"Pastor Dave could give me a reference, if you want him to." For some reason, Austin desperately wanted her to agree, but he hoped he didn't sound desperate enough to scare her off.

When Valerie laughed, music poured over his soul. "I don't think that'll be necessary. Sure, I could use your help. It'll keep me from having to ask a bunch of guys until I find one who's willing."

Their loss is my gain. "And I can pick up the cabinets for you. I have a truck."

"That would be wonderful." A relieved smile settled on her face.

"I probably need your receipt, especially if George isn't there when I pick them up."

Valerie dug in her purse, pulled out the slip of paper, and handed it to him. "When do you work again? Maybe I'll come by the store to see you."

"Oh, but I—"

"Austin!" greeted a masculine voice and a feminine voice in unison.

Valerie had watched the couple make their way across the crowded restaurant. How quickly it had filled up after she and Austin arrived. When the two did a simultaneous double take while passing the booth where Valerie and Austin sat, she almost laughed. Their movements were as synchronized as their words.

Valerie wondered who they were, but evidently her dining partner knew them.

Austin rose in one fluid motion. "Terry and Sherry." He said it almost as if it were a one-word name. "I want you to meet Valerie Bradford. She goes to Word of Love, too."

When he glanced at her, Valerie gave him a questioning look. "They go to church there, too?"

He nodded. "Yeah, but they usually go to the late service." He gave a sweeping glance around the restaurant. "There doesn't seem to be anywhere else to sit. I hope you don't mind if they join us."

That suited Valerie just fine. Maybe the buffer would keep her thoughts from straying into areas they shouldn't. She had never been so fascinated by a man, and she didn't know what to think about that.

After the other couple was seated, Austin gestured for the harried waitress to stop by their table. Soon their drinks were taken care of and they also were eating plates of food from the buffet.

"It's almost like two different churches meeting at the same place." Sherry smiled at Valerie. "Terry and I occasionally go to the other service so we can get to know more of the single people in the church."

Valerie couldn't hide her surprised look. "But I thought—"

"They're twins." Austin looked as if he was trying not to laugh.

That explains the syncopation. "Twins? Interesting."

The meal proved to be a pleasant time of conversation. Valerie enjoyed watching the interplay between Austin and the other two. Even more, she was amazed by all of the ways

193

the siblings were alike. Now that she knew their relationship, she saw other similarities. Brown hair with a hint of curl—even though Terry wore his much shorter, both of them had a visible cowlick on the left side of their forehead. Sherry cleverly disguised hers with a style that swept that direction. Their hazel eyes sparkled with life. Even though Sherry enhanced hers with mascara, Valerie could tell they both had very long eyelashes. Many of their gestures were alike. Soon they were taking bites of their food at exactly the same time, often eating the same thing. Valerie knew it was unusual for boy/girl twins to look so much alike since they were fraternal instead of identical. Being intrigued with the twins helped take her attention from the man who sat across from her. . .but not for long.

Austin studied Valerie as she discovered each new thing about Terry and Sherry. He'd known them so long they were no longer a fascination. They were just good friends, and he now knew them well enough to see the vast differences between them that weren't evident at their first meeting. When he finished eating, he leaned back in his chair and took part in the animated discussion of everything from the merits of Word of Love Church to the best place to go hiking in the Pisgah National Forest.

Not until he was in his SUV headed home did he remember that he never got a chance to tell Valerie the truth about what he did for a living. Next Saturday when he went to her house to help her install the cabinets, he needed to do that first thing. Total honesty was always best in any kind of relationship, and he had to admit to himself that he wanted a relationship with her—if it was okay with the Lord.

Valerie looked forward to Saturday more than she wanted to admit. Austin was just a guy who worked at the Home & Hearth Superstore. Of course, he did go to her church, so they might become friends, but no more. However, her heart seemed to want more.

Because they were going to work on the kitchen today, she'd eaten a cinnamon roll off a paper plate and drank her milk from a Styrofoam cup. She was throwing them in the trash when she heard his truck pull up. Actually, it sounded as though two vehicles stopped in front of her house. She hurried toward the front door.

Austin closed the door of a midnight blue SUV just as she stepped out on the porch. Home & Hearth must pay better than she realized. She turned her attention toward the large truck backed into her driveway. She couldn't read the writing on the open door because she was viewing it at an angle. The vehicle didn't have any writing on the sides as many commercial vehicles did.

"Where did you get the big truck?" With one hand, she shaded her eyes against the bright morning sunlight.

The tall auburn-haired man sauntered toward the house. "Borrowed it from a work site. Borrowed two of the workers, too. We can get this stuff unloaded faster that way."

Austin was right; with three men working together, soon all of the cartons of cabinets stood in the middle of her kitchen. Thankfully, these old houses had large rooms. Valerie had moved all of the chairs into the dining room and pushed the table against the far wall. With the merchandise, the room felt crowded for the first time in her life.

Valerie went to get her purse so she could pay the helpers. She wasn't sure how much she should give each one, but they had helped a lot. By the time she reached the front porch, the truck was pulling into the street.

"I wanted to pay them for helping."

Austin turned when he heard Valerie's comment. "They don't expect anything from you," he told her. "I took care of it."

Valerie huffed out a big breath. "You shouldn't have. You're doing enough as it is."

She pivoted and went back inside. He followed her, hoping she wasn't mad at him. When they got to the kitchen, she gave him a tour. He decided to tell her what he did later in the day, so they could enjoy their work time together. Somehow, he knew that waiting even this long to be totally honest with her might upset Valerie. It would be harder to get the work done if she was, and possibly she wouldn't want him to stay and help.

Within an hour, they had removed the old cabinets and sink. Austin had figured it would take longer, but they worked well together. Their conversation centered on the activities they enjoyed at Word of Love. Now Austin wished he had become a part of the singles' ministry. He might have met her sooner.

Valerie told him a lot about her grandmother and why she had come to live with her while she was in college. He felt that she was holding something back about that time in her life, and whatever it was had hurt her greatly. Maybe someday she would share it with him. When her grandmother died last year, Valerie inherited this house since she had taken care of the older woman for several years. He liked everything he was learning about this woman. Was she the one God intended for him? He wanted to find out.

"So, Austin, what do you like on pizza?"

Valerie stood before him with a pad and pencil in her hands. Smudges of dirt adorned both of her cheeks, which failed to diminish her beauty. Even though she had pulled her abundant blond hair into a ponytail high on her head, fluffy curls framed her face.

He stopped and took off his tool belt, laying it on one of the cabinets. "What do you like?"

A twinkle ignited in her eyes. "I asked you first."

"I haven't met a pizza I didn't like, so whatever you order will be fine with me."

She stood with the pencil poised over the paper. "All the guys in the singles' group love pepperoni, but I don't like it. How about if we order a half and half?"

Austin crossed his arms, thoroughly enjoying their bantering. "And what sissy thing will be on your half? Pineapple?"

She laughed and wrote as she talked. "Half pepperoni and half mushroom with pineapple." She raised the pencil, then made an emphatic period at the end of her sentence.

Laughter burst forth from him. He wanted to pull her into his arms.

Where did that come from? His earlier thoughts had caused a shift in his paradigm. He'd better be careful. He didn't want to move from the path of God's perfect will for his life. Maybe it was a good thing lunchtime had arrived.

"Point me toward the bathroom, and I'll wash up while you

call the order in." He didn't want her to pay for his lunch, but she had insisted. Of course, a little pizza wasn't much to pay for all the labor, but he didn't want to take anything from her.

The afternoon proceeded much as the morning, and at the end of the day, all of the lower cabinets were hung. While he cleaned up the mess he'd made, Valerie ran her hands over the cabinets and her new sink, exclaiming how much she liked them. With each word, his heart expanded.

On the way home, Austin remembered that he hadn't told her the truth about who he really was. How could he have gotten so wrapped up in their interaction that he forgot to explain she had assumed the wrong thing that day at Home & Hearth? The truth had to come out, but he wanted to tell her face-to-face—not over the phone.

Chapter 3

Austin yawned. He'd had a hard time falling asleep last night. Working with Valerie invigorated him in more ways than he cared to enumerate. What was it about this woman that seemed to burrow deep inside him? He really didn't have time to spend ruminating over her. After church this morning, he'd be leaving for several days. A new project in Fayetteville needed his oversight. He'd probably be gone all week. Austin knew he'd have to hustle so he could come home next weekend. No way would he miss working in Valerie's kitchen on Saturday.

While he dressed for church, his thoughts jumbled together. One minute he would concentrate on the blueprint of the building, but soon a pair of laughing brown eyes intruded. Blond curls fell across Valerie's forehead in the vision, and she'd swipe them back with her forearm. How many times had she done that yesterday? Finally, she'd gone upstairs and tied her hair back with a bandanna. He'd teased her about the cloth belonging to her boyfriend.

A becoming blush had painted her cheeks. "I don't have a boyfriend. Why, Mr. Hodges, are you tryin' to find out more about my personal life?" Valerie had affected a strong Southern drawl that had left them both quaking with laughter.

Austin shook his head to dislodge the memory and pulled on a denim jacket. He usually dressed up more for church, but since he planned to leave after the service, he didn't want to take time to change into traveling clothes. At least no one would notice, since people wore everything from casual to what his mother called "Sunday best."

Valerie woke with a start. *What time is it?* She glanced at the clock radio on the nightstand beside her bed: 9:00. She would be late for church. After jumping from under the covers, she remembered she wasn't going to the early service. For some reason, Valerie wanted to check out the late service. Of course, she knew that a tall man with deep auburn waves would be there, too. She almost felt shameless chasing a man like that.

Well, she wasn't really chasing him. She just wanted to thank him for his help. *Right!*

Four carelessly tossed outfits later, Valerie settled on one. After putting the finishing touches on her hair and makeup, she grabbed her purse and headed for her car, finally backing out of the driveway. She would barely make it to church in time for the start of the service.

While she stepped through the open doorway from the vestibule into the sanctuary, her eyes scanned the crowded room. Not a single auburn-haired man in sight. Valerie couldn't keep her spirits from sagging. Whether Austin was here or not didn't matter. She'd come to worship the Lord, hadn't she?

Pasting a smile on her face, Valerie made her way down the

aisle and slipped into the first vacant seat. It took all her effort to concentrate on the service, and she was glad she did. Pastor Dave's sermon from Hebrews 6 reminded her that God would always be pleased with the extra things she did for her students. Many of them came from families that couldn't afford much, so she used her own financial resources to give them the best education possible.

No one needed to know that even though the message lifted her spirits, heavy disappointment at not seeing Austin roosted like a vulture in her heart. When she arrived home, she wanted to avoid the kitchen. The memory of Austin's laughing face and strong arms awaited her there. After changing into jeans, a sweatshirt, and sneakers, Valerie picked up a kid's meal with burger and fries but rewarded herself with a large chocolate malt. She took the food to a nearby park and ate a solitary meal under the spreading branches of a tall elm tree.

Valerie threw the wrappers into a trash container. She walked along the paths of the park, enjoying the mostly native shrubs. Many of them were budding or in flower. Splashes of variegated greens, pinks, and whites, with a few blues and reds mixed in, provided a kaleidoscope of constantly changing shapes. Pleasant fragrances laced the gentle breeze. If anything could lift her spirits, these gardens would. *If only Austin were here to share them with me.* Valerie rejected that thought. The man probably had a girlfriend. . .or even a fiancée. Spending so much time thinking about him was only setting her up for possible hurt. She hurried toward her car, intent on preparing dynamite lesson plans.

After a week of amazingly smooth teaching days and miserable nights fighting her attraction to an employee of Home & Hearth, Valerie woke early on Saturday. Since she hadn't heard from Austin all week, doubt had become her constant companion. Would he return to finish the job or not?

While she brushed her hair back and secured it into a ponytail, her ears were attuned to every sound outside her window. Finally, she heard the SUV pull into her driveway, and the vulture released its hold on her heart, which began a quick *rat-a-tat-tat* in her chest. Valerie took a deep, calming breath and skipped down the stairs. She reached the door just as the ring of the doorbell pealed through the hallway.

Should she let him know how eager she was to see him? Probably not. After slowly counting to thirty, she opened the heavy wooden door. "Austin, how good to see you." Did that sound gushy?

A slow smile spread across his face, ending with a twinkle in his gray eyes. "I've been out of town."

Her heart lightened even more. If she wasn't careful, it could float right out of her chest. "I'm glad you're back." Valerie pushed open the screen door.

Austin gestured for her to go back into the living room in front of him. One hand caught the screen door, and he closed it carefully, without letting it slam. If Gram were alive, she'd like this polite man. She could almost hear her say, *"He might be a keeper."*

His long-legged stride quickly took him to the unfinished kitchen. Austin stopped in the doorway and crossed his arms, tucking his hands into his armpits. With a tilt of his head, he studied what they had accomplished the week before. "It looks pretty good, doesn't it?"

Valerie nodded, not sure whether she was agreeing about

the kitchen or the man. "Would you like me to make coffee before we start?"

"Nah, I already had some."

She liked the sound of his rich baritone voice filling her home. After rubbing her palms down her jeans, she stepped around him. "Well, we'd better get started on these."

"Okay." He followed her toward the cartons against the wall. "Say, I—"

"I went—"

They spoke in unison, then stopped with wide grins.

"Go ahead." His gaze probed deep into hers.

"I was just going to say that I went to the second service Sunday, and I didn't see you there."

A loud laugh burst from him. Valerie couldn't imagine what was so funny.

"And I went to the early service. I thought we could worship together before I left for my out-of-town business trip." He stuffed his hands into the front pockets of his jeans. "Maybe go out for brunch again."

This time, Valerie joined in with his laughter.

The day flew by for Austin. No matter how much he tried to slow down the work, the hours wouldn't cooperate. At least they didn't get all of the upper cabinets hung. Maybe because they spent so much time laughing and sharing stories from their growing-up years. He couldn't remember ever telling a woman so much about himself.

Valerie stood across the room with her hands on her hips surveying the completed work. "Those white cabinets really brighten the room, don't they?"

Austin moved to stand beside her. Even after all the work, a faint fragrance of something flowery wafted from her. He took a deep breath. "They look good, if I do say so myself."

When she glanced up at him, her face held a serious expression. "You were so right. I never would have been able to do this by myself. Whatever was I thinking?"

"Maybe you weren't." He accompanied the comment with a quick laugh.

Without conscious thought, he reached to pick a fleck of sawdust from one of the curls that had worked out of her ponytail and now hung beside her face. That was a mistake. The strand of hair wrapped around his finger the same way being with this woman wound around his heart. He didn't want to let go, but the startled expression in her eyes told him he had better untangle it. "You had sawdust in your hair."

She wrapped the errant strand around her own finger. "Thank you. . .and thank you for all your help. Will you have time next Saturday?"

That sounded like an eternity to him. Did he dare ask her for a date? "Of course. I never leave a job unfinished." He stuck his fingers into his back pockets. "Um, I'm planning to attend the late service tomorrow. If you're going to that one, I'd like to take you out for lunch."

Valerie started gathering the small amount of trash on the floor. "That would be nice, but I should buy your lunch since you've done so much for me." She straightened and turned a questioning expression toward him.

He cleared his throat. "Actually, I was asking you for a date, and I always pay for dates."

Her mouth formed a perfect O before she bit her lip. "A date?"

"Is that a problem?" He held his breath.

She took a moment before answering. "No problem at all," came out on a whisper.

During the service, Austin tried to concentrate on the sermon. Valerie sat beside him, and even though they weren't touching, he could feel her presence. He hadn't considered that calling their lunch a date would change him so much. Since church attendance preceded lunch, the whole morning felt like a date. He'd even given Valerie a ride to church, which magnified the feeling. He hoped no one asked him anything about Pastor Dave's message.

Austin couldn't remember any woman ever tying him in knots this way. *Lord, what does it mean?*

After the last amen, Valerie reached back to pick up her purse and Bible. "That was a good sermon, wasn't it?"

Since Austin had never heard Pastor Dave preach anything but good messages, he agreed. "Where do you want to go for lunch?"

She clutched her navy Bible close to her chest. "Since you invited me, you choose the place."

Austin wanted it to be nice, but he didn't want to overdo. "Have you tried the Italian Inn over on Creek Road?"

"No, but I've been meaning to."

Since the crowd in the aisle was thinning out, he urged her in front of him. They made it to the SUV without anyone stopping them to talk. The trip to the restaurant didn't take long, and they filled the time by continuing their discussion of their growing-up years. Austin felt as if he'd known Valerie a long time, yet everything about the relationship was new and fresh.

Because they were near the front of the line, before long the hostess seated them at a table near the windows, which looked out across a tree-lined chasm. The colors of spring spread around and below them.

They both ordered the special of the day, and Austin didn't even care what it was. He just wanted this time with Valerie.

She reached across the table and lightly touched his hand. "I've wanted to talk to you about something, Austin."

"Okay." *What is this all about?* He leaned back in his chair to listen.

"I really appreciate all you've done for me." She stared straight into his eyes. "We've gotten to know each other pretty well, and I feel I can say this to you now."

From the serious sound of her voice, he knew whatever she had to say must be important. "Fire away."

"I'm sure you're good at your job at Home & Hearth," she began.

His heart dropped into the pit of his stomach.

"But you're so talented that you could work for a builder." Putting her elbows on the table, she leaned toward him. "You might even work your way up in that business and have a better future."

Now is the time. He had hoped to be able to weave it into a conversation. He cleared his throat, trying to think of the best way to start.

"Austin!" called a familiar feminine voice from across the restaurant.

Not again!

His best friend Scott accompanied his wife toward the table. "Hey, buddy."

Austin looked around, finally noticing how much more crowded the place was than when he and Valerie had entered. Quickly, he rose from his chair and stuck out his hand toward Scott.

After shaking his hand, Scott clapped him on the shoulder. "Who's this?" He looked straight at Austin's companion.

"Valerie Bradford, this is my best friend, Scott Preston, and his wife, Lisa. I've been helping Valerie install new cabinets in her kitchen."

She shook hands with both Scott and Lisa.

"It looks pretty crowded." Lisa frowned. "I really wanted to try this place."

Good manners won out. "Why don't the two of you join us? It hasn't been long since we ordered. If that's all right with you?" He nodded toward Valerie.

"Sure."

He signaled the waitress, who was quick to take their order.

"Hey, man." Scott sounded excited. "We're going to move into the new house this week."

Lisa leaned forward. "We couldn't have done it without all your help. Thanks for getting all the things I really wanted."

That statement must have reignited Valerie's zeal. "I've been trying to tell Austin his talents are wasted working at Home & Hearth."

Thankfully, Valerie didn't see the questioning expression Scott and Lisa each shot Austin. With a barely perceptible shake of his head, he let his best friend know that he shouldn't tell her anything. Scott quickly moved his arm, probably toward Lisa's hand under the table.

"He should work for a builder," Valerie plunged on. "He might have a better future. You know, work his way up in that business."

Austin knew the moment Lisa realized what was happening. She glared at him but pressed her lips together and didn't say a word.

Oh, what a tangled web we weave. . . The words his mother often repeated while he was growing up beat a rhythm in his mind. He hadn't meant to deceive Valerie, and he hadn't actually told her a lie. He just hadn't told her the whole truth. But he wanted to be the one to explain to her, not have her hear it from someone else. And he wanted it be in private, not in front of a crowd.

Chapter 4

Austin didn't have a good week. He was able to finish what he needed to at the work site, and he would be able to stay in Oak Ridge several weeks when he returned. These out-of-town trips to job sites grew tedious, and the long nights in the hotel ate at his soul. Why had he been such an idiot? Why didn't he tell Valerie the whole truth when he realized she thought he worked at Home & Hearth? He couldn't come up with a good answer to either question.

Most nights, he spent a long time praying. Over and over, he rehearsed different ways to approach the subject with Valerie. The imagined scenarios always had bad endings. Perhaps he should've made time to tell her on Sunday, but when they finished having the meal and fellowship with Scott and Lisa, Austin had to leave. Or he thought he did. The Prestons even offered to take Valerie home so he wouldn't miss his flight. He wondered about the conversation in their car, but that was all in the past. What he had to do was face the future.

Finally deciding that he should wait to tell Valerie until

after they finished hanging the cabinets—in case she didn't take it well—Austin made it to the airport with time to spare. He didn't want the news to upset their budding relationship. *Lord, when the time comes, please give me the right words.*

Valerie knew Austin was out of town this week. When she wasn't in class, her thoughts often revisited their times together. She had never felt about any man the way she did about Austin. Some kind of connection existed between them, but she wasn't sure exactly what it was. Of course, a girl could hope. There wasn't anything about the man she didn't like—his looks, his personality, and most important, his faith. After her background, she needed a man she could trust completely.

She spent extra time with the Lord asking Him what He wanted her to do. In all probability, she and Austin would finish hanging the cabinets this Saturday. They wouldn't have any reason to spend time together after that, but her heart didn't want to accept this fact. *What am I going to do?*

On Saturday morning, Valerie awoke early after a restless night. She usually slept later on the days she didn't have school or church—but not today. After a leisurely breakfast, she dressed. Funny how long it took for her to pick out what to wear. They were just going to work in the kitchen—anything would do. But she donned her most becoming sweatshirt because it brought out the chocolate brown of her eyes, and the flowers decorating the front made it feel festive.

When the SUV stopped in the driveway, she rushed down the stairs and opened the door. Austin glanced up at her and smiled, but something was different about him. She wasn't sure what, but he didn't seem to be as carefree as before. Maybe things hadn't gone well at work this week. She hoped Home & Hearth wasn't going to ask him to transfer to Fayetteville. The thought of not seeing him again, or even as often, made her heart react with a painful squeeze.

Austin reached for the handle of the screen. "Did you have a good week?"

Valerie gave him her most dazzling smile. "Yes, did you?"

"It was interesting, to say the least." His cryptic comment increased her feeling that something wasn't right.

Valerie and Austin worked together as a team the way they had before. Even their easy banter returned, and they finished the job by noon. Austin started cleaning up the mess, and Valerie enjoyed the fact that their time together was extended, even if it would be for only a few more minutes. She was going to miss having him around. The man had engaged her heart. She'd tried to prevent it, because she knew their time together would end with the job.

She placed the last of the cardboard in a large trash can. "I want to thank you again for all you've done for me." She couldn't read the expression that flitted across his face. "I'd like to pay you something for your time."

Austin held up his hand as if to ward off her next words.

"I know, I know—you don't want me to pay you." His intense scrutiny made her nose itch, so she rubbed it with her forefinger. "I could make you a home-cooked meal."

He shook his head. "There's only one thing I want." He reached out and took one of her hands in both of his. "Let me take you to dinner tonight."

"But—" She hoped he didn't notice her trembling.

"I'll pick you up at seven." A twinkle lit his eyes. "Wear something nice."

She laughed. He had no idea she had tried to do that this morning. "This sounds like another of your 'dates.'"

"It is."

Maybe she'd worried too soon. The chance of a different kind of relationship developing between them gave her all kinds of delightful ideas.

Valerie spent all afternoon trying to decide what to wear. She also gave herself a manicure and pedicure while she mulled over everything in her closet. After her shower, she took great pains styling her hair and putting on subtle makeup. Even though she had decided on an outfit three different times, she stood once again in front of the closet and questioned her choice. Uncertain whether Austin desired a more serious relationship, she tried hard not to overwhelm him. But she did want to look nice. Finally, she stepped into a slim black skirt and topped it with a rust-colored silk sweater. The outfit set off her coloring in a special way. Gold and pearl hoop earrings and a matching necklace complemented her outfit.

She cocked her head from side to side. *Not bad, if I do say so myself.*

As usual, Austin was punctual. The appreciative once-over he gave her made all of her preparations worthwhile.

Tonight, Austin wasn't driving the SUV. Instead, their chariot was a well-preserved, high-end sedan. Maybe he'd borrowed the car from someone because of their date. Valerie wouldn't spoil the evening by commenting on the vehicle.

Within fifteen minutes, Austin maneuvered the car under the porte cochere of a very upscale restaurant. This date must be important to him. She hoped he wasn't going to spend too much of his hard-earned money. A new thought entered her mind. Maybe Austin was a manager or something like that. She hoped so, but just in case, she would be careful not to order anything too expensive.

The maître d' seated them at a secluded table as Austin had requested when he made the reservation. He didn't want an audience while he told her the whole truth.

Valerie perused the menu bound in burgundy leather, then closed it. "I'm not very hungry. I just want a Cobb salad."

He knew what she was doing, so he ordered for both of them. "We'll have the prime rib, cooked medium, with the special house dressing on the salad." He remembered her telling him that prime rib was her favorite.

She opened the menu and peeked at it once more. Her eyes widened.

Austin reached across the table and took her hand. "I never invite a woman to a restaurant I can't afford."

A becoming blush stained her cheeks.

After the waiter brought them a basket containing a variety of breads and made sure they had plenty to drink, Austin finally broached the subject that had been bothering him all week.

"Valerie, I brought you here because I need to talk to you about something."

She put the whole-grain roll she'd taken from the basket on her bread plate and slipped her hands into her lap. An eager expression lit her eyes. He hoped what he had to say wouldn't dim it.

"When we first met, I know you assumed that I worked at Home & Hearth. Right?"

Her eyes narrowed, and she tilted her head. "Yes. . .don't you?"

"No."

Confusion flared in her eyes. "But you were wearing one of their shirts."

Austin shook his head. "I may have had on a shirt the same style and color, but I don't work there."

Betrayal stole across her expression.

"I was there buying knobs for Lisa's kitchen cabinets. The ones she liked best are a Home & Hearth exclusive."

Austin wanted to take Valerie in his arms. She looked as though she would need protection from what he was about to say to her. With a wary expression in her eyes, she seemed to shrink against the plush chair.

"So what do you do, Mr. Hodges?" Her brittle words sounded as if he were an ax murderer or something just as bad. She shrank even deeper into her chair.

"Actually, I own a company that constructs commercial buildings. I went to Fayetteville to oversee the start of a shopping mall there."

Instead of his words soothing her as he had hoped, her anger flared. "Just when were you planning to tell me?"

"That's what I'm doing right now." He hoped his expression conveyed how he felt.

Her spine stiffened, and she leaned forward. "And how do I know I can believe you now, since you've lied to me for so long?" Strong emotion laced the words.

"Wait a minute, Valerie." Once again, Austin held up his

hand, hoping to stem the flow of her anger. "I never told you a lie. You just assumed I worked there."

"And you didn't tell me any different." She clenched her fists on the table. "Isn't that lying by omission?"

He nodded. "Yeah. Probably is, and I'm so sorry. I didn't even realize you thought that until later."

"Why would you do a thing like that?" Her brows knit into deep grooves. "I thought you were a Christian. At least, you acted like one while we were in church."

That hurt—a lot. Austin took a deep breath against the pain. "I'm more sorry than I can tell you for all this." The expression of hurt and anger on her face stabbed like a sword into his heart. "I just wanted to help you and get to know you."

"Under false pretenses?" Valerie's voice sounded shrill, but at least she wasn't raising it.

Before he could answer, the waiter approached the table with their entrées. She kept her eyes trained on her lap while the man set the plates, with a flourish, in front of them. When she glanced at the dish with the attractive display of food, revulsion painted her expression. He hoped she wouldn't get indigestion from eating it.

"Valerie. . ."

She never looked at him or acknowledged he spoke.

Finally, Austin picked up his fork and tried the steak. As usual, he could cut it with that utensil instead of needing a knife. He placed the bite in his mouth, and it seemed to swell instead of diminish while he chewed.

Valerie acted as if she were alone at the table. Instead of consuming her food, she mangled it with her fork and pushed it around the plate.

Austin couldn't think of a single thing that would salvage the evening. Finally, he signaled for the check. When he arose to pull out Valerie's chair, she got up so fast she almost turned the chair over before he could reach it. She marched out the door and toward the car with her spine as stiff as a tree trunk.

"If you don't feel comfortable riding with me, I can call you a cab."

She shook her head and waited by the passenger door. After he unlocked and opened it, she slid in and buckled her seat belt. On the ride home, Austin turned on the radio, trying to dissipate the heavy atmosphere in the vehicle. The music only added to the miasma.

How could I have been such an idiot? Valerie slammed the car door behind her and ran up the steps to her porch. She glanced over her shoulder to see Austin standing beside his open car door. The look of sorrow on his face would have affected her if the last hour hadn't happened. Now she felt crushed. Pictures from her past, with snatches of this evening interspersed, flashed through her mind like a video in fast-forward mode.

Fumbling with the key, she finally opened the lock. After entering, she leaned against the closed door, and a torrent of watery sobs released like a dam breaking in a flood. She hadn't heard the car start, so she went to the living room window and peeked out. The scene blurred through the tears pooling in her eyes. Austin still stood where he had been when she opened the door to the house, but his head was bowed.

Surely the man wasn't praying for her. How could he after all he'd done?

Valerie slumped onto the couch and clutched a pillow to her chest. Sobs poured out of her but didn't wash away any of the pain. She hadn't had many relationships. Maybe that was why she was so gullible, thinking that he cared for her. He had called it a date, but he only wanted to dump this load—weighted with his previous dishonesty—on her. A load she wasn't prepared to carry.

The man could have been honest from the beginning. If he had, would she have let him help her with the cabinets? *Probably not.* She wouldn't have a new kitchen, but was it worth the pain? *Definitely not!*

Valerie knew that no one really died of a broken heart, but how long could she live with this agony eating at her?

Chapter 5

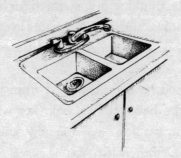

Austin couldn't leave until he prayed for Valerie. Even after he got in the car and closed the door, he crossed his arms on the steering wheel and leaned his forehead against them. *Lord, please comfort Valerie and help her deal with the hurt I saw in her eyes.* When the lights—in what he assumed was her bedroom upstairs—went on, he started the car and headed home.

He paced like a caged lion all around his house, not able to settle anywhere for long. Finally, he pulled out his Bible and started reading Romans 8. Several verses jumped out at him, so he reread the words: *"But hope that is seen is no hope at all. Who hopes for what he already has? But if we hope for what we do not yet have, we wait for it patiently. . . . And we know that in all things God works for the good of those who love him, who have been called according to his purpose."*

Austin let the words sink into his spirit. "Are You trying to tell me something?" He liked to speak out loud to the Lord. "Have I been rushing ahead instead of waiting for what You planned?"

That's exactly what he'd done. He felt a special attraction

to Valerie that went beyond the physical. He even thought she might be the woman God created for him. But what had he done? Sorrow filled Austin.

"Lord, I did it again. I didn't trust You and let You work things out according to Your will. If I had trusted You, I wouldn't have let the lie of omission continue."

Austin knew better. Hadn't he walked with the Lord long enough to know that he could trust Him? Especially with something as important as this?

"So what do I do now, Lord? Have I really blown it for good?"

Trust Me. The words dropped into his heart and mind.

"I know I have to trust You on this, but I really feel a need to let Valerie know how sorry I am I hurt her."

Maybe he should call her tomorrow. He listened with his spirit to see if the Lord would tell him to wait. When nothing but the peace of the Lord filled him, he knew he should apologize to her.

The last few weeks of school were always hectic, and this year was no exception. Valerie pulled into her driveway at five-thirty, thankful to be home. She had two students who needed extra help before the final tests, and she was glad to give them everything that would make them successful, even if it made her day extra long.

Each day this week and next, she planned to bring home some of her personal items from the classroom. She hadn't realized how heavy her box was until she carried it up the steps to the porch, so she set it on the nearby wrought iron table and unlocked the door. Before she went back for the extra things, she noticed the light on her answering machine blinking. She wondered who it was, but she'd listen to the message after she retrieved the supplies.

The red light was a beacon that called to her, but she took the box into the storeroom beside the kitchen. Just walking by the doorway reminded her of Austin's laughing presence for three Saturdays. Three short days that seemed like so much more. Of course, they did go out to eat a few times, too.

Her heart was divided. Attraction to the man warred with the knowledge that she shouldn't trust him. He was too much like her father, who only said what would get him what he wanted. So many times she wanted to shout at her mother for believing the man while he manipulated her. By the time she was twelve, Valerie had vowed that she would never let a man be less than honest with her. Getting away from the hurt her father caused everyone in the house had spurred her to move to North Carolina and live with Gram.

Pushing aside those thoughts, Valerie went to the machine and punched the PLAY button.

Austin's voice filled the room as much as his memory danced through her mind. "Valerie? I guess you're not home. I'll call later."

She glanced at the counter on the machine. Four calls— were they all from him?

"Valerie? I didn't know you stayed this late at school."

Should she listen to the other calls or just erase them? They could be from someone else.

"Valerie? Maybe you had to pick something up on the way home."

His voice played through her heart, wreaking havoc with her senses. One more call. *Please, please, please don't be from him.*

"Valerie? I really want to apologize to you. I'd rather do it in person, but if this is the only way, here goes. I was an idiot not to tell you when I first realized what you thought. My thinking was muddled or I wouldn't have let it go on so long. Can you possibly find it in your heart to forgive me?"

Tears streamed down her face as she listened. He sounded so sincere, but she hadn't had any indication he wasn't being honest with her all the time they worked together or when they went out.

Her phone could be set up with caller ID. Gram hadn't needed it, but now that the phone was in her name, it was time to utilize that feature. She retrieved the directory and dialed the phone company business office and ordered the service. Valerie hoped Austin wouldn't call back until it was activated. Maybe she should let all of the calls tonight go to the machine. She could pick up during the message if it wasn't him.

The next day, one of the seniors who helped in the office stuck her head into the classroom. "Miss Bradford?"

Valerie waved her in. "It's all right, Brenda. The students are taking a practice test."

"Mrs. Jones sent you this note." The girl placed a white envelope on Valerie's desk before going back into the hall.

After a quick scan of the room to make sure her students were still working on their papers, Valerie slit the envelope open.

"Please come to the office when you have a break," she read silently.

She wondered what the summons meant. She hoped none of the parents wanted another conference. Some of the ones last week weren't pleasant. She hated this time of year when the parents thought their children should be making better grades than they had earned.

The noon bell rang, and the students filed out. Valerie didn't have lunchroom duty today, so she headed to the office. As she approached, she saw a large, gorgeous bouquet of yellow roses—her favorite. Evidently, someone else liked them, too. For a moment, she wondered if today was Mrs. Jones's anniversary—or were the roses for someone else?

"Valerie," the school secretary said with a smile, "I almost didn't tell you to come this soon. I was enjoying your roses so much."

My roses? Why had she called them Valerie's roses?

"These came for you awhile ago. I didn't want to take them to the classroom in case you were giving a test."

"I was." Valerie stared at the large arrangement. "Who could've sent them to me?"

Mrs. Jones laughed. "Why don't you read the card and find out?" She pointed to the small envelope almost lost among the blossoms.

Valerie didn't want anyone to know just how much these flowers affected her, so she picked up the vase and carried it down the hall. The scent of roses surrounded her, making her want to press her nose into each partially opened bud. As she passed other classroom doors, some of the teachers gave her questioning looks, but she didn't stop.

She set the delivery on her desk and went back to close the door before extracting the envelope. On the way to the room, a memory had invaded her thoughts. At one point during the time she and Austin installed the cabinets, they had talked about flowers. She remembered telling him that yellow roses were her favorite. Surely they couldn't be from him, but she knew before she opened the card.

> *I'm so sorry, Valerie. Let these flowers convey my sincere apologies to you. I'll be calling you.*
>
> *Austin*

She started counting the perfect buds. Four dozen. They must have cost him a fortune. Then she realized she was thinking about Austin who worked at Home & Hearth, not the real Austin who owned a company. Tears made trails down her face, and she didn't care if she wiped them off or not.

Austin was at his wit's end. He'd sent flowers. He'd called numerous times. Yet he hadn't heard a word from Valerie. Austin still felt the need to talk to her in person, and the Lord hadn't given him a check in his spirit to tell him not to pursue this need.

He thought about going to the early service, but he didn't want to force himself on her in public. Waiting for her to pick up the phone each time he called dragged out his agony. Surely she went home sometime.

After a couple of weeks, he knew the schools were out in Oak Ridge. Of course, the teachers had several more days to finish out the year, but now those days should have ended. The schools looked deserted.

One evening, Austin drove by her house. Lights were on in several rooms, but no other cars were in the driveway, so he pulled into the next block and parked by the curb. He punched the speed-dial number for Valerie's home and waited. After four rings, the machine took over, but he didn't leave a message. Austin waited ten minutes, in case she was indisposed when he called before, then punched the number again. A repeat of the last time.

Then a thought hit him. Maybe she had caller ID and wouldn't answer his number. *Lord, what am I going to do?* Time for outside help. Austin called Pastor Dave and made an appointment with him for the next day.

"Come in." Pastor Dave urged Austin toward the conversational furniture grouping on the opposite side of his office from his large desk.

His secretary followed the men into the room and set a tray on the table in front of the two chairs. Austin would welcome the coffee but wasn't sure he needed any of the cookies brimming with nuts and chocolate chips. The chocolate made him think of Valerie's eyes.

"Thank you, Hannah." Pastor Dave poured two mugs of coffee and handed one to Austin. "You sounded serious last night. Is there a problem?"

Austin laughed. "You might say that. I'm probably the problem."

After taking a sip, the pastor set his cup on the tray. "How's that?"

Even though Austin didn't enjoy it, he told the whole story, trying not to leave out anything. As the words poured forth, he recognized that they made him sound almost like a boy in junior high trying to show off for the girls. Wasn't that what he'd done—showed off his knowledge and abilities to Valerie? He craved her approval.

"If she has caller ID, can you blame her for not accepting your calls?" The man got right to the point.

"Not really." Austin squirmed in the comfortable chair. "What I did sounded immature while I told you the story."

"It wasn't your finest hour. That's for sure." Dave's voice held a hint of humor.

Surely he wasn't laughing at Austin, but maybe he needed to be laughed at.

"So how do you feel about this now?" Did pastors have a class at the seminary on how to ask questions? Dave always knew the right ones.

"Kind of stupid. I wish I could go back to that Saturday last month when we first met. Of course, I didn't realize then that she thought I worked at Home & Hearth. Maybe I'd like to go back to the moment I realized she thought that. If I could do it over, I'd be honorable."

"Lofty words, my friend. But don't be too hard on yourself." Dave leaned forward with his forearms on his thighs. "What is the underlying reason you want to go back?"

Austin rubbed his eyes with one hand while he thought about it. "Is this confession time?"

"Confession is good for the soul, isn't it?" A sense of expectancy emanated from the man of God.

"All right. I felt drawn to her in a way I'd never experienced before." Austin hoped that would satisfy him, but the silence lengthened. "I even thought maybe she was the one God had created for me—my helpmate."

Dave leaned back. "And you don't think that anymore?"

"I don't know. I'm still drawn to her on many levels, and I still want her to be"—he made quotation marks in the air—"the one."

"Maybe she is." A smile spread across Pastor Dave's face.

"I'll never get a chance to find out now." Austin knew he sounded discouraged, but he didn't care at this point. He needed all the help he could get.

"There's some scripture I've had to learn to live by. 'But hope that is seen is no hope at all. Who hopes for what he already has? But if we hope for what we do not yet have, we wait for it patiently.' This verse is talking about waiting on the Lord. Maybe she is the one for you, but your timing was off. You ran ahead of the Lord by manipulating your experiences with Valerie. You might have to wait on the Lord to bring it to pass."

Austin nodded. "Were you looking over my shoulder a few nights ago when I was reading in Romans? God made that section come alive in my heart. I believe you've just confirmed it. So I'm to wait on the Lord, but I can still hope. How long will that take?"

"That, my friend, is the million-dollar question. Only God knows the answer."

Chapter 6

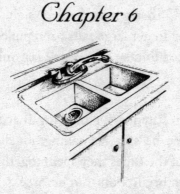

Austin's gaze probed Mother's Kitchen and Pancake House trying to locate Terry and Sherry Reeves. He'd spent so much time obsessing about Valerie that he hadn't touched base with his other friends. When Terry called asking Austin to meet the two of them for lunch, he gladly accepted.

Two hands raised simultaneously in a booth across the room. Twin waves signaled the siblings' location.

After making his way between the tables, Austin slid onto the bench beside Terry. "So what's up?"

Sherry frowned at her brother. "Didn't you tell him what we wanted?"

"I guess I forgot." Terry seemed unconcerned about his lapse. He turned toward Austin. "Are you still going to help us with the seventh and eighth grade camping trip?"

"How many times have I missed it?" Austin leaned his elbows on the table. "So where are we going this year?"

An incredulous expression flushed Sherry's face. "Did you forget you offered to let us use your property in the Blue Ridge Mountains?"

Austin laughed, then turned toward Terry. "You're right. She's so gullible, she'll fall for anything."

"Oh, you two." Sherry huffed a deep sigh. "I knew you were kidding." She dug in her large purse and pulled out a notebook and pen. "We need to take care of the last-minute details."

Each day, Valerie listened for the ring that signaled Austin's persistence. When he stopped calling, loneliness became her companion. All of the times they spent together—until the last dinner—had been bright points in her weeks. Now that school was out until August, she had time to work on other improvements in the house she had inherited. Too many reminders of Gram filled each room. Even though Valerie would keep some of her grandmother's things to display around the house, she wanted to make it into a home with her own personality.

As she entered Home & Hearth to choose colors of paint, she couldn't help remembering her first encounter with Austin. Why did that man flit into her thoughts so often?

When she finished buying gallons and gallons of paint in a variety of colors and carting them to her car, exhaustion weighed Valerie down. She swung out of the parking lot and noticed the coffee shop just down the block. A mocha latte sounded good, even if she'd have to drink it by herself. She needed to unwind the knots that had developed in her muscles during her marathon shopping spree.

Valerie chose a table by the window so she could enjoy the lush foliage. She loved all the colors in the summer landscape, even the greens. She took a sip of the hot beverage and sighed.

"That sounded soulful."

She turned her attention from the window to the woman who stood beside her table. "Sherry. I haven't seen you for a while." Valerie noticed the steaming cup in her new friend's hand. "Are you with someone, or would you like to join me?"

"Why, join you, of course. We need to get better acquainted." She set her cup down and pulled out the chair across the table. "This would be an excellent opportunity. I suppose you're completely finished with school for the summer. Right?"

"Now I'm concentrating on sprucing up the house."

"That's right. Austin helped you replace kitchen cabinets. What else are you doing?" Sherry blew on the hot liquid in her cup before taking a quick sip.

Valerie fought the tug on her heart at the mention of his name. "Gram hadn't had the house painted in several years, and the colors she used were darker than I like. I'm going to paint all the rooms in lighter shades."

A bright smile lit Sherry's face. "I love to paint. How about if I help you? That'll give us time to really get to know each other. Nothing like working together on a big job to bring out every facet of our personalities."

The house was a large two-story, and help sounded like a good idea, but Valerie hadn't thought about asking anyone. "I'd appreciate it. I could make sure we have a good lunch the day or days you come over."

"I'll bring something, too."

Valerie shook her head. "I'll let you help if I feed you. I'm not taking advantage of your offer any other way."

"Sounds good to me. When do we start?" Sherry took another sip of her coffee. "Now it's cool enough to enjoy this hot brew. My brother drinks it so hot it'll scald his mouth, but I don't."

"I don't, either." Valerie tasted her latte; it was just right, so she took a bigger sip. "I'm not in a hurry. I want to get the whole house done before school starts again, but I don't plan on painting every day. And I don't have any other plans."

Sherry cocked her head as if a new thought struck her. "You're free all summer?"

"Mostly." Valerie nodded. This would be her first summer without having to help Gram, so she wanted to take it easy. She wondered where her friend was going with this conversation.

"I have an idea." Sherry dug in her shoulder tote for a pad and pen. "Terry and I are in charge of the seventh and eighth grade camping trip for the church. We drive into the Blue Ridge Mountains and camp out, instead of spending the week at a regular campground. The kids love it."

"Sounds like fun to me, too." Valerie took another sip of her latte.

A huge grin spread across Sherry's face. "I hoped you'd say that. I need another woman to help with the girls. Pastor Dave and his wife always go, too, so we'd have three women that way."

"I just love Margie. I'd like to spend more time with her." The idea was taking a strong hold of Valerie's imagination. "Being with young teens will be a change from the high school students I teach."

Sherry started scratching words into her notebook. "Then it's settled. That was easy. I was afraid I'd have a harder time getting someone else to go."

"How many others have you asked?"

"You're the first one. Woo-hoo! Wait till I tell Terry."

Valerie glanced around to see if anyone else noticed all the commotion Sherry was making. Of course, if Valerie was going to spend time with teenage girls, she'd better get used to noise. "So exactly when is this trip, and how long does it last?"

"Now she asks." Sherry lifted a page. "We'll be leaving next Sunday afternoon about 3:00 p.m. And we won't be back until Saturday afternoon."

Valerie gulped. She had thought maybe a long weekend, but this trip would take a whole week. Oh well, she did have all summer. They could start the painting job when they got back.

"What do I need to do to get ready?" *What have I gotten myself into?*

Sherry looked down at the list in front of her. "The church bought tents several years ago. That way they could control the quality, and they're top of the line. The money the kids pay for the trip covers the food and supplies. All you'll have to bring are your personal things."

"That sounds easy enough." Valerie had never been on a long camping trip. Surely it wouldn't be much different from the times she'd gone to campgrounds when she was in the youth department herself.

"Just remember"—Sherry jotted something else down— "we won't have modern conveniences. No electricity for your blow dryer. The kids will have to dig latrines when we get where we're going. And we'll all have to pitch in with the cooking and cleaning up."

Valerie hadn't thought about that. No electricity. No bathroom. "If we don't have electricity, how do we heat the water to wash dishes?"

Without blinking, Sherry replied, "In a big iron pot over the campfire."

Having second thoughts, Valerie asked, "Is it too late to back out?"

Sherry frowned and shook her head. "We won't force you to come, but even without the modern conveniences, the camping trip is wonderful. We'll be up close and personal with nature. I've seen more varieties of rhododendrons and wild azaleas on these trips than anywhere else. And this time of year, the dogwoods and red buds will be in full bloom. Looking out across the mountains is a breathtaking sight."

Valerie began to catch Sherry's enthusiasm. *How hard could it be anyway?* "Okay, I'm still in."

"You'll need a sleeping bag. If you don't have one, I'll try to borrow one for you."

The only times Valerie had ever used a sleeping bag were when she was a lot younger. She might still have it in the attic. "I don't really think the Sleeping Beauty kind I slept in at Grams when I was little is what you're talking about, is it?"

"No." Sherry laughed. "For a minute there, I could just see you showing up with that one." She took another quick sip of her drink. "You'll need a good one. Nights get really cool up in the mountains, even in June. I'll borrow one for you. At least we won't have to carry everything in our backpacks." Sherry stared out the window. "I'm trying to remember which year it was. . .maybe three years ago. The guys picked a camping spot way up a mountain with no road to it. We lugged everything in large backpacks. I thought I wouldn't make it with my share." She turned back toward Valerie. "I told them if they wanted to camp someplace like that again, I wasn't going. They'd have to find another woman to head up working with the girls. They've been better about choosing an accessible spot since then."

Valerie was thankful she hadn't been involved with that trip. "So they're taking most of the supplies in a vehicle."

"It's the only way to camp, in my opinion." Sherry laughed. "And since they didn't want to find someone to take my place. . ."

When Valerie arrived at the church on Sunday afternoon, teens and parents swarmed the parking lot. Six large vans stood waiting as well as a pickup that had an enclosed trailer hitched to the back. Evidently, the pickup bed was fully loaded, because a tarp stretched across the top.

As soon as Valerie stepped out of her car and dragged a large cylindrical bag from the backseat, Pastor Dave came up to her. "Here, let me help you with your duffel bag." He hefted it onto his shoulder. "I like a woman who travels light."

Valerie laughed. "Well, that's not all I brought." She picked up a large zippered tote bag. "Where are we taking these?"

"I'm hoping everything will go in the trailer. It makes the ride more comfortable if we don't have to make room in the vans for any luggage." After the bags were stowed in the rapidly filling trailer, Pastor Dave turned back to Valerie. "Since you're a teacher, are you licensed to drive students on field trips?"

"The district wants all teachers to obtain that kind of license, just in case."

The pastor looked relieved. "Good. Now I don't have to try to find another person to drive. Of course, you could drive the pickup instead of one of the vans. That way you wouldn't need a special license."

"Does this mean I have to keep order in the van *and* drive?" Things were sounding less desirable by the minute.

"Actually, it's not so bad. I'll take all the more rambunctious kids in my van." He scanned the parking lot. "Most everybody is here, so we can start loading the vans. You can take the eighth grade girls. I think they'll be the least amount of trouble. They've been on the trip before, and they know the rules. The adults will stay in touch with walkie-talkies, and if there's any problem, we'll all stop."

Valerie took a deep breath. "That sounds better than trying to manage a trailer behind a pickup." She looked around the parking lot, wondering which other adults were going with them.

Terry and Sherry soon had the young people rounded up and started assigning them to vans. Parents talked among themselves or leaned against their cars watching the whole circus. When all the teens were in the vans, the only people standing near them were Terry and Sherry, Pastor Dave and Margie, and Valerie. The numbers didn't add up. Seven vehicles, five drivers. *Now what?*

Pastor Dave directed Valerie to one of the vans. Before she reached the door, a car screeched up and let out two young men. They looked to Valerie as if they might be college students. One of them jumped into the cab of the pickup, and Pastor Dave pointed the other one to a van full of boys. Soon the caravan wound out of the parking lot. Valerie's van was third from the front.

"Miss Bradford?"

Valerie glanced in the rearview mirror.

At the back of the vehicle, a girl with red corkscrew curls waved her hand. "Will it bother you if we sing on the way?"

Valerie raised her voice. "Not a bit. Just don't get too loud in case someone calls me on the walkie-talkie. I want to be able to hear it."

The music started at the back of the conveyance and rolled forward. The usual youth choruses rang out, but soon the girls started singing some of the popular contemporary songs often played by KSON, the local Christian radio station. Valerie knew some of the words, but these teens knew every word.

Actually, the music was a pleasant background to the scenic route they took. Valerie's gaze often drifted toward the mountains they were driving through. Sometimes the mountains looked like the rolling waves of the ocean. Muted dark greens morphed into bursting colors as they passed through the forested slopes. The farther they went, the steeper the climb. They weren't on the Blue Ridge Parkway. Instead, the caravan snaked around twisting two-lane mountain roads.

After they had been driving for about two hours, Terry's voice called through the walkie-talkie. "A good place to stop and take a quick break is coming up on the right. Everyone let me know you hear this."

"Sherry here." She drove the lead van.

From the second vehicle came the words, "Margie here."

Valerie pushed the button. "Valerie here."

Similar responses continued down the line. Just as they finished, Valerie rounded a curve that revealed a store, complete with outdoor displays of mountain crafts and quilts. She planned to enjoy this stop.

After the "quick break" that took an hour, the trip changed. Within a couple of miles, they turned off the main highway onto a narrow, blacktopped road that eventually gave way to a well-maintained dirt road. Then it became a rough track.

Nearly an hour after leaving the fascinating store, they pulled into a large, almost flat meadow surrounded by dense woods. Valerie felt as if they had completely left civilization. Her bottom hurt from bouncing over all the bumps in the last section of road. She'd be glad to get out of the van and stretch her legs again. She hadn't realized how much she had tensed her muscles until they came to a full stop.

"You girls stay in the van until I ask Terry and Sherry what we do now." Valerie stepped down, and her foot landed on a rock and slid sideways. She pitched forward toward the hard ground.

Strong arms wrapped around her. "Be careful." The warm masculine tone overwhelmed her with memories.

Valerie looked up into the warm gray eyes she had tried to forget. "Austin, what are you doing here?"

"I might ask you the same thing." He let her go and crossed his arms over his chest, a usual posture for him.

Valerie couldn't help noticing how his muscles bulged beneath the bright red T-shirt he wore. She had a hard time catching her breath. They must be at a higher altitude than she realized. "Sherry asked me to help with the girls."

"And I'm helping with the guys." Austin's laugh pealed across the meadow. "I guess no one thought to tell us that the other one was coming."

Valerie tried to gain some reasoning power. This was the man who hadn't been completely honest with her. She missed seeing him, but she needed to guard her heart, so she hurried around him toward where the twins stood between their respective vans. "So what do we do now?"

Sherry turned toward her. "I saw Austin help you when you got out of the van. Wasn't it nice of him to bring some of his men up here early and set up all the tents?"

How could Valerie disagree?

"He even sent a couple of the college boys he employs during the summer to help drive the vans. Some of the guys will stay around to help any way they can. One of them is even the camp cook, but we'll have to help him."

So that's where the young men had come from. "Why would he do that?" The words burst from Valerie before she could think.

"Actually, he owns this land, and he offered to let us camp here this year." Sherry's voice held such a strong note of admiration for the man that Valerie wondered if she was interested in him—maybe in a romantic way.

Why did that thought bother her? And why hadn't anyone told her he would be here? Valerie seriously wondered if she would have come on this jaunt if she had known. Maybe if he stayed with the boys and she stayed with the girls, they could keep out of each other's way. If not, this would be a very long week.

Chapter 7

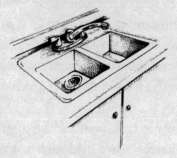

After helping everyone settle into tents, Austin climbed one of his favorite trails. He stopped at a lookout point and sat on the flat rock shelf that jutted over the wooded valley.

"Lord, I've stopped pursuing Valerie and rested in Your care. Now here she is, and we'll be spending the week together. It's going to be hard to stay away from her, so You'll have to give me constant directions. I'll try to listen for them better than I did before." Of course, he couldn't keep from hoping she'd forgive him.

From his perch on the side of the highest peak on his inherited property, Austin let his gaze rove over the vista spread before him. He knew why this part of the Blue Ridge Mountains reminded his ancestors of the Scottish Highlands they'd left years before. A couple of years ago, he'd stood on a craggy hill in Scotland.

Taking a deep breath, Austin heaved himself to his feet and started down the steep path. A smile crept across his face, and his heart lifted. Valerie was somewhere at the end of the trail. At least he could see her for the next few days. He hoped, if nothing else, they could at least become friends again.

He arrived at the campsite and searched the area until he found her helping put together the evening meal. Hunger gnawed at his stomach, accompanied by a desire for more than just the food.

"Hey, Austin." Pastor Dave waved him over.

He jogged toward the two men who had been deep in conversation when he returned from his jaunt. "What's up, Pastor?"

His friend greeted him with a clap on the shoulder. "Terry and I were just trying to nail down the schedule for tomorrow. We were discussing whether or not we should divide the group and alternate activities. What do you think?"

Austin crossed his arms and thought about it for a moment before answering. Sounded like a good idea to him. With fewer kids to worry about at one time, the activities would go more smoothly. "I agree."

"Then it's all set." Terry marked something on his clipboard. "I'll let the women know." He trotted off toward the cooking crew.

Austin started to follow, but Pastor Dave put a hand on his arm to restrain him. "I need to ask you something. How would you feel being paired with Valerie tomorrow?"

Is he kidding? Austin tried not to sound too eager. "That would work."

Supper was a noisy affair, and Valerie used the time to try to get to know some of the girls. She wasn't sure what would transpire this week, but she would put her whole heart into it. These young people deserved her best.

After they finished eating, Terry called everyone over to an area where large logs lay arranged on the ground like seats in an amphitheater. The kids clustered in clumps with their friends, and the adults lined the back row. All but Terry.

"Here's what we're gonna do." He glanced down at the clipboard. "Tomorrow we're gonna divide into two groups. Since there are more seventh graders than eighth graders, Pastor Dave, Margie, Sherry, and I will take the larger group horseback riding in the morning. Austin and Valerie will go mountain climbing with the other kids. Then in the afternoon, we'll switch."

Valerie took a deep breath. She couldn't remember how long it had been since she climbed a mountain. She hoped she wasn't too out of shape.

She would also be spending most of the day with Austin. How would that work? Of course, she would be in charge of the girls. She and Austin wouldn't necessarily have any interaction. *I can do this.*

Of their own volition, her eyes drifted toward the man. He was staring straight at her, and the expression on his face revealed that he hadn't been sure of her reaction to the news. Valerie gave him the best smile she could muster.

For Valerie, morning took forever to arrive. She couldn't remember how long it had been since she'd slept on the ground. Even with the thickly padded sleeping bag beneath her, the ground was far too hard. Finding a comfortable position had taken a long time, and then her thoughts had taken over and kept her awake for hours longer.

She crawled out of the tent, fully clothed. All of her friends would be surprised to hear that she'd slept in the clothing she wore yesterday. But what if one of the girls needed her during the night? If that happened, she wouldn't want to go outside in her pj's and robe.

Valerie didn't see anyone else moving around in the soft prelight of dawn. The sun hadn't risen above the mountains surrounding them, and mist shrouded the area. Everything smelled fresh and new. She stretched, trying to get the kinks out of her back. Valerie yawned and wanted her toothbrush right away, but she didn't know where to find the water to brush with. Maybe she could just use the toothpaste and spit it on the ground. After pulling her duffel bag away from the side of the tent, she rummaged inside.

Footsteps rustled the leaves behind her. She turned. Austin stood staring at her, with his hair rumpled and reddish-golden stubble dusting his cheeks and chin. For a long moment, she saw a virile man who did something to her equilibrium instead of the man she had come to know at their last encounter.

"Miss Valerie?" Shanda crawled from the opening of the tent.

Valerie looked back at her charge, but she still felt the heat of his presence as he watched for a moment longer before turning to go.

During the mountain excursion, Austin's appreciation of Valerie increased. Not only was she good with the teenage girls, but her lithe body had been created for the intense exercise. More than once, she encouraged one of the girls who lagged behind the others. Sometimes Austin wished he had chosen an easier slope for them to climb. Evidently, many of these teens never did anything more strenuous than walking around the mall. Valerie was just as good with the guys as she was with the girls. No wonder she was a teacher—probably an excellent one.

Austin heaved himself up over the ledge at the top of the trail. A small meadow spread behind him where they could rest before they started back down. That trip would be even trickier than going up. They'd really have to hold on to the trees and be careful climbing over exposed rocks so they wouldn't fall and roll down against an obstacle.

He reached over the edge and gave the girl behind him a helping hand. One by one, he pulled them each to safety, ending with Valerie. Just touching her hand shot a spark of heat all the way to his shoulder. He wondered if she felt the jolt, too, but she didn't give any indication she did.

"All right, everyone." He looked at the teens, who sprawled all around the grassy area. "Be sure to drink plenty of water while you're here. That's why we brought those canteens. With this altitude, you need to replenish your fluids before we start down."

Two boys scuffled off to the side, and one of the canteens sailed through the air and slid over the edge of the last rock they'd climbed to reach the meadow.

"Oh no!" One of the teens hurried toward the ledge. "I didn't mean to do that."

"Did you see that, Mr. Austin?" Anger painted the other boy's face red. "He threw my canteen away."

Austin started toward that boy, planning to calm him down before he helped retrieve the missing item. Before he reached the teen, a scream rent the air. He whirled to see two feet disappear over the ledge. Austin rushed to the spot. Mark, the other teen, hung a couple of feet below the top, holding on to a small tree that grew sideways from a split in the rock. His scared eyes looked like blue saucers in his pale face.

"Valerie, help me!"

The other teens crowded around.

"Everyone move over there and sit down to give Mr. Hodges room to do whatever he needs to do." Valerie's authoritative tone calmed the kids down a bit. "What do you want me to do, Austin?"

Quickly, he threw himself down on his stomach. "Sit on my legs to keep me from moving."

Without question, she complied.

"Mark, you're going to have to listen closely and do what I say."

The teen's eyes darted down toward the empty air below him.

"Don't look down!" Austin captured Mark's gaze with his. "You have to trust me. I'm gonna ask you to let go with one hand and reach out for mine." He thrust his arm down toward the teen as far as he could reach without going too far over the edge. Thankfully, it would be enough.

At his words, Mark's grip only tightened on the limb. He began quivering. So did the small tree.

"We need to do it quickly." Austin tried to convey with his eyes how important speed would be. "We don't want to stress the tree too much."

Austin didn't see how the boy could get any more scared, but the fear in his eyes intensified. "Now give me your hand. Keep a hold on the tree with your strongest one."

Slowly, one of Mark's hands released and lunged toward his leader's outstretched palm. Austin grabbed the boy's wrist. That way his grip wouldn't slip. Mark followed his example and gripped Austin's wrist.

"Good. Now let go with the other one."

The teen's attention wavered, but he quickly looked back toward Austin. "I'm really scared."

"That's okay. So am I."

Mark finally released his death grip on the tree and swung the hand toward Austin. When both wrists were firmly clutched, Austin slowly drew the boy up toward the edge. Even though the teen looked thin, Austin felt every ounce of the boy's weight on his own shoulders. When Mark was close enough, Austin slipped one arm around his body and eased him onto the grass. Valerie got up from his legs, and Austin missed her touch. They had worked together so well.

Tears filled Mark's eyes, and he swiped at them with one hand.

"Okay, everyone." Valerie's voice sounded breathless, but then it firmed. "Drink up. We'll need to start down soon, and we won't be able to use our canteens until we reach bottom. Remember, we'll have to hold on to the trees and rocks for safety."

Austin would have to remember to thank her for the distraction. He was able to talk to Mark in private.

"I was—really scared—down there." The boy's deep breaths broke up his words.

"It's okay to be afraid sometimes." Austin studied the teen's face. "I've been scared before."

"But what happened was my fault." Mark seemed to be

gaining control of his emotions. "I was just being stupid—fooling around."

Austin nodded. "Yes, you were, but we all sometimes do things that aren't wise."

"When was the last time you did something stupid?" Mark's tone told Austin he believed it was a very long time ago.

"I did a very foolish and prideful thing a couple of months ago. Something I shouldn't have, because it hurt another person." He placed his arm across the teen's shoulders. "We learn from our mistakes, and I'll never do anything like that again. I'm sure you'll be more careful from now on, too."

A tremulous smile chased away the tears in Mark's eyes.

"That's why we need to keep in close contact with the Lord and let Him show us what to do." Austin almost gulped on these last words. Who was he to preach to others when he made so many mistakes himself? He sounded just like Pastor Dave.

Instead of dragging as Valerie had feared, the week galloped by. The young men who worked for Austin did a lot of the labor around the camp so the counselors could concentrate on the kids. She enjoyed every minute, except not having a hot shower every day.

Perhaps God wanted her to be here for her own good, in addition to helping with the young people. Every moment she spent with the teens and Austin helped her see how wrong she'd been about him. He was nothing like her father had been. Yes, he'd made a mistake, but she'd blown it way out of proportion. She thought she had outgrown that tendency, but

God showed her that she had a long way to go before she even came close to perfection in that area of her life.

Now she wished she could figure out some way to let Austin know she wanted to pursue some kind of relationship with him. She watched him as he talked to Pastor Dave while the rest of the group packed up personal belongings. All week long, he'd demonstrated his strength of character in many ways. Why hadn't she recognized that part of him?

Austin glanced at her before turning to stride across the uneven ground toward where she zipped up her duffel. She stood and waited for him.

"I've just made arrangements with Pastor Dave for you to ride with me going back to town. I hope you don't mind." He waited for her reply.

"That's okay with me." Suddenly her heartbeat accelerated.

"I'd like to show you something before we go back." His penetrating gaze seemed to search her heart and soul.

"Sure. Whatever you want." She picked up her duffel, but he took it from her along with her tote bag and led the way to his SUV.

They drove a different direction from the camp, more around the mountain than down. On the other side, the road started a steep descent, but Austin handled the vehicle as if he were driving on flat ground.

"So where are we going?" She kept her eyes on the lush vegetation growing in the forest surrounding them, looking for the splashes of color indicating rhododendrons or their cousins, the azaleas. Their blooms were glorious in June.

The truck broke through the edge of the wooded area, and the road widened. "My ancestors settled this land generations ago. Now it belongs to me." Austin made a sharp turn onto another road. "I'm taking you to the home place."

They rounded a bend, and Valerie gasped. A lovely older home perched regally on a knoll, with grassy land spread around almost like a royal train. "That's the home place?"

The area was well maintained, and the large two-story house sparkled in the sunlight.

"Yeah. I thought it was time for us to talk." A smile lit his gray eyes and went straight to her heart.

They hadn't been driving very long. "Do you mean that a shower and other amenities were only a few minutes from camp?" She tried to look disgusted, but when he laughed, she joined him.

"It wouldn't be a camping trip if we came up to the house to bathe. But you can take a shower now, if you want."

The offer sounded inviting, but she wasn't sure she'd feel comfortable showering in his home.

When they stopped in front of the house, a motherly-looking woman wrapped in a voluminous apron came out on the porch. "Austin, I see you and the young lady have arrived. I'll have a nice lunch for you in about an hour."

He opened the door for Valerie and helped her down. "You might want to bring your duffel inside. . .if you want to clean up." He reached for the bag and brought it with them.

"Well, come on in." The woman held the door open.

"Marta, this is Valerie Bradford. Marta is my housekeeper here on the farm."

"Not that he's here very often." The older woman shook hands with Valerie. "Always traipsing all over the state working on those big buildings. And then he stays in Oak Ridge a lot of the time, too. At least I have my own family to cook for."

After partaking of Marta's abundant meal, they retired to the den, where his housekeeper brought a tray with coffee and shortbread cookies.

Austin finally convinced Valerie to make use of one of the guest rooms while he cleaned up. He wanted them both to feel comfortable when he broached the subject close to his heart.

Valerie sat on the couch with one foot up under her. Her hair hung in damp ringlets.

"I'm sorry I didn't have a blow dryer for you." He wished he could see what those wet curls would feel like wrapped around one of his fingers.

She reached to fluff her hair.

"You look lovely." He stopped, not wanting to scare her away before he said what was on his mind.

"Not like a wet dog?"

"Never like a wet dog."

"So what did you want to talk about?" She eyed him speculatively.

Austin leaned forward, placing his elbows on his knees. "I have a confession to make." She seemed to perk up, so he continued. "I was drawn to you from the first moment I met you. And I didn't want anything to stop a relationship from developing between us."

Her eyes grew large, but she sat still.

"When I realized you thought I worked at Home & Hearth, I should've told you the truth immediately."

She nodded agreement.

"I actually tried to a couple of times, but we were inter-rupted. First by Terry and Sherry, then by Scott and Lisa."

Valerie seemed to ponder those words. "I remember you were starting to say something each time—so that's what it was."

"Then I decided to take things into my own hands." Austin didn't realize how hard it would be to say these words. He wanted her to respect him. "I didn't trust God to make things right and I didn't want to upset you before we finished the cabinets. . .so I deliberately held the information back."

"Why would you do that?" She sounded hurt, even now.

"Because my feelings had been growing, and I was afraid I'd lose you if you found out I hadn't been completely truth-ful." Here he was, a businessman who owned a company and a family farm and on whom many people depended for their livelihood, but she made him feel like a shy little boy. "I had hoped you were the woman God had prepared for me, and yet I couldn't trust Him to bring it about. I was wrong. Can you ever forgive me?"

She fiddled with the fringe on one of Marta's colorful afghans and took a moment to answer. "I have something to confess, too. I blew everything out of proportion. Yes, you made a mistake, but it wasn't that big of a deal. My only defense is that it reminded me of the hard times with my father, who was a manipulator. I lumped you with him. I shouldn't have, because you're not the same kind of man, but my past colored my feelings. God has shown me that even though I thought I had forgiven my father, I hadn't really. And that unforgiveness spilled all over you."

Hope leaped in Austin's chest. "So does that mean I'm forgiven now?"

"Yes, and yesterday in the evening worship time at camp, I truly forgave my father."

Austin leaned back and rocked in the large maple chair. "I finally realized what I was doing and decided to trust God with the whole problem."

"Is that why you stopped calling?"

Did he hear disappointment in Valerie's question? "So you noticed." He chuckled. "Yes, I had to trust Him, even if a relationship with you never happened. But do you think it might work out?"

With a sweet smile, she nodded. "I hope so."

"This has been some week, hasn't it?" Austin stood and extended his hand to her. "Let's go for a walk."

Valerie wasn't walking—she was floating, or at least it felt that way. Never letting go of her hand, Austin led her out the back door and across the yard to an apple orchard. They wandered through the trees, talking about their family histories.

Finally, he stopped and turned to face her. "Valerie, I believe you're the woman God created for me. I want to marry you, but I'll give you all the time you need to get to know me better."

"Oh, I think I know you well enough to know that you're the man God created for me." She reached up and placed a quick kiss on his cheek, then became embarrassed at how forward she'd been.

Austin pulled her into his arms, and she rested her head on his chest. "Father, thank You for bringing Valerie into my life. Help me love her and cherish her the way You intend for me to. We give our future into Your hands."

When his voice died away, Valerie looked up at him and smiled with her whole heart. He lowered his face toward hers, and when their lips met, her toes curled, her world shifted, and she had to cling to him to keep from melting into a puddle.

Epilogue

Four months later

Austin stood at the front of the sanctuary of Word of Love Church, listening to the prelude music. Scott and Terry stood beside him. The three men watched as first Sherry, then Lisa, walked slowly down the aisle on the white runner.

The "Wedding March" pealed from the organ, and the doors at the end of the aisle opened wide. Austin had eyes for nothing except his lovely bride. Valerie had opted not to cover her face with her veil. She told him she didn't want any more secrets hidden from each other. That's what had caused their problems, and she didn't want to start their marriage hiding anything from him.

Can you help me? The first words Austin ever heard from Valerie played through his mind. Yes, he planned to help her for the rest of their lives. And she'd helped him learn to trust God more completely. Together they would forge a strong family built on that trust.

LENA NELSON DOOLEY lives in Hurst, Texas, with her husband, James, and enjoys her two daughters and her grandchildren. Aside from writing, Lena has been a speaker to women's groups and retreats and at writing seminars and conferences. Lena appreciates any opportunity to spread the gospel through mission work and writing. Visit her Web site at www.LenaNelsonDooley.com.

CAUGHT
RED-HANDED

by Yvonne Lehman

Dedication

To David Lehman for sharing his knowledge of security.
And to Michelle Cox, Debbie Presnell, and Ann Tatlock
for taking the time to read this
and giving their invaluable input.

You are to live clean, innocent lives
as children of God in a dark world
full of crooked and perverse people.
Let your lives shine brightly before them.
PHILIPPIANS 2:15 NLT

Chapter 1

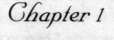

L aurel Jones, with her hands around a potted plant, was leaning far into the back of her minivan when she saw the movement outside the passenger-side window.

It's just the wind moving the branches. There was no good reason for anyone to be standing back there at the burlap-balled trees next to the vinyl shed.

No *good* reason.

That thought made her freeze like she was a DVD and someone pushed the remote's PAUSE button. But she knew she had to make sure, without being obvious, whether or not someone was out there.

Neither lifting her face nor turning her head, she shot a glance through the window.

Yes. Someone stood there. She wasn't exactly in the most offensive position to cope with an attacker. Her hands eased away from the plant, and she backed out of the minivan.

Slowly straightening, she took a step back, and in her peripheral vision she saw the figure take a step forward.

She knew the gates of the fourteen-foot high chain-link

fencing were closed and locked. A few managers or security personnel might still be inside the Home & Hearth Superstore, but they would be too far away to hear if she screamed.

A pickup truck was parked next to her van. *Does it belong to someone inside the store or to this person sneaking around in the dark?* The time was way past nine o'clock since she'd stayed awhile talking to her supervisor. The overcast sky didn't help, either, having turned the night into a blend of darkness and shadows.

She'd have to depend on the rush of adrenaline that provided supernatural strength she'd heard accompanied danger. Her purse, with her cell phone in it, lay right inside the back of the minivan, but it contained no weapon. The van keys were above her head in the slot on the raised back door.

What to do? Possibilities invaded her mind just as a streak of lightning lit up the sky.

Reach up and jerk the keys out? He'd be there by then, maybe even cover her hand as she reached, or he'd wrestle the keys from her. Should she wait until he came near her, throw the plant at him, jump into the van, and slam down the door? She could then dive over the seat and press the LOCK button.

No, that wouldn't work. All he'd have to do is take the keys out of the slot and use the remote to unlock the doors. That would be like an invitation for him to drive her somewhere.

Maybe she could pretend not to be afraid and talk him out of whatever he had in mind.

Running wouldn't help. No one would hear or get to her in time even if she made it to the doors of the building. Anyone inside would be in an office anyway, not on the floor. To run through the vast parking lot up to the interstate might mean worse trouble. Who would stop for some girl out at night waving wildly at them?

The "who" part made her tremble.

She would simply have to use her wits, which seemed to have taken a vacation. But he was coming closer. His pace was slow, and he seemed to sway slightly. *Is he drunk?*

That could be in her favor. If he were drunk enough, she might be able to shove him. If he wasn't. . .

Pray.

Yes, pray.

Lord, help me.

Thunder sounded, and she jumped. A large drop of rain splattered on her nose.

He limped closer. She picked up a plant, ready to throw it at him if he came too close.

He stopped at the back tire. "I didn't mean to surprise you."

Trying not to sound scared, she said, "No. It was the thunder."

She set the plant right inside the van, watching his every move. He didn't move except to fold his arms in front of him. A man didn't walk around late at night dressed in dark clothing, with a brimmed cap obscuring part of his face, and stand in the shadows for no reason.

When she reached down for another plant, she saw the medical cast on his left foot. A guy in college had worn one like that after he sprained his ankle. Great! She could outrun this man. Unless he reached up and grabbed the keys. She couldn't outrun the van.

And what might he have in that boot? Duct tape? Rope? A

knife? She shuddered, all her senses alert as she put one plant after another into the trunk.

"Quite a few plants you have there," he said, as if something was wrong with that.

"Yes." She felt more drops of rain. With her left hand she picked up her purse. With her right she slammed down the door. Her next move would be to snatch the keys. She'd be ready to whack him with the purse if he grabbed for her. Then she'd shove the metal cart into his legs.

"I'm. . . ," he said, and his other words were drowned out by sounds of the storm.

Thunder rumbled and lightning streaked the sky just as a cloud burst and the rain poured. When he looked toward the sky, she jerked out the keys. His hands dropped to his sides. He took a step forward. She stepped aside, ready to shove the cart if necessary.

She didn't know what he'd said after "I'm" and didn't care. She didn't want to know who or what he was or how he felt.

"Whoa," he said as the rain fell harder. "Would you mind giving me a ride around to the other side of the lot where my car's parked?"

Laurel stared, totally shocked. Something about his tone of voice sounded as friendly, serious, and polite as if he were a friend from church asking for a ride home. Her moment of sympathy quickly switched to caution. She remembered having seen a program on TV about a good-looking, intelligent serial killer who had lured young women into his car by pretending to have a broken arm.

Without answering, she sloshed around the cart, careful of her steps lest she slip in the water, soaking her shoes, or lest he run toward her, which wasn't likely unless he was faking the foot injury.

Uncertain whether the beating of her heart or the thunder was shaking the earth, she reached the front door, jerked it open, and pushed the LOCK button. She jumped into the driver's seat and slammed the door shut.

Whew! Saved by the storm.

Thank You, Lord.

She and friends had discussed what they'd do if someone tried to force their way into their vehicle. The general consensus was not to acknowledge it but take a chance to get away. Could she really just drive away if he pulled a gun? She was afraid to look but didn't think he was at the window. If she had to shove him and the cart away with the van, so be it. Maybe that's how he got the injured foot in the first place—sneaking up on women late at night.

Laurel realized she'd been operating on an unnatural calm. But she mustn't give in to nerves or weakness until she was safely out of there. Despite the shaking of her hand, the key finally connected with the slot and slid in. Now all she needed was for the engine to catch. It did.

Looking into the rearview mirror while backing cautiously, she saw the white glow of the backup lights and then the scarlet tint from the brake lights illuminating the man in black, hobbling toward the building. Holding on to the handle of the cart, he pulled it behind him.

Why is he taking the cart toward the building? The only reason she could think of was that he would be stealing the plants sitting outside the building. Maybe he wasn't a killer but a thief.

With that downpour, he'd be totally drenched. Served him

right. He shouldn't have been out there scaring people in the first place.

She cautiously steered the van across the water-swamped parking lot. The *slop-slosh* sound of the wipers against the heavy rain pelting the windshield matched the beat of her heart as she headed in the direction of the interstate. Each glance in the rearview mirror revealed a figure, like a dark wavy blot silhouetted against a gray building, fading in the distance.

First thing tomorrow, upon arriving at work, she'd report this incident.

"Of all the stupid stunts to pull."

Marc Goodson berated himself for behaving so unprofessionally. As head of security at H&H, he was supposed to be catching thieves red-handed, not hanging around outside looking like a criminal or a pervert.

He'd expected to find the guys he'd suspected of stealing lumber and had been out beside the shed, concealed by the trees, to discover whether that pickup truck was the vehicle for transporting the stolen goods from H&H. But upon seeing Laurel Jones, he'd let surprise overwhelm his good sense.

What was she doing with all those plants? He couldn't accuse her of anything until after he checked to see if she paid for them. He didn't easily become surprised and certainly never allowed some female to cause him to be tongue-tied.

When he'd tried to introduce himself, the storm had interfered. But his name probably wouldn't have meant anything to her anyway. Then he'd stupidly asked her for a ride.

By the time he reached the other side of the building, he

decided not to unlock and enter through the private entrance but slogged and squished to his black sports car parked opposite the door. Feeling like a drowned rat—and a humiliated one at that—he shook himself like a wet dog, which did no good in the heavy downpour.

He managed to get into the driver's seat, his foot feeling as heavy as concrete in the cast. Trying to ignore his plight as much as possible, he slammed the door shut, found a napkin and wiped his hands with it, then took his cell phone from the inside pocket of his jacket.

Edgar Banks, his assistant who was waiting for a report, answered on the first ring.

"Just to let you know everything's all right," Marc said. He almost laughed aloud at that. "What I mean is my suspects weren't out there tonight. I'm going home."

"You'll get 'em sooner or later," Banks said. "You always do."

Maybe. Apparently the thieves were smarter than to risk losing their lives in an electrical storm. "See you tomorrow." He flipped the cover of the phone shut and returned it to his pocket.

"What's wrong with me nowadays?" he questioned aloud. First he'd broken a bone on the side of his foot when a guy had resisted arrest—decided on *fight* instead of *flight*—and he'd had to wrestle the fellow to the floor. Marc had a few sore knuckles, but the other fellow's nose would never be the same.

It wasn't often Marc had to use physical force. In fact, he was only allowed to do so in self-defense. Now, besides having a broken bone on the side of his foot, he'd misjudged the events he'd expected to occur tonight. And if Miss Jones spread the word, the thieves would know he was onto them.

Thirty minutes later, he drove his car into the garage of his grandmother's house and pushed the remote to lower the door. While it grinded shut, he eased out onto the concrete floor.

All he needed now was to slip and break his other foot. Or to get electrocuted when he switched on the garage light, because any minute the automatic one would go off and he'd be in a pickle in the darkness—much like he'd been back at the store.

After switching on the light, he found a towel and wiped the rainwater from the leather car seat. He tossed the towel aside, opened the laundry room door, and sat on the threshold to take off his shoe and set it on the concrete. Next, off came the cast. The Velcro and nylon, attached to the rubber sole, should dry overnight—once he'd wiped out the inside.

He remained seated as best he could while removing his clothing, feeling as he thought a snake might feel while shedding its skin. The process was slow, wet, and cold.

Inside the laundry room, he tossed his clothes, except for the jacket, into the washer. His once-white undershorts were dyed a navy blue hue, and he suspected the skin on his backside was the same color—the color of his mood at the moment.

When he walked into the kitchen, he saw the flashing light on the wall phone. His mood worsened when he listened to the message that said his grandmother was doing well but wouldn't be able to talk with him tonight. He missed her most when the weather was cold or stormy.

Twenty minutes later he sat on the couch in dry clothes and with one of his grandmother's afghans around his shoulders. It felt good on a night when he'd been soaked clear through to the bone. The warm bath had helped. And now hot coffee warmed his insides.

After a while he heard the signal that the washer had done its job. He'd put the clothes in the dryer later. Maybe the humming would help him sleep. He'd need something to still that feeling of having totally messed up tonight.

He switched on the TV, but another picture was playing on his mental monitor. He kept visualizing the young woman who'd recently come to work at H&H.

He'd wanted to find the right time to meet Laurel Jones for reasons that had nothing to do with the work situation. Tonight had been neither the right time nor the right way.

Chapter 2

Laurel had slept fitfully. One minute she felt like a victim. The next she felt like a villain.

She couldn't stop thinking about the man in the storm. Something about his voice caused her to rationalize and think that perhaps the man in black had simply been looking at the trees and really had come around to help her.

But she needed to face facts—not some obscure feeling of guilt or what-might-have-been.

To get her mind on something else, she stood on the back deck with her hands wrapped around the aromatic cup of hot coffee with its slight odor and taste of coconut creamer. After another sip of the delicious brew, she lowered the cup to the wooden railing and took in a deep breath of the fresh pine-scented morning air.

The vegetable garden looked like chocolate pudding decorated with strips of little green spinach shoots. In the flower beds around the deck, a few blossoms of pansies had been beaten to a pulp, but most of the spring shoots were intact. The boxwoods, rhododendron, and English laurel were hardy plants that could withstand not only April showers but the late May downpours like that of last night.

After breakfast she'd take the potted plants to the basement. That thought brought with it a stab of loneliness as she remembered how she and her mom used to work together with plants. Would her efforts make her mom proud?

A laugh of irony almost escaped her throat at that thought. Her mom had expected right things from her, but Laurel had never had to prove her worth. She felt a smile then. The sun shot brighter rays across the sky as it rose farther from behind the distant mountains.

"Laurel?" her dad called.

After lifting the cup for the last drop of her wake-up brew, she opened the screen door and walked into the kitchen. Her senses were further awakened by the sizzle and aroma of bacon. Her dad looked over his shoulder and smiled. "Hey, doll."

"Good morning, Dad." Laurel walked over, put her hands on his shoulders, and leaned against his back for a moment. She thought of the many times she'd given her mom and dad a quick hug or a hasty adieu. It had never occurred to her that she might lose either of them.

"Sleep well?" he asked.

She moved to the countertop and leaned against it where she could see his face. "I had strange dreams."

He turned the bacon with tongs and put the round spatter screen over the skillet before facing her. "What about?"

"I don't remember, but they awakened me with the same kind of feelings I had at Home & Hearth last night."

"The storm?" He laid down the tongs and spread his hands in a helpless gesture. His face, beneath a bald head that only enhanced his good looks, took on a concerned expression. "Honey, why didn't you tell me you were upset last night? Just because I'm lying in bed with the TV on—"

"Dad," she interrupted, "I know I can talk to you anytime. But I didn't tell you for the very reason you'd get on your high horse and call the police or go out in the storm yourself."

"Police?" he blared before she got the entire sentence out of her mouth.

"No big deal now." She pointed to the skillet. "Better watch that bacon."

"Yeah," he said, "the pancakes, too. They're ready to be turned."

"I'll do it." Laurel walked over to the electric griddle where the pancakes had bubbled. She turned each one. "I'll tell you about it over breakfast. But only if you promise to let me handle the situation."

He grumbled while putting the bacon on a platter. "Sure, Laurel. My only daughter, who can't sleep, has nightmares because of something that happened at work, talks about calling the police, and I'm to promise to stay out of it. Now, what kind of dad would that make me?" He set the platter near the griddle.

"The kind who knows his daughter is a grown woman and can do a few things herself." She raised the edge of a pancake and saw that it was brown on the bottom and began lifting them all onto the platter.

Her dad took orange juice from the refrigerator and glasses from the cupboard, all the while muttering something about a grown woman. "Like your mom used to say, Laurel—you'll always be my baby girl."

She nodded, feeling a sudden swell of emotion. "I hope so,

Daddy." She set the platter on the island and moved to a cabinet to get the bottle of maple syrup. Setting it down, she faced him. "And if this is too big for me, you'll be the first one I call."

They sat on their stools and her dad asked the blessing. Almost as soon as she opened her eyes, he said, "Now tell me about it."

Laurel did.

She let her dad rant and rave until she felt he had most of it out of his system. "Where was security?" he spouted. "What kind of place is that anyway?"

"Dad. . ." She tried to use a consoling tone. "H&H is the kind of place that gives you a discount on your building materials. It's the kind of place that gave me a part-time, temporary job. And the kind of place that sells me plants at a greatly reduced price."

He snorted, his red face turning a lighter shade of pink, which she hoped meant he had sufficiently vented. "It's the kind of place that's going to hear from me about safety."

Laurel lifted a piece of bacon onto her plate. "Dad, you promised to let me handle this."

"When did I do that?"

"When I asked if you would, you said, 'Sure.' "

"No, no," he rebutted. "That was a rhetorical answer."

"Dad, questions are rhetorical—not answers."

His eyebrows lifted, his head ducked slightly, and he gazed at her. His tone of voice grew quiet. "You're all I have, hon."

"But I'm a big girl now."

He nodded. "So was your mom."

She wished he hadn't said that. Sometimes they could talk about her mom and even laugh about a former funny experience.

But other times, like this, a great loneliness welled up, threatening to bring tears.

In the light of day and feeling safe while sitting across from her dad, she wondered if she'd overreacted last night. "The man didn't really do or say anything wrong. Maybe he was a customer who left late and—"

"Laurel." Her dad's terse tone and steady gaze held a world of meaning.

She exhaled heavily. "I'll talk with security about it."

He nodded, pointing his fork at her. "And you don't leave that place alone after dark."

She promised. "If I leave after dark, I'll have security walk me out."

"And you will report this."

"Yes, Dad. As soon as I get to work."

"Looks like we might have a wedding in the store." Charlie Simmons set his tray on the table and settled into the chair across from Marc in the food court.

Marc stared at the manager of the Home & Hearth Superstore. "You've got to be kidding."

"No joke," Charlie said. "Just a minute and I'll tell you about it."

Marc waited while Charlie bowed his head of brown hair intermingled with gray and said a brief thanks for the food. After his "Amen," he began unwrapping his burger. "I got a call this morning from a woman. We set up an appointment for her and her fiancé to talk with me about it." He looked pleased. "They met at the store."

Marc scoffed. "Looks to me like H&H is turning into a dating service instead of a home supply store." He removed the plastic lid from his salad, although he felt his appetite wane at the turn of the conversation.

During the three-block drive to the mall, the discussion between him and his middle-aged boss had centered around Marc's work as security agent of H&H and the considerable amount of money Marc was saving the store by not only catching shoplifters but also uncovering inside criminal activity.

"Don't knock it," Charlie said after washing down a bite of burger with a drink of his milkshake. "Those newspaper articles about couples meeting in our store keep bringing in more customers. They'll make a purchase to keep from being too obvious about looking for a mate. Some of them will end up getting married and setting up a home, and that's what our store is all about—beautifying the home. After all"—he popped a french fry into his mouth, chewed, swallowed, and then grinned—"love makes the world go 'round."

Marc could have said love also makes it fall apart. But such a statement could lead to questions Marc didn't care to answer. He gave a short laugh. "It's interesting, watching the security monitors and seeing men and women run into each other's cart or wait in the aisles until a member of the opposite sex appears."

Charlie grinned. "How do you know some of those couples aren't married to each other?"

"Easy," Marc said. "Married couples stand there and argue about wallpaper, paint, or appliances. Singles are on their best behavior, dressed up, and smiling."

Charlie wadded up his burger wrapper and tossed it onto

the tray. "If I'm not being too personal, Marc, I'd say you have something against marriage."

Marc shrugged. "Never been in that state of anxiety."

"See. There you go." Charlie settled back against his chair. "At your age—what is it, twenty-nine?—you should be thinking about settling down. But you sound like a guy who's been bitten."

The snap of the plastic lid as his fingers fastened it on the remains of the salad seemed to punctuate Marc's words. "I'm in no hurry."

"Mmmm," Charlie scoffed. "So you'd rather watch customers walk the aisles of H&H Superstore than watch some pretty young woman walk down the church aisle toward you?"

Without commenting on Charlie's remark, Marc chewed on a whole-wheat cracker. He would have stopped this line of talk long before now with anyone else. But he and Charlie had hit it off from the time Marc had been interviewed for the job, and they'd both been open about their faith.

However, Marc didn't care to talk about his past private life. He drank his coffee and listened to Charlie praise the state of marriage and tell stories about his children.

Sometimes he thought Charlie was too good to be true with his reputation of being a fine Christian family man. But Marc was well aware of a public persona that could be different from one's private life. His own family had taught him that.

"Mark my words," Charlie said after finishing his milkshake. "One of these days you'll get caught." He stood and took hold of his tray.

Pushing his chair back, Marc laughed. "Charlie, you just gave another reason for *not* getting married. You referred to it as 'getting caught.' Now, who wants to live like that?"

"Anybody who falls in love," Charlie said, as if Marc should have known the answer.

Marc shook his head and dumped the remains of his lunch into the trash bin.

Chapter 3

Laurel had worked all morning in the basement, treating the plants that had fungus, neglect, or insect problems. She was as adamant about trying to keep plants alive and healthy as some people were about their animals. She felt they had a right to live their beautiful, productive lives and enrich the lives of others.

"Yes," she said as she watered a geranium that had only the problem of being thirsty. "Here's a nice, long drink for you. And when you're stronger, I'll find a good home for you." She smiled, remembering her mom had said plants needed talking to and touching, just like humans.

Later in the day, after having babied her plants, she arrived at H&H thirty minutes early to let Mindy, the manager of the Garden Shop, know that someone had been sneaking around outside last night and that she needed to report the incident to security.

Showing concern, Mindy advised her in much the way Laurel's dad had—not to be outside alone after dark.

Laurel agreed with that. "I should be finished by three

o'clock, but in case I'm not, I wanted you to know that I'll be in the security office."

"That's fine, Laurel. Take your time. We don't want anything happening to you. You're a natural with plants." Mindy touched Laurel's arm. "For your information, head of security is called 'Deacon' behind his back. He's known for preaching morality while having somebody arrested."

Now, that sounded to Laurel like someone who'd take care of this matter properly. "Thanks," she said and smiled. She admired Mindy for having become a manager while being only a couple of years older than she. Mindy's expertise lay in the business aspect of things rather than in a great knowledge of plants.

But for now, Laurel reminded herself to concentrate on what she should say to "Deacon." So engrossed in her thoughts, she suddenly found herself in the center of the aisle and ran head-on into someone.

"Oh. I'm"—her breath caught—"sorry."

Looking up into the unusually handsome face and feeling the strength of his hands on her shoulders, she easily could have said, "I'm delighted." Something about him seemed familiar. Did she know this man? Maybe from her dreams—daydreams, that is. She could get lost in those blue, blue eyes.

Suddenly, those newspaper articles about people meeting at H&H didn't seem so ridiculous. Oh, but this good-looking man wouldn't need to go to a store to find a girl. He'd have to go somewhere to hide from the line of women chasing him.

Hoping he couldn't read her mind, she stepped back, and her gaze moved to the floor. The first thing she saw beneath the dress pants was a foot cast.

"Y—you," she could only whisper as she wrenched away from him.

"Please, wait," he implored with an outstretched hand. "You don't understand."

She was already several steps away from him when she heard the words. She was afraid she understood all too well. Seeing the manager ahead, she strode to him. "Pardon me," she said, interrupting his conversation with a customer. "This is urgent."

"Just a moment," he said to the customer and moved to a more private spot with Laurel.

"You see that man down there? Pretend you're not looking. The one wearing the foot cast?"

"Yes," the manager said.

Her breath came in short gasps. "Watch him. I don't want to be anywhere near him, and I'm on my way to tell security about him."

"What's it about?"

"He was outside in the dark last night, and now he's in here. He's either a thief or he's stalking me." She hurried away toward the security office.

"A thief or. . .stalking?" Marc could hardly believe the words he was hearing from Charlie.

Charlie grimaced. "You know why she'd say that?"

"Yes," Marc admitted, "I do." He was careful about his reputation as a responsible security agent and needed to be trusted. Never had he been accused of anything close to being a thief or a stalker.

Marc didn't think Charlie would believe that about him.

But after coming to work in security two years ago, Marc was the one who uncovered a theft plot masterminded by the head of security. His own undercover work had led to his promotion. Any kind of accusation, however unfounded, could cause others to wonder if he were any more trustworthy than the former security agent.

Now, a young woman whom he suspected was the daughter of a man who had shown utmost trust in him was labeling him not only a thief, but a stalker. Marc took a deep breath and exhaled. "Can we go into your office and talk about it?"

"Sure," Charlie said. "But get that look of horror off your face. You know I trust you, Marc, and I know you have a reason for being outside after dark last night." He grinned. "What I'm finding interesting is that some woman has you riled up. She's gone to report you to security." Charlie laughed as they entered his office. "Think of the irony of that."

Marc could see the irony but not the humor. He couldn't laugh or even smile about such a thing. He sat on the couch and watched while Charlie moved to a table in the corner and filled two foam cups with coffee.

"Cream, right?" Charlie asked.

"Yes, thanks." Marc appreciated Charlie's trying to put him at ease. He handed Marc a cup and sat in a chair behind the desk. After taking a sip, Charlie set his coffee down. "Okay," he said and grinned. "What did you do to that poor girl? Are you trying one of those meet-at-the-H&H-store romance meetings?"

Marc didn't want to kid around about this situation. "You know I dislike things like that going on here, Charlie."

"So you've told me." He chuckled. "But you have to admit, she's one attractive young woman."

Marc was well aware of that even though she usually wore casual slacks and a plain shirt covered by a blue hip-length H&H smock. Today she wasn't wearing the smock. She was early. He knew she came in at 3:00 p.m. His usual hours were 9:00 a.m. to 5:00 p.m., unless he had some particular investigation going on that required him to work different hours.

Marc crossed his right leg over his left knee. He related his reason for being outside the night before. He expected to see two guys loading up that truck. Instead, he encountered Laurel.

"And a few minutes ago," he explained, "I was going to the Garden Shop to introduce myself and apologize for last night when we. . .ran into each other." He gave a short laugh. "I should say she ran into me." He pointed to his boot. "I mean, I'm forced to take it slowly, and she had a good gait. Slammed right into me."

"Fate," Charlie said. He tilted his head and spoke as if thoughtful. "No, let me change that to. . .blessing."

"Blessing?" Marc snorted. "She's reporting me to security for being a thief and a stalker." Marc felt Charlie was enjoying the entire situation way too much.

"Then you'd better get to your office so she can report to you." Charlie's eyes held amusement.

Marc glanced at the wall clock. "Can't do that right now. I have a doctor's appointment to see if I can quit wearing this thing." He tapped his cast. "I'm anxious to get back on the exercise machines." He finished his coffee and stood. "I came in for the express reason of explaining to Miss Laurel Jones that I was outside last night because of security reasons and in here today because I work here." He tossed his cup into the trash can.

"Best wishes," Charlie said as Marc headed for the door.

Marc looked back. Was Charlie wishing him the best in regard to his foot or to the situation with Laurel Jones? Both, maybe. He sighed. "Sometimes we just have to face the. . ." *Not music.* "Verdict," he muttered and opened the door a few inches to peer out like some kind of sneak.

This was ridiculous. He wasn't afraid to approach a muscular thief twice his size and had a broken bone in his foot to prove it. Physical fear had nothing to do with this situation, however. And he understood all too well the psychological side of it. Could he never get over this feeling of having to constantly prove himself trustworthy?

Glancing around—lest she run into him again and accuse him of something else—he hobbled as well as he could out a side door and headed for his car.

Edgar Banks would likely inform Miss Jones that Marc was head of security and that's the reason he would have been outside last night and the reason he was in the store this afternoon.

Marc did manage a short laugh as he got into his car and stuck the key into the ignition. Then Miss Jones could apologize to him.

Yes, that's the way it would. . .should happen. Let her be on the defensive.

For a moment he sat grasping the steering wheel and looking straight ahead. No, he really didn't want her to be on the defensive. Last night he should have yelled out—even above the thunder and the rain and the lightning—that he was security and would protect her. . .not scare her.

This was not simply a laugh-away store matter. He didn't take kindly to being called a thief and a stalker. He could

279

understand her jumping to conclusions, but they were the wrong ones. He'd have to set it straight. The possibility of a lawsuit—as well as his reputation—was at stake. Yes, he must apologize.

But maybe inside H&H wasn't the best place to do it. This called for an off-duty, personal call.

Chapter 4

Laurel could hardly believe the attitude of the short, redheaded security person who introduced himself as Edgar Banks.

After telling about her scare last night caused by the guy in the trees, she watched his facial expression change from serious to something akin to amusement. "Now, tell me again what he looked like."

"He was wearing dark clothes and had a baseball cap pulled down concealing his eyes. It was dark and stormy, so I didn't get a good look last night and I was scared. But," she said, "I saw him perfectly clearly awhile ago. He's tall and sort of. . .well, good-looking, and he was wearing a foot cast, like that man was wearing last night."

Edgar drummed his fingers on the desk. After a moment he looked across at her. "Did he try to harm you?"

"No. But he scared the daylights out of me. I didn't know what he had in mind, being out there in the dark and walking toward me."

"Did he say anything threatening?"

Laurel tried to remember. "He asked if I needed help."

"You, um. . ." Banks cleared his throat. "You found that threatening?"

Something about this man's manner was making her think she'd jumped to foolish conclusions. "At the time, yes," she said. "Something in his voice didn't sound too friendly when he asked that."

Banks avoided looking directly at her. His teeth played with his lower lip, and he smoothed his red curls. . .uselessly. They still looked unruly. The way his gaze didn't quite meet hers made her think he thought she was nuts.

He cleared his throat again. "Did he say anything else?"

"When it started pouring rain, he asked for a ride. He said his car was parked on the other side of the lot."

Edgar looked at her then and nodded thoughtfully. "You found that threatening?"

She shrugged. Edgar Banks was making her feel foolish. "I don't know. How can I say if he wanted a ride or was just trying to get into my vehicle?"

"I understand why you might have felt you shouldn't trust him. Um, he didn't say who he was?"

She shook her head. "I think he might have, but there was a loud rumble of thunder just then and the downpour came. That's when he asked for a ride."

"So he really didn't try to harm you or say anything unseemly."

"Well, his just being out there was. . .weird."

"Why is that?"

"Out in the dark late at night?" She felt like screaming. This man didn't seem very perceptive.

"Well, Miss Jones, you were out in the dark late at night."

Laurel gasped. "I was loading plants."

Edgar nodded. "And you said there was a truck beside your vehicle. Then later he pulled the cart toward the store." His eyebrows lifted. "Maybe he had something to load, too."

That seemed possible. Amazing how another opinion could put an entirely different spin on things.

"You suppose, ma'am, you were just surprised and scared and thought the worst?"

Laurel could honestly say, "I suppose, but. . .he was in the store today and ran straight into me."

"Ran?" Edgar asked. "With a cast on his foot?" He looked at her with a tolerant expression as though he were the head of the complaint department and she was saying nothing more than why she was returning a defective item.

"Well," she hedged. "Maybe he didn't exactly run. I suppose I was thinking about what to say when I came in here and wasn't watching where I was going. But why would he be here in the store today after what happened last night?"

Edgar gave her a straightforward look. "The same thing you're doing here. Maybe he works here or maybe he's shopping. Oh." He grinned. "Maybe he's looking for romance."

"Romance?"

Laurel felt it was time for her to leave. Either Edgar wasn't very astute, or she was out of her mind and imagining things. Romance—of all things!

She thought of the dark, mysterious figure of last night. Then of the tall, serious-looking, handsome man with intense deep blue eyes she ran into this afternoon. That combination didn't spell romance to her. It spelled. . .danger.

"No offense, Miss Jones," Edgar said. "I'm old enough to be your father. But if I were a younger man like your mystery man in the cast, I'd feel like coming to H&H with romance on my mind if I'd encountered you." He raised both palms and leaned slightly back as if warding her off lest she attack him. "Like I said, no offense. I'm a happily married man. But you seem to jump to conclusions, and I'm just trying to give you a compliment."

"Thanks," Laurel said blandly. She could have added, "No thanks," but she felt Edgar was just trying to placate her by being overly complimentary.

"And, Miss Jones. . .it's best you don't talk to anyone else here about your suspicions. You're an employee, and if you falsely accuse anyone, we could have a lawsuit on our hands." He paused, quite serious. "Have you told anyone else?"

The question rendered Laurel speechless for a moment. The impact of what Edgar Banks was saying began to register. She'd been here less than a week and was being told she could cause a lawsuit. The mystery man could claim that he was trying to meet her, or that he'd been looking at trees, then saw her loading plants and offered to help. He could say anything and she could prove nothing.

Feeling on the defensive, she said she'd only told her dad. "Oh, I did tell the Garden Shop manager."

"Mindy," he said. "How much did you tell her?"

Laurel tried to remember exactly. "I just said someone was out there last night and I needed to tell security."

"You didn't mention the cast?"

After a moment, Laurel shook her head. "No, I just said a man was out there and scared me to death. I told her about the incident quickly, wanting to come in here and report it, then get to work by three o'clock."

She followed his glance to the wall clock. The hands had neared three o'clock. She stood. "I won't say anything. But this bears looking into."

"Yes, ma'am," he said. "We have security cameras throughout the store, even outside, and after hours we have a staff security person on duty."

"Where was this person last night?"

She wondered if he was trying to cover inefficiency when he paused for a moment, then said, "Security cameras aren't as clear as we'd like during a storm."

She left the office, thinking she had no idea why anyone would call that man "Deacon."

Walking back toward the Garden Shop, Laurel kept a keen eye on the aisles in case the man was lurking somewhere, looking for her or looking for. . .romance.

The idea!

She refused to admit that something had stirred inside her when she looked up at him and he held onto her shoulders. It was like. . .she knew him—or wanted to.

But that could be explained away, because she did know him. She knew him as the sneaky prowler of the night before.

And how in the world could she think of romance with someone who appeared to be a pervert, a thief, or a stalker? That was about as tasteful as eating cheesecake topped with boiled okra.

Tonight she'd have security walk out with her, and if that man—good-looking or not—showed up, she'd threaten to have him arrested if he approached her again.

"What?" Marc said after returning to H&H from his doctor's appointment. He'd envisioned that Edgar would have told Laurel Jones he was neither a thief nor a stalker. "Why didn't you tell her that was me and I'm security?"

Edgar got a helpless look on his face. "You said you'd be out there expecting to put an end to one of your cases, and I didn't know but that she might be part of it. I didn't want to tip your hand."

Feeling frustrated, Marc took a few steps away from Edgar, turned, and paced back toward him. "So you didn't mention that I'm security?"

"Nope. Not a word. I think I made her realize how ridiculous her charges were. But I said we'd look into it. Didn't want to chance messing up your investigation." He grinned. "Or your chances with the new employee who attracted your attention."

Marc scoffed. "You're out of your mind."

"Now, Deacon. Don't lose your religion over this. I noticed your interest the day that pretty girl started working here. Several times you've said, 'There's Firefly again.'"

"C'mon, Ed. You make it sound like I spend my days watching her."

"No, I don't mean that. I just mean you've mentioned her several times. Even given her a nickname."

"That's done around here, Ed; you know that. You're called Red instead of Ed." Marc shrugged. "It's just that Miss Jones lights up when she's talking to a customer. She talks with her hands, and the name Firefly just came to mind. She's quite animated when working with a customer. And they always buy and go away happy." He could kick himself for trying to explain himself to Edgar as if he were on trial.

Marc didn't speak aloud the thought that passed through his mind. He'd frightened Laurel twice already. How was he ever going to get this worked out? Or could he?

This didn't seem to be the day or the time for another run-in with Miss Firefly. "I'll be here a little while longer, Ed," Marc said. "I want to check some receipts."

"For your information," Ed said, "she and Mindy seem to have become quite chummy. During a break, the two of them went down to Lumber and talked to Spike, then they went to Appliances and talked to Sparky."

Marc felt he was in a dilemma. How could he convince Laurel Jones that he was an honest fellow but she should beware of becoming friends with the threesome he suspected of illegal activity? No way could he tell that to an employee.

Then a worse thought struck him. Suppose she was already mixed up with that threesome? Suppose she had been stealing plants last night?

Surely not.

No?

It happened in the best of families. He knew because it had happened in his. His dad had been a leader in the church and a respected businessman.

The business partner/accountant of Marc's dad came to Clovis Goodson, saying he had "borrowed" some money when he got in a tight spot. He didn't report everything on his taxes to make up for it, was in trouble, and asked for a chance to make it right.

Marc's dad gave him that chance. But the IRS found the discrepancy and wasn't interested in excuses. Although the partner admitted he was the one who'd done wrong, Marc's dad admitted he'd known about it and didn't report it. Being a partner and knowing of the illegal act of trying to cover up embezzled funds, Clovis Goodson lost his business, his home, his wife, many of his friends, his reputation, and his freedom for many months—all because he'd tried to be lenient with his friend.

That memory was as clear for Marc as it had been almost a decade ago. Maybe even clearer now, because then he'd experienced the ordeal emotionally. Now he could be more objective. He thought he might even be able to understand his dad's trying to protect his friend and partner.

Marc was in the business of catching thieves red-handed. But the last one in the world he'd want to catch would be the daughter of Harlan Jones.

Chapter 5

Laurel thought she'd have no problem remembering the nicknames of Mindy's two friends. They looked nothing alike. Mindy introduced the lanky, dark-haired fellow with spiked hair as her boyfriend. Sparky was his friend, shorter with thin light brown hair and a round face. He was stocky and muscular and appeared rather hyper the way he spoke fast and shifted from one foot to the other as though he couldn't be still.

"Maybe we could double-date," Mindy said after they returned to the Garden Shop. "Me and Spike, you and Sparky. That is, if you like him."

Like him? The guys were pleasant enough. Mindy had mentioned Laurel's scare the night before, and the guys said they'd walk her out and make sure she was okay when she left work.

She hadn't dated in a long time. In college several guys and girls had gone to ball games, movies, and other functions together as friends. She belonged to a singles' class at church, but no one really appealed to her beyond friendship.

Despite his nickname, neither did Sparky—nor Spike. During the past few years, she'd had no time to allow a serious relationship to develop. She'd been busy trying to get her education and dropping out of college for a semester to help care for her mom.

Spending those last months with her mom had helped ease the pain of losing her.

During supper break, she and Mindy ate together at the mall food court. Later, at closing time, Spike, Sparky, and Mindy walked from H&H with her. Laurel glanced around, wondering if security was watching.

About twenty minutes past 9:00 p.m., Laurel drove into the carport and saw the kitchen door open before she could exit her vehicle. She figured if she'd been a minute late, her dad would have been on the phone calling 911. Although unnecessary, his protectiveness gave her a warm feeling.

"I'm home safe and sound." She patted his arm then walked past him and was immediately engulfed by the aroma of baked cookies. A plate of them sat on the table. "Mmmm. You've been baking again."

"Your favorite—chocolate chip." He closed the door. "Sit down and tell me everything. I made a pot of coffee."

She tried to downplay the fact that the man had showed up at H&H that afternoon by first telling her dad about her conversation with Edgar Banks and his assurance that the store had both security cameras and security personnel.

However, he was livid when she relayed that she'd run into the man again. "Security is going to hear from me." His fist on the table rattled the cups and plate.

"Careful," Laurel warned. "You're going to shake the chips

right out of those cookies."

"I promise you this—I'll be at that store tomorrow and I won't be waiting for that man to find me or you. I'll find him, and what I'll shake out of him won't be chocolate chips, believe you me."

She believed him.

"But, Dad," she said, "we might be making too much of this. He could be a customer who went to H&H two days in a row. We've done that."

Although he still had fire in his eyes, he was listening.

"And we've sometimes been the last ones to leave a store."

"True," he said. "And if they wanted to check us out, they could. Just like I'm going to check out this situation."

Laurel knew she couldn't change her dad's mind and wasn't sure she wanted to. What if the man had simply been caught in the rain after dark because he moved slowly? Or maybe he had bought some plants and needed to load them on a cart, like she had done. Or what if he was looking for. . .romance? Would this turn out to be something they could all laugh about later?

There they were again—those mixed feelings. No wonder that good-looking serial killer had been so terribly successful in luring young women into his car. . .if they'd had notions as foolish as she was having.

She read for a while to take her mind off the man in the cast. He returned, however, as soon as she switched off the lamp and stared up at the dark ceiling. Finally, she resorted to mouthing church songs and letting the tunes occupy her mind until she felt sleep overtaking her.

All of a sudden she was being stalked by a man in dark clothes. She was in an empty building with many hallways, doorways, and recesses. The doors were all locked. She moved into a cubbyhole, peeked around, and saw the dark figure turn down another hallway, so she ran to the next recess.

She neared the end of the hallway, where an EXIT sign hung over a door with a push bar. There was a side door between her and the exit. When she stepped out of the recess, she saw the dark figure at the end of the hallway. He began walking at a fast pace toward her.

When he was midway up the hall, the door next to her opened and someone yanked her inside. "You're safe," a voice said. "I'll drive you home."

The handsome man smiled, and his eyes looked kind. She felt safe standing close to him with his hands on her upper arms. She was ready to thank him. But she glanced down and saw the cast on his foot.

Laurel sat straight up in bed, awakening with a scream in her throat.

What was going on?

After many deep breaths, she settled back on her pillows. Maybe dreams didn't always mean anything, but she knew this one occurred because of the fright she'd had that dark, stormy night. But why that feeling of being safe and then discovering her rescuer was her stalker? Or. . .her stalker was her rescuer?

Later that morning, Laurel did what she loved most, which was help her dad's landscaper work at his new development that he'd bought after her mom died. He'd gone from being a builder to a developer but still helped out with the carpentry at times.

So did she.

He'd taught her at an early age how to drive a nail into a thick board with only a couple of whacks. Her love, however, was not just planning a landscape but helping it materialize. She'd worked for several hours during the morning, raking and picking up rocks and throwing them into a pile, and wheelbarrowing roots and debris, all the while thinking the workers could be neater with pieces of wood and nails.

She returned home to eat lunch and take a shower before going to work. Realizing she could use a good manicure but lacked the time, she applied lotion to her hands and massaged it into her palms, which were still red from the morning's work, despite the fact that she'd worn gloves.

All of a sudden she stopped rubbing in the lotion. Her breath caught as a memory of another time when her palms were red began to trickle into her consciousness. That was like a lifetime ago. Well, she supposed it really had been. It was before her mom became ill. Before she died. Before Laurel even knew tragedies and suffering could touch her life. That had been childhood, an ideal existence.

Her mind traveled back in time to when she was thirteen. Her mom had taken Laurel and her friend Katie to a development where a house was being built. While her mom talked to the buyer of the house about interior design and paint colors, Laurel and Katie decided to inspect the premises.

Going around to the back of the house, Laurel had almost run into a piece of discarded wire mesh, the kind workers put down on gravel driveways before pouring concrete. To dodge it, she tripped over a piece of wood, fell face forward into a mound of dirt and rocks, and caught herself with her hands.

She sat up, ready to cry. She stared at her hands, red from the fall and from the mud. Before she knew it, a carpenter laid down his hammer and rushed over to her. "Here. I know what to do about that. Come over to the spigot."

He had gorgeous blue eyes and a nice voice. He turned on the faucet and led her hand under the water. "My mother always did this for me when I got hurt. She'd say the water would wash the hurt down the drain."

Not only the water, but the gentle, caring sound of his voice eased the pain.

After the water had washed away the mud, he said, "Let me see." He held her wrists gently as she stretched out her hands for his inspection.

He'd stared at her hands, pink from the fall but otherwise not damaged. "Hmmm. I think you'll live."

She wasn't supposed to be too friendly with workers or men she didn't know. She simply stared into his smiling eyes, not knowing what to say. She couldn't remember any man ever having touched her except her dad.

He stood. "Be careful." He went back inside the frame of the house and began pounding a nail into a board, seemingly oblivious to her and Katie.

She told her mother about it at the site. Later during supper, they mentioned it to her dad. Laurel had been afraid her dad might be angry that the man had held her hand under the water and helped her, since she'd been warned about safety measures.

Her parents assured her that it was all right, that some men were kind but sometimes it was hard to judge that.

"What's his name?" Laurel had asked.

"A worker," her dad replied.

Laurel asked how old he was, and her dad sort of barked that the worker was out of his teens.

"I didn't say thank you," she told her parents.

"He told me about it," her dad said. "I thanked him for you."

For the rest of that summer she had a crush on "that curly-haired older man." A couple of other times her mom took her and Katie to the development. When they saw him, they'd giggle. Since Laurel didn't know his name, she thought of him as her carpenter.

Then it seemed her mother had all kinds of projects for her to help with and plans for her summer. Almost before she knew it, August came. She returned to school.

She forgot about the incident until a few years later. She'd been washing out a glass in the sink. When she shoved the dishcloth into it and turned it, the fragile glass broke and cut her hand.

Her mom had rushed to her and told her to wash the soap off with clear water. "Let the hurt wash down the drain," she'd said.

Being a teenager, Laurel had balked, remembering the incident with the man at the work site. "Moooom, I'm not a child."

"No," her mom agreed, holding Laurel's hand under the stream of clear water. "But it's a nice phrase, isn't it? And I know this hurts." Her mom wrapped a clean towel around Laurel's hand.

What hurt was the fact that her mother remembered what Laurel had told her years before, which seemed to be an invasion into Laurel's private memory of her special carpenter. That had been her very first crush on an older man who looked like a movie star.

Now that she thought of it, that had been her only crush on such a man.

Laurel remembered those words of advice again a couple of years ago, when her mother was terminally ill, then again after her death. Laurel had stood in the shower crying and praying the hurt would wash away, down the drain. Only time had eased the grief and the pain of missing her mom.

Why did she think of that now?

She touched her left wrist with her right hand and remembered the man's caring touch, his gentle voice, his blue, blue eyes in a suntanned face surrounded by unruly dark curls.

Suddenly, she knew.

This man—whatever he was. . .thief, stalker—reminded her of her first teenage crush. Young she had been, but the feelings had not been trivial.

Her villain's face wasn't sunburned, nor was his dark hair unruly. But his voice held a mesmerizing quality. And his eyes were Carolina sky blue.

Was it possible that the stalker could be. . .her carpenter?

Chapter 6

Marc got out of his sports car and hobbled toward the house where workers were on the roof, putting on gray tiles. He recognized the stance of Harlan Jones, straddling the roof with his hands on his waist.

Jones apparently saw Marc, judging from the way he hurried down the roof, scampered down the ladder, and dodged around building materials on the ground.

Marc wondered what kind of reception he'd get from this man who had been like a dad to him one summer—and a friend after that. He was finding his answer as Harlan looked at the cast, then lifted his gaze to Marc's face. The look in his eyes resembled the surprised and suspicious look Marc had seen in the eyes of Laurel Jones.

Harlan offered no welcoming hug.

"Sir, could we go somewhere and talk?" Marc asked.

"You bet," came Harlan Jones's quick answer almost before Marc finished asking the question.

The absence of a warm greeting from Harlan told Marc all he needed to know about the relationship between this man and Laurel Jones. She was still his young daughter who had walked in the development where he worked one summer so long ago.

Harlan's long strides led him to the front of the house, where he picked up one of several boards that were on the ground and laid it on the frame for steps.

Marc wasn't sure he should take a seat beside Harlan, but the man gestured for him to sit. Marc did, but he missed the smile and hug from this man who'd befriended him one summer when he'd needed it most.

"Been awhile," Harlan said stiffly.

"Over two years." Marc was wondering how to broach the topic he'd come to discuss. Harlan probably was wondering the same thing, judging from his flushed face, which Marc suspected had something to do with a fellow in a foot cast who had scared his daughter.

"How's the police business in Charlotte?" Harlan snapped.

Marc felt Harlan's eyes boring into his, reminding him of the way the electric drill lying behind them could bore a hole through a two-by-four lickety-split.

"I'm not on the force anymore."

"What're you doing?"

"Something more secretive," Marc said. "Instead of confronting criminals outright, I have to figure out who's doing what—when and how. Sometimes it gets to be a sneaky business."

"Detective?"

"In a sense. I'm head of security at a store out in west Oak Ridge."

"Security?" Harlan's word came slowly, as though he might be onto something. "What store?"

Marc stuck his booted foot out in front of him and turned his head toward Harlan. "Home & Hearth Superstore."

The crease that had knitted Harlan's brows together began to smooth out. Speculation replaced the questioning in his eyes, and a look of irony settled on his face. His gaze flitted to the cast and back to Marc's face. A trace of a grin touched his lips. "So you're the man Laurel saw prowling around outside the store after dark."

Marc nodded. "I know that's what it looked like, but I was out there expecting to catch a couple of guys I've suspected of stealing from the store."

Harlan's brow wrinkled. "If you know, can't you arrest them?"

"It's simpler if I catch them in the act—red-handed, so to speak. I want enough evidence without having a court case or chancing the store being sued." Marc gave a short laugh. "Not good for business."

"Laurel says you approached her twice. Why didn't you simply tell Laurel who you are?"

Approach wasn't exactly the right word. Marc took a moment to think of how to say it tactfully. "First," he said, "I was surprised to see Laurel. I knew she was about the age of your daughter, but Laurel was just a kid the last time I saw her. I don't think my name would mean anything to her."

Harlan nodded his understanding.

"But even if she were your daughter, she's still an employee. I couldn't just blurt out that I was outside trying to catch a thief. Sorry to say this, but I didn't know if she was stealing the plants. . .or what."

Harlan reared back. "You thought Laurel was a thief?"

"No. Yes. I mean. . .I didn't know."

Harlan began to laugh.

Marc stared at him, uncertain whether his laughter was a prelude to something more threatening.

Finally, Harlan stopped laughing. "That's what she thought about you." He cleared his throat. "Sorry. I can see you don't think this is funny."

"No, sir," Marc replied immediately. "I was on my way to introduce myself and apologize for scaring her the night of the storm when she ran right into me. Then she ran from me. She reported me to the manager and my assistant as a thief and a stalker."

Rearing back, Harlan asked, "Is that causing a problem for you?"

"Not with the manager and my assistant." He glanced at Harlan. "The manager is a fine Christian man, and we've become friends. He knows my family history and, like you, doesn't blame me."

Harlan nodded. "Good."

"And my assistant didn't want to tell Laurel anything that might hamper my investigation. You see, Laurel's supervisor is under suspicion simply because she's a friend of two guys I suspect. That's not the kind of thing I can tell Laurel, her being an employee. She and her supervisor seem to get along great."

"Can you tell me what you suspect the two guys of?"

"Sure. The receipts aren't matching up with some missing material. A couple of builders have come in and bought new appliances, saying theirs were stolen."

Harlan was nodding. "I thought it might be something like that. I'm a developer now, but we builders used to confide in each other about materials being stolen from our work projects. A lot of times we had reasons to suspect some of our workers or store personnel."

"Let me assure you," Marc said, "most all the personnel at H&H are honest. But there are always those few who cause trouble. A store like that is a perfect setup for criminal activity. A builder comes in and buys materials and the workers know where it's to be delivered. All they need is a pickup truck and a dark night and a house in a secluded area. I can't go to the site, since I'm not a police officer anymore. I have to catch those on the grounds who are stealing. And I can't accuse without evidence."

"I see your dilemma," Harlan said. "That might explain why your assistant didn't tell Laurel who you were and implied you might be looking for romance."

Marc gasped. "He never should have said that."

"Are you married?"

"No."

"Spoken for?"

"No."

"But you're not looking for romance?"

"Well. . ." Marc was at a loss for words. Finally, he found some. "I'm not the kind of guy to walk the aisles of the store looking for it—like those couples in the newspaper articles."

"She's not a kid anymore, you know."

Marc turned his head away for a moment, lest this man read on his face or in his eyes that he was well aware of that fact. "She doesn't trust me, and she's run from me twice. I. . .um. . .don't suppose you could put in a good word for me?"

"Nope," Harlan said.

Turning his head quickly, Marc stared at Harlan, who grinned. "That's your job. But maybe I can help you out a little."

Marc stood when Harlan did.

"We got off on the wrong foot when you walked up here," Harlan said. "Pun intended." He spread his arms. "Now let's have a proper greeting."

When Harlan hugged him tight and slapped his shoulders, Marc felt like it was old times. He was still in the good graces of this man, whom he admired more than anyone.

When Harlan stepped back, Marc thought the big man wiped at a tear. "Come to supper tonight," he said. "I grill a mean steak. You remember where I live?"

Oak Ridge Estates wasn't an easy area to forget. "Same place?"

"Yes. It's like Carolyn is all over the place. I'm not ready to leave it."

Marc saw the look of loss on his face. He hadn't known of Harlan's wife's illness until it was all over. On one of his visits from Charlotte, he'd stopped by a site. The two of them had gone to Harlan's house and talked about it.

Marc had called Harlan when he'd returned to Oak Ridge two years ago and discovered he'd gone to Europe with his daughter for the summer. Having been busy with his grandmother's affairs, Marc hadn't tried to contact him again.

"It's Laurel's day off," Harlan said. He turned and picked up the electric drill from the porch. "We usually eat around six. Come early, if you like." He nodded toward the step.

Marc straightened the step and Harlan opened a box of screws. Marc held the board in place. The years seemed to fade away. Marc welcomed the whine of the drill, the metallic odor, and the wisps of sawdust as the nails went into the wood. Marc picked up one board after another, and with the two of them working together, all of the steps were attached in no time flat.

Harlan Jones was a developer now, he'd said. Years ago, he'd been a builder. Marc knew he'd always think of Harlan Jones as being a developer and builder of a young man named Marc Goodson, who almost a decade ago had needed someone to show faith and trust in him.

Hearing footsteps on the back deck, Laurel looked up from her crouched position and loosened her grip on a pot of black-eyed Susans. The first thing she saw through the railings were three tennis shoes and a foot cast.

The shock of it sent the Susans rolling down the slight incline and her careening to her backside. She barely caught herself before rolling down the hill herself.

This had to be a dream. There she was, in shorts and a grimy T-shirt—not to mention dirty, sweaty skin and hair wet from the sun's rays. No way could this be reality, because that would mean she'd been frightened twice by the same man while she held a potted plant in her hands.

The stalker had a grimace on his handsome face and a look of uncertainty in his blue eyes. He didn't move, but her dad walked to the railing and looked over. "You all right, Laurel?"

She gave him her best "whadda ya think?" look. Did he think she always fell on her backside while a pot of flowers rolled down the hill?

While her dad chuckled, she was thinking there were several options here.

One, she was having a nightmare.

Two, the stalker had found out where they lived and was holding her dad at gunpoint to get to her.

Three, her dad had tracked down the stalker and was going to kill him right before her eyes.

Four, she was totally out of her mind.

The villain simply stared and had the decency to look ill at ease.

"Honey, I told you we had someone coming for dinner."

Yes, and she'd asked if the guest was male or female and he said male. So she figured she'd finish planting the black-eyed Susans and get cleaned up while her dad grilled and conversed with his guest.

"Daaaad," Laurel said threateningly.

He straightened and held up his hands. "Okay. I guess my little joke didn't go over too well."

"Joke?" she shrieked.

"Okay. Okay." He gestured toward the unmoving man. "Laurel, this is Marc Goodson. He worked for me one summer. . . oh, about ten years ago. We've kept in touch a few times through the years. He has a perfectly good explanation about this little misunderstanding."

Now what was she expected to do? Walk up and offer a dirty-gloved hand to him? Go up there looking like a wet dog? And smelling worse? After all, she did use fertilizer when planting.

Deciding to let him take the initiative, Laurel knelt and took a plant out of a pot near her. He was walking across the deck when she set the flowers in the hole and lifted them again to put in more topsoil and a little phosphorus.

When he walked down the slope to where she knelt, her heart pounded as it had on the night he'd frightened her.

She felt frightened now—when he stooped down and knelt close to her.

She knew her dad wouldn't have brought him here if he didn't have complete trust in this man. To trust him or not wasn't what frightened her. The problem was, when Marc Goodson softly said, "I'm sorry I've caused you any concern," his voice had the quality that brought back the memory of when she was thirteen years old, with a crush on an older man.

Yes, this was her carpenter.

"I need—" She needed to put things in perspective. "I need to plant the Susans and then get cleaned up. I'm a mess."

Chapter 7

A mess?

Marc already knew that Laurel Jones was a very attractive woman. And he couldn't imagine a more adorable one than when she'd fallen back on the yard, gazing at the pot of yellow flowers rolling down the hill as if it were a catastrophe. He'd wanted to run and pick her up and brush the dirt off and tell her not to think badly of him.

As she brushed the dirt off herself, he hobbled to retrieve the pot. She thanked him and snatched it from his outstretched hand. Not once had she asked about his foot, but she examined the plant as if it were some injured child. He could readily see what took precedence.

After apologizing, rather than make a nuisance of himself, he walked back up onto the deck where Harlan was putting steaks on the grill.

The two of them talked while Laurel planted the Susans, picked up her empty pots and tools, and disappeared down around the corner of the house. About twenty minutes later, she came from the kitchen and out onto the deck. She was wearing denim shorts and a white tank top, both complementary to her tan. Her sun-streaked light brown hair fell freely along her face and down to her shoulders.

He started to rise from the lounge chair where Harlan had insisted he sit and prop up his foot. He was determined to show Laurel he respected her.

"No need to get up," Laurel said.

"At least let me say that I'm sorry we got off on the. . . wrong foot." He cleared his throat. *How stupid can I get?*

She didn't say his apology was accepted. But she did smile before gliding over to her dad and touching his arm. "Want to eat inside or out?"

"Outside," her dad said. "I hope there won't be too many bugs."

Her hands moved to her hips. "I happen to like bugs."

"Great," Harlan quipped. "I'll give you the steak the fly just landed on."

She laughed, so Marc did, too. He'd never given much thought to whether or not he liked bugs. But if Laurel liked bugs, he could learn to like them.

As she headed for the screen door, Marc asked, "Can I help?"

She paused and looked over her shoulder. "No. You need to take care of that"—she grinned—"left foot of yours."

Ah, maybe she hadn't thought his remark too stupid. She did smile before going into the house. Could she mean he had a chance to start over with her?

When everything was ready, they sat at a round table with an umbrella shading them from the evening sun rays. While they ate the steak, salad, and rolls that Harlan took from the grill's warmer, Marc told Laurel about his job at H&H and explained his reason for being out back during the night of the storm.

"I was on my way to explain to you the next day when you. . . when we ran into each other." He hoped she accepted his explanation as valid.

"I'm sorry I misjudged you." She caught her napkin as it threatened to blow away in the sudden breeze. "Should I tell Mr. Banks that I want to withdraw my complaint?"

"No. If anything, he should apologize to you. Edgar could have told you what I was doing outside H&H that night."

"Why didn't he?" She looked at him curiously, lifted her tea glass, and took a sip.

"He didn't want to say anything that might hamper my investigation. If he had told you, then you might have relayed that information to someone in your department, who could in turn tell someone else, and before long all the employees would think they were under suspicion."

"Oh." Laurel set down her tea glass. "I'm beginning to get it." Her eyes widened. "Instead of you being a thief as I suspected—among other things—you thought *I* might be a thief?"

"Well, no. . . I. . ." He got the impression she didn't quite believe him.

Harlan chuckled and said he needed another steak. "Anybody else?"

Laurel said, "No thanks," at the same time as Marc. Then she turned to Marc and continued, "Looking back, I remember that you said, 'Got a lot of plants there, don't you?'—almost like you were accusing me."

"No. You see, I had this mind-set of catching someone that night, and then I encountered. . .you."

She gave him a sideways glance. "Did you check to see if I paid for the plants?"

He was about to lose his appetite. "It's part of my job."

Harlan returned to the table and filled the ensuing silence. "Laurel, why don't you show him what you do with those plants?"

She didn't answer but instead turned to look at Marc.

About to swallow hard, Marc decided that might be easier to do with a sip of tea. He picked up his glass. He felt as though he was between a rock and a hard place. If he said he wanted to know, she might take that as his admission that he was suspicious of her. If he said he didn't need to know, then he might miss an opportunity to see her again.

After a drink, he set his glass down and said, "I just saw you planting flowers. That's a pretty good indication."

She shook her head. "That's not what I do with them."

Marc nodded. "They're for landscaping where your dad's building houses?"

"I have bought plants for that," she said. "But that's not what these are for. These were looking unhealthy, and I bought them at a reduced price."

"Speaking of landscaping, Laurel," Harlan said, "it's best you don't come around the development where we're building right now. Marc and I are working on a way to catch some of those thieves he's talking about."

Laurel perked up. "I'll be glad to help."

"Sorry," Marc said. "You're an employee at H&H. I can't enlist your help for this. I'd appreciate your not mentioning anything. Just act normal."

"Normal?" Her gaze moved upward for a moment, then she looked at him and smiled. He felt as though a butterfly had gone down his throat and was beating its wings inside his chest.

"Oh, I should have asked," she said. "What happened to your foot?"

He told her about the scuffle at H&H. "It's healing just fine," he added. "I don't have to wear the cast all the time now. The doctor advised me to wear it when I'm at places where the walking might be. . .precarious."

"Ah," Harlan teased. "Today you didn't want to be one of those biblical fools who step in where angels fear to tread, huh?"

"Something like that," Marc said.

Actually, it had been exactly like that. He wouldn't have had to wear the cast to the Joneses' house. But he wanted to appear as the same man who had caused her concern and yet somehow alleviate that concern.

He glanced at Laurel but couldn't tell if she thought his comment was light, serious, or ridiculous. He watched her look at her plate, poke a bite of steak into her mouth, chew, and glance at him with what seemed to be a challenge in her eyes.

Okay, so she was wasn't going to make anything easy for him. But that did seem to be a smile on her face after she swallowed and then picked up her glass of tea.

Harlan mentioned he'd like to work out a few details about the plan he and Marc had talked about. Laurel took that as her cue to take their plates into the house and make herself scarce.

After their discussion and not wanting to wear out his

welcome, Marc said he needed to go. When he and Harlan reached the front porch, Laurel was kneeling on a tarp, picking dying blooms off colorful pansies in a flower bed.

Harlan thanked him for coming and went back inside. Marc walked down to where Laurel knelt. "I hope everything is cleared up and there are no hard feelings."

"No hard feelings." She stood.

"By the way, what *do* you do with those plants?" He quickly added, "Not because I think you're a thief."

"You're really interested?"

Interested? Is there a double meaning there? "Definitely."

"Are you free in the morning?"

In case this wasn't just small talk on her part, he decided on a detailed answer. "My normal hours are 9:00 a.m. to 5:00 p.m. But since I'm my own boss to a great extent and sometimes investigate after hours and weekends, I can take off during the week if I like."

"Then I could use some help with the plants."

"What time should I pick you up?"

"Unless you have a pickup truck or a van, I'll need to take my van."

"I don't," he said.

"Then meet me here. Why not come early enough for breakfast?"

"Oh, you're a cook, too?"

"Nope." She grinned. "But Dad is. Eight o'clock sound okay?"

"Sounds perfect. I'm glad we got to do this, Laurel. Thanks for a nice evening."

"You're welcome." She smiled. "See you in the morning."

He nodded and turned to leave, then stopped. "Oh, any particular way to dress in the morning?"

"Jeans would be fine. Oh, and wear the cast."

Lifting his hand in farewell, he headed toward his car. Her remark must mean that whatever was to occur in the morning would be a precarious situation. But he hoped her invitation meant, too, that with Laurel Jones, he was on the right foot.

Laurel found her dad on the back deck, cleaning the grill. She put her hands on her hips. "That was some little surprise you pulled, Dad."

"Sure was. I hope you didn't hurt yourself when you. . . ahem. . .fell for him." He laughed.

"That is *so* not funny."

His eyebrows moved upward. "Oh? You mean. . .there's something serious going on?"

"Serious? Dad, I've never even talked to him before the night in the storm." Her thoughts went immediately to when she was thirteen and he washed the hurt from her hands. No, she hadn't talked to him then. He had talked and reassured her.

"You talked to him when you ran into him inside the store," her dad reminded her.

"Talk? We didn't talk. He tried, but I stuttered and stammered."

He chuckled. "That's how I felt when I first met your mother—had never been so tongue-tied in my life."

Laurel gasped and laid her hand on the back of a chair. "You've certainly changed your tune from when I first told you about him."

"Well, sure," he said. "That's before I knew who he was."

Laurel hoped her dad didn't realize she was fishing for information when she said, "You told me he used to work for you, but. . .how well do you really know him?"

Laurel went over to the railing and looked down at the black-eyed Susans she'd planted earlier—the place where Marc had knelt down beside her, much as he'd done about ten years ago.

"It's hard to say," her dad began. "You can be around some people for a lifetime and not really know them. With others, it's like instant camaraderie."

Laurel knew the feeling. She turned and faced her dad's profile.

He looked up from the grill and stared ahead as if looking into the past. "Let's see. . .I think it was when Marc had just finished his sophomore year at college. I took him on as a carpenter. He was eager to learn, and I knew there were some family troubles. . ."

"What kind?"

A look of sadness came into her dad's eyes. "I don't need to repeat the details," he said. "But his dad lost his business, then Marc's mom and dad separated. Marc moved in with his grandmother."

"That must have been hard." Laurel could empathize with anyone whose life was affected by the loss of a loved one, whether by death or a difficult situation.

"Yes," her dad said. "Marc felt the emotional impact of it. I was kind of like a dad to him that summer. He was a good kid. I liked him."

Laurel realized that Marc would have been going through that difficult time when she was thirteen. Yet he'd been kind to her when she hurt her hands. He must have a caring heart. She leaned back against the railing. "So you kept in touch with him through the years?"

Using the wire brush, her dad scrubbed hard at a particular spot on the grill. "He always took the initiative. I wanted him to know I was there for him, but I didn't want him to feel obligated just because I befriended him that summer."

"Why didn't he keep working for you?"

"That wouldn't have been convenient for him. I don't know if I can keep all the facts straight—it's been a long time—but I do know his mom moved to Charlotte. At some point his mom and dad got back together. Marc transferred from UNCA to NC State." He shrugged. "Through the years there's been a lot going on in his life."

"Like what? Did he ever marry or anything? I mean. . ."

Her dad looked at her and smiled. "No. He never mentioned anything personal like that when he e-mailed me occasionally. He always sent a Christmas card with a brief note about his schooling or a job."

Laurel suspected Marc might have been like a son he would have liked to have. She could imagine the two of them working together on some kind of building project. "Did he ever come to see you?"

Her dad laid down the brush and began to wipe the grill with a cloth. "A few times. Once during his college break and one Christmas when he came to pick up his grandmother and take her to Charlotte."

"But not here?"

"He was here a couple of times. After he found out your mother died, he came and we talked for a long time. Before that, he came at Christmastime. That was the year you went to meet. . .what's-his-name's parents."

"Dad," she chided, "his name is Darren."

He shook his head. "He wasn't right for you."

"I knew that. I told you we were just friends."

"Well, anyway, I didn't invite Marc here while you were still a teenager. Not after that time when you hurt your hand."

Laurel gasped. "Dad! That was a decade ago. How can you remember something like that?"

He faced her directly then. "When a worker, or any man for that matter, is near my daughter, I don't forget it. Besides," he said more calmly, "I was on the roof and saw what happened. And Marc told me about it. So did you and your mother." He spoke with determination. "I didn't invite him back then because I wasn't about to expose my thirteen-year-old daughter to some twenty-year-old college guy no matter how moral she and he might be."

"Dad, that's silly."

"I knew that. But I couldn't chance anything with my beautiful girl. Besides, your mother thought you took a fancy to him. That's the summer she decided you needed to go to equestrian camp."

Laurel gave a quick laugh. "I wondered how she came up with that. I don't think I'd ever even mentioned anything about riding a horse." She paused. "But I loved it. Anyway"—she shook her finger at him—"now I get the idea you're pushing me toward Marc."

He scoffed. "How did you come up with that?"

"Oh, just a few things." She walked over and sat in a chair at the table. "First, you brought him home. You didn't monopolize the conversation." At that, he gave her a warning glance.

Ignoring that, Laurel continued. "You left us alone out front. You did everything but come right out and invite him to see what I do with my plants."

"Sneaky, aren't I?" He grinned.

"Right. You're no more obvious than the nose on your face."

"Did it work?"

"No." She enjoyed the look of chagrin on his face. If he kept cleaning like that, he'd have the grill shining like a new nickel. "But. . . ," she said, and his head turned toward her. "He did mention he was curious about what I do with the plants."

"Soooo?"

"So. . .since I've decided he's neither a thief nor a stalker, I want to make sure he's not walking the aisles of H&H looking for romance."

Her dad reared back and laughed. "You could do worse."

She huffed. "Well. That's not too high a recommendation."

"What I mean is, from all I've seen, he has integrity and a great work ethic. I like Marc."

Laurel laughed then. "Dad, I remember the time you didn't like any of the guys I liked, and I didn't like the ones you liked."

"And now?"

Laurel stood and walked over to the screen door. "We'll see," she said noncommittally. "By the way, he's coming in the morning for breakfast. So fix something impressive."

His brow wrinkled. "Well, aren't my pancakes and bacon always impressive?"

She nodded. "As long as I'm not the one who has to cook it, it's impressive."

He dad looked at her and quipped, "Yep, I'd make someone a good wife."

She knew he was kidding, but he had made "someone" a good husband. However, since her mom died, his social life had almost come to a halt. An intriguing thought occurred. She opened the screen door and was ready to jump into the kitchen considering what she was about to say. "Dad. . ." She waited for his full attention. "Have you ever thought about going to H&H, walking the aisles, and bumping into some woman's cart?"

He drew back his arm, threatening to throw the greasy cleaning cloth at her.

"Yiiii!" She yanked the door open and jumped into the kitchen.

Separated by the screen door, they both laughed. Laurel watched him a moment longer as his smile faded and he stared at the grill. How nice it would be if her dad had someone special in his life besides her—or even Marc—to smile about.

Chapter 8

Accustomed to rising early, Marc was ready long before 8:00 a.m. Not having to make breakfast gave him extra time to sit at the kitchen table with a cup of coffee and read the *Oak Ridge News*.

Just as he picked up his cup, a front-page headline caught his attention. "What?" The coffee almost sloshed out on the table. The headline read DIFFERING OPINIONS ON FINDING LOVE AT OAK RIDGE'S HOME & HEARTH SUPERSTORE.

Oh no. Would this never stop? Wasn't it enough that the opposing articles appeared in the Asheville papers? Whatever became of customers going to H&H for home improvement supplies?

"I don't think it's good for business," Marc said to Harlan about thirty minutes later when he sat in the Joneses' kitchen while Harlan cooked and Laurel set the table. She looked very attractive in denim shorts and a tank top, her hair pulled back in a ponytail.

But he needed to concentrate on the conversation. The article had been the first subject that came up after Marc arrived.

"How's it bad for business?" Harlan asked.

Seeing Laurel's curious glance, Marc wanted to be careful how he answered. "Not that I have anything against romance," he said. "But newspaper reporters are taking differing opinions. If H&H is asked for the store's opinion, customers may feel they have to take a stand. Then we could lose half our customers. If we say, 'No comment,' we could lose even more."

"Who would be the H&H person to comment?" Laurel asked.

"Probably the manager."

"How does he feel about it?"

"He's all for anything that brings people into the store. But I don't think he sees beyond that." Marc scoffed, "There's even a couple planning a wedding at H&H."

"Now that's interesting," Laurel said. "How do you feel about all that, Marc?"

"That's not the place—" he began and saw her stiffen slightly. Not wanting to be misunderstood, he added. "But like I said, I have nothing against romance."

She gave him a searching look before turning away and taking orange juice from the refrigerator. "Here," he said, standing up and wanting to change what seemed to be a touchy subject with her, "let me do that. If I invite you to my house for dinner, I have a feeling the cooking will be my job." He grinned. "I should say, my pleasure."

He saw Harlan's head turn toward him then. "I mean," Marc said, "when I invite the two of you."

Harlan and Laurel laughed as Marc poured the juice. Harlan set scrambled eggs, pancakes, and bacon on the table. After Harlan asked the blessing, Marc was glad the conversation moved to topics that didn't require an opinion. That is, until the subject of sports came up and they engaged in light banter about who would win the state basketball championship—Carolina or NC State.

After Harlan left for work, Marc walked down to the basement with Laurel. He wanted to make sure he hadn't offended her by his earlier remarks. "I'm not too keen on people intentionally meeting in a store. But," he said emphatically when they reached the bottom of the stairs, "if it happens naturally, then that's fine." She stood still, looking up at him. She no longer reminded him of the child Laurel, but of a beautiful, desirable woman.

Watch it, he warned himself. He'd started to lean closer to her. What happened to his resolve to keep his thoughts and emotions under control? For several years he hadn't wanted to be serious about a woman. As the years passed, he'd accepted the fact that most women his age were married, divorced, or widowed. Why such thoughts anyway? Deliberately looking around at several tables laden with pots of plants, he whistled. "So this is your. . .flower shop?"

She laughed. "Yeah. Over here are some that need pampering. Those are some I'm taking care of until the landscaper can get them planted." She gestured from one table to another. "These are ready for me to put foil and ribbons on, and these," she said, walking over to a table near the garage door, "these are ready to go." A light came into her eyes. "But all this is nothing compared with what I have planned for the future."

"What's that?" He wondered if she had anyone in particular with whom she hoped to share that future. He stood near her, watching as she straightened a bow that was tied around a flowering plant in a pot wrapped in green foil.

He saw the excitement in her eyes when she turned to face him. "I'd like to start my own landscaping business after I finish school. I have one more semester at State. I'm majoring in Horticultural Science and Agricultural Business Management."

Marc thought he understood. "So your interest in plants is what brought you to H&H?"

"One reason," she said. "I wanted a job where I could have a part in supporting myself without letting Dad foot the bills for everything, although he's willing." She shook her head. "It's hard for him to let me grow up. We've depended on each other so much since Mom died. So I also wanted a job doing something I like and to sort of carry on a project my mom started."

"With plants?"

She nodded, setting a plant on silver foil, and with movements as deft as those of a carpenter with a hammer and nails, she brought the green side of the foil up around the plant and asked him to hold it.

While he accommodated, she cut a piece of ribbon from a roll and wrapped it around the foil, just beneath his hands. "Mom used to take fresh flowers or potted plants to people who didn't have any in the hospital where she volunteered," she said while making a bow. "She loved working in her flower beds, and from the time I was little, she and I would often take cut flowers from her gardens to sick people."

He moved his hands away after she patted the bow and gave the plant a satisfied nod. "So that's why you had all those from H&H?"

She nodded and reached for another plant. They repeated the wrapping process. "When the plants look wilted or have brown spots, the customers don't want them and H&H reduces the price. So instead of chancing their being thrown away, I decided to buy them and treat them, and if they're healthy again, I'll take them where they can be enjoyed."

"To the hospital?"

She shook her head. "Not these. My singles' class from church had a praise and worship time at the Oak Ridge Retirement Center the weekend I returned from college. A few of the patients had no flowers or plants. That's when I decided to bring some."

"Wonderful idea," he said. "I think my church would be interested in a worthwhile project like that. I'm sure there's the same need at other retirement and nursing homes."

Her eyes lit up. "Oh, Marc, that's a great idea. I could write up a note of instruction about each plant, letting the residents know whether they should set a plant in full sun on the windowsill or give them partial sun and how much water is needed. I could even take plant food the residents could share."

Her excitement was catching. "Like a community project," he said. "That would give them another reason to mingle."

"Exactly." Her face glowed with pleasure.

He glanced around the room. "You already have quite an array."

"Yep." She grinned. "But not as many as H&H."

He laughed lightly. "Well, not yet."

She pointed to a stack of plastic trays. "We can put the foil-wrapped plants in these. Each tray holds six. Incidentally," she said, glancing at him, "the plants you saw me loading are on the table near the stairs. These are some I brought home after my second day of working at H&H." She tilted her head in a saucy way. "You didn't catch me loading those, so you might need to hone your security activities."

"Yes, looks like I need to watch you more closely." He knew that wouldn't be difficult.

He saw her smile. But was she smiling about what he said or about the plants on the table?

From the moment he stepped through the door of the center, Marc felt as if he was in a different world—a world where older men and women greeted him and Laurel with hugs, smiles, and welcoming words.

He relaxed and particularly liked being called "Laurel's young man." He listened to old men tell a few jokes, and he told a couple of his own.

Laurel looked in on some residents just to say hello and ask about their plants. She and Marc gave plants to new residents. She even exchanged a healthy plant for a puny one in the lobby.

Being in the line of work where he had to be cautious, suspicious, and always on the lookout for criminal activity, he could readily see his need for this kind of positive interaction. And he couldn't think of a more vivacious, cheery person than Laurel Jones to provide it.

"That was one dumb joke you told," Laurel said after she and Marc were back in the van and heading toward the main road.

He placed his hand over his heart. "Mine?"

"Yeah." She lowered her chin and her voice, trying to mimic him. "What's the definition of a chicken crossing the road?" She shook her head and gave the answer he'd given. "Poultry in motion." She groaned.

"Well, they laughed, didn't they?"

"Yes, because it's so silly."

Marc scoffed. "No sillier than the man who said a boiled egg is hard to beat."

Glancing over at him, she grinned. "You know I'm joking with you."

"Sure. And I've heard the saying that you only joke with people you like."

"Seriously, though—"

"What? You mean that wasn't serious? You don't like me?" Not wanting to risk her giving a negative reply or saying she was involved with someone else, he quickly said, "Now I'm joking."

Her head turned toward him as she executed a turn from the center grounds and drove onto the main road. She gave him a quick glance. He wondered if the bit of color that came into her cheeks meant she was pleased that he implied he joked with her because he liked her.

"They really enjoyed your being there, Marc. I've been told that some of them rarely have visitors. A few never do." Her tone of voice lowered. "And I liked having you there with me. Thank you."

"You're entirely welcome. It was good for me to do things I'd like to do for my grandmother. Of course, I do things for her, but she can't always respond."

"She's. . .ill?"

He nodded. "She's in Asheville at the home for Alzheimer's patients."

Laurel's genuine concern led to his telling about his return- ing to Oak Ridge a couple of years ago. Bittersweet memories crowded his mind. "My grandmother discovered she was in the first stages of dementia and needed someone to help settle her affairs and be with her for as long as she could stay in her home. I wanted to do whatever I could for her."

"I understand that."

"I know. Your dad said you even dropped out of college to be with your mom."

"I'm glad I did. Even in her last days, she would sit on the deck and watch me take care of the flower beds."

"That sounds nice." After a considerable silence, he spoke again. "Speaking of flower beds, that reminds me. I keep promising myself that I'm going to do something about the weed beds at Grandmother's house." He shrugged. "Frankly, I have no idea how to begin. But I do know she used to like those little pink and white juicy plants. She had them in pots on the front porch. They're long gone now." He scoffed. "I think they probably needed water."

Her glance toward him indicated as much. "That sounds like begonias. And yes, they're succulent plants that need plenty of water. Would you like for me to get a begonia for her?"

"Yes." He liked her suggestion. "Would you like to go with me to give it to her?"

"I'd love to. So do you live in her house or just take care of it?"

"I live in it. It's legally mine since I'm the administrator of her affairs. But to me, it's still Grandmother's house."

"Where is it?"

"In east Oak Ridge."

At the next road, Laurel turned and headed east. "Tell me where."

Laurel had to remind herself to look away from the warmth in his blue eyes. She had her hands full just contending with the morning traffic. She looked straight ahead. *I'm sitting here with. . .my carpenter. And I think he likes me.*

Following his directions, she drove into a residential area of white frame houses and pulled into a driveway. After they were out of the vehicle, she shook her head at the conglomeration of cramped boxwoods and weed-choked bushes. "That is a pitiful excuse for a flower bed."

"Too far gone, huh?"

"Not gone far enough." She waved her hand over it. "Get rid of the whole mess and I'll see what I can do."

"Great. I'll clean the beds out in the evenings and you can plant in the mornings. That way we can work together." When she gave him a quick look, he added, "Separately."

After they drove away from the house, Marc told her he hoped his grandmother could come and see the yard after they finished. "She still has what they call 'a good day' now and then, and they let me bring her home. But those days," he said with a touch of sadness in his voice, "are few and far between. My dad can barely take seeing his mom like that. It's heartbreaking to him and Mom that Grandmother doesn't often recognize them or communicate with them."

"Even if she can't respond, Marc, this can be your tribute to her. It's kind of like my putting flowers on Mom's grave. It's an act of doing something to show that I appreciate what she means to me."

He nodded. "I already feel good about it, and we haven't

even started. But," he said at her quick glance, "I'll start digging today."

Then he made a request she never thought she'd hear from an employee of H&H. "Don't buy the plant from H&H. And it's best if you don't mention our plans to anyone at the store or that your dad is a developer."

"Oh, man"—she turned into the driveway of her house—"I'd love to know what's going on."

"You will—soon, I expect. Be patient."

Patience wasn't exactly her middle name, but soon she felt content sitting on her back porch, drinking coffee, and talking quite personally. She told of having been rather serious about a young man when she was a freshman in college. They drifted apart, however, when so much of Laurel's time was taken up with her mother.

Marc told her about his dad's and mom's problems. Even now, he found it hard to talk about. "They got back together after Dad was released from jail. But my mom just couldn't face the humiliation of continuing to live here." Marc took a deep breath. "Well, I've burdened you with that."

"It's not a burden. I want to know about you, Marc."

He looked thoughtfully at his cup, then back at her. "I'll tell you this, Laurel. My parents' situation soured me on marriage for a while. Then I was busy trying to find a career where I needed to prove that I wasn't like my dad but was trustworthy. It took awhile for me to realize I didn't need to try to make up for my dad's mistakes." He laughed lightly. "I could make enough of my own."

She smiled at him. He looked beyond her, as if at a memory. "I've dated occasionally, but I wouldn't let myself get serious about anyone."

Laurel wondered if he was saying he still didn't want to be seriously involved with anyone.

"Strange, isn't it," he said. "If that hadn't happened with my parents, then neither your dad nor my grandmother would have played such an important part in my life."

He was beginning to believe in the saying that some good came from the worst of things. He gazed at her. "And you and I probably wouldn't be sitting here—"

He started to reach for her hand, but just then his cell phone chirped, so he reached into his pocket to answer it. "Yes, thanks," he said to the caller, then stood. "I need to go. Business calls."

She stood, too, and he touched her shoulder briefly. He could honestly tell her, "This morning has meant more to me than I can even say."

Yes, Marc. To me, too. But were you trying to say you're glad that we are. . .sitting here together? Or were you warning me that you don't intend to get seriously involved?

Chapter 9

On Monday, Laurel used the account of Franklin, her dad's landscaper, at a home improvement store in Asheville for the purchase of bushes. Early on Tuesday, long before the sun would rise high in the sky, she headed to Marc's house.

Marc came out with a cup of coffee for her. She looked up at him from beneath her floppy-brimmed hat, aware of how incredibly handsome he looked dressed for work in a suit and tie.

She took off a glove and reached for the coffee. After a sip, she set the cup beside her water bottle. "You've done a lot of work here," she said. "I don't think you left any of the boxwood roots."

"I tried."

"Thanks." She leaned on her shovel. "This is good dirt."

"Yeah." He grinned. "It looks good streaked across your forehead there."

She wrinkled her nose. "There'll be more dirt on me before I'm finished."

He smiled. "It's your color." His gaze moved to the bushes she'd taken from her van. "What are those bushes?"

"Azaleas," she said. "They're evergreen. And these are nandina. These green leaves will turn deep red during the winter."

He nodded with approval. "Oh, feel free to use the house. When you leave, just lock the door."

She left a couple of hours later, having finished getting the bushes in sooner than she'd expected. His loosening up the soil had made the job easier than if she'd had to dig holes in hard ground.

"It's looking good," he said the following morning when he brought coffee to her. "What's the plan for today?"

"The next rows will be for black-eyed Susans and gaura. Oh, and the gaura is also called whirling butterflies. They look like butterflies when they sway in the wind. These are both perennials."

"Sounds beautiful," he said. "Um, is perennial the same as deciduous?"

"No," she explained. "Deciduous means they lose their leaves. Perennial means the plants either endure from one season to the next or die off during the winter and come back with new growth in the spring."

He smiled. "Perfect. I'll never have to bother with the flower beds again."

"Sorry, that's not how it works," she said. "Somebody will still have to pull the weeds and put down the mulch. And I'm going to plant a few annuals. That means they won't last through the winter."

She finished the work on Thursday and stopped by early on Friday for his reaction to her addition of white polka dot vinca and red salvia.

"Perfect touch," he said. "It's really beautiful." His blue eyes looked into hers for a long moment. "I believe you're a real landscaper."

"Oh, I had to prove it?" She lifted her chin. "When are you going to prove you're a good security agent and catch your crooks?"

"It's up to the police now. We just have to wait."

That intrigued her further, but then he asked if she had receipts for the plants. She retrieved them from her pocket. His close scrutiny and frown made her ask, "Is something wrong?"

"Yes. You didn't include a fee for your labor."

While looking into his eyes, the thought "labor of love" crossed her mind, but she said, "No charge. I did it for your grandmother."

"Thank you."

His smile and warm blue gaze made her feel rather like a gaura. Before she could whirl, however, he said, "Oh, by the way, one of those newspaper reporters called and wants to interview me. I'm hoping to have time for that by next week. She wants a statement of how I feel about couples finding romance at the store."

"I thought you said they'd probably interview the manager."

"I expected that. But Charlie is married. She wanted to interview a spokesman from the store who is single."

"Well, Marc, what are you going to tell her?"

She thought he'd never answer. Finally, he grinned. "You can read about it in the paper."

That was what her dad said on Sunday afternoon after she returned from having lunch with a couple of friends from her singles' class at church. "It's done. The thieves finally bit."

She sat down, eager to know. "Tell me about it."

"Not yet. The arrest was just made. We want to make sure this is all done right before it's talked about." He was nodding with a satisfied look on his face. "If all goes well, it should be in tomorrow's paper."

It was—even made the front page. Two young men, Leon "Spike" Riddle and Marvin "Sparky" Cobb, were arrested Sunday morning at a small appliance store in south Asheville. Having been under suspicion by the police, they'd been watched and apprehended after taking new appliances from a new house at Cottonwood Development. Riddle and Cobb were followed by the police and apprehended when they took the items from the truck and took them inside the appliance store. No mention was made of the H&H store.

Her dad explained there had been quite a thieving racket going on with other developers in Oak Ridge and Asheville. "We banded together, and three of us had our builders go to H&H for materials as a ploy to find out if Spike and Sparky had anything to do with it."

"How did the builders set them up?"

"It would be more accurate, Laurel, to say they set themselves up. Marc has known for some time those two fellows have been stealing from the store. And it began to look like an even bigger operation was taking place. We builders legitimately bought materials that we could use, and the police agreed to stake out the developments."

"So this has been going on for a while?"

"Oh yes. But there has to be more than suspicion. There has to be evidence. We builders always report any theft. The police knew they stole from an Asheville house Wednesday night. Friday they went to a development in Skyland and stole lumber.

The police wanted to find out if there were several bands of thieves or the same crooks stealing from several different developments. Sunday morning, they stole a washer and dryer, still in the boxes, from my development at Cottonwood."

"On Sunday, of all days. It's like. . .stealing at Christmastime. Somehow that seems worse."

"Exactly, Laurel. But it's what Marc expected. He said broad daylight is a crook's best time to steal. The work sites are deserted. If people do pass by, they're probably on their way to church and don't want to think of anyone stealing on Sunday. If they were seen late at night, then they might be suspected of stealing—but not on Sunday morning.

Marc called that afternoon and gave her a few more details. "The appliance store where they took your dad's washer and dryer is in south Asheville." She heard his pause. "The store is operated by the brother of your supervisor."

"Mindy?"

"But. . .does that mean she's mixed up in this?"

"I don't have evidence of her being involved directly, but I feel sure she knew what was going on. I try to be careful about judging someone just because a friend or relative is mixed up in something crooked. But I did question her."

"How is she taking all this?"

"She wouldn't talk about it. But that's another reason I'm calling. She quit, Laurel."

"Oh, I hate that. She seemed interested when I talked to her about coming to the singles' class at church. I guess there's no chance now."

"There's always a chance, Laurel. Just as I didn't forget the words of your dad and my grandmother in that difficult time, she won't forget what she should be doing. Maybe she can start over. She does have a good work record here. Which brings me to another point—how would you like to take her place and work days instead of evenings?"

The impact of what was happening with Mindy hit her hard. "I'll have to think about that."

"I understand. Take your time. You have tomorrow off. Think about it. Pray about it."

Laurel had a heaviness in her heart all day. She was glad the crooks were caught. But she felt sad, thinking about how people who had good minds, potential, and opportunity used it in negative instead of positive ways.

She did her laundry and cleaned the bathrooms. Still bothered that evening, she decided to do what she had done many times in the past.

"Hi, Franklin." She walked up to where he was working. "Want some help."

Franklin had taught her a lot about plants, much that she couldn't learn in a classroom. He had to leave early. She told him to take her van and she'd keep the truck. "I'd like to stay and work for a while. If you're going to be here in the morning, I can bring the truck by early enough for you to have the tools."

She worked until long after the sun had set and darkness approached. The recently installed street light shone on the area, allowing her to see well enough to rake out stones and roots until she finally felt tired.

Knowing where the key was for workers who needed to get in when the builder wasn't around, she took that, unlocked the back door, and went inside. She washed up as best she could in the light coming through the small bathroom window.

When she reached for the paper towels, her hand brushed against the key. It dropped with a clinking sound on the tile floor. After drying her hands, she got on all fours and felt around for the key. Just as she started to rise, she heard a step and caught her breath as a bright light shown into her eyes.

"Hey," she yelled. Whoever had the light swung it down out of her eyes and muttered something that sounded like, "What is—"

Blinking away the bright spots before her eyes, she saw a pair of shoes and brought her fists down hard on one of them.

"Owww!" The person stepped back and stumbled away from the door. She heard a louder yelp, a thud, and a couple of grunts as she slammed the door shut. Yes! There was a lock on the bathroom door. The paper towel roll wouldn't make a very good weapon. Maybe she could climb out the window or at least raise it and hope someone would hear.

"Laurel Jones," she heard then, "will you stop this foolishness and open that door? It's me—Marc."

Laurel felt relief and laughter welling up inside. She made her voice sound serious. "Why did you shine that light in my eyes?"

Sounding close to the door, he answered, "I didn't know you were in there."

"You didn't see the truck?"

"Yes, but I didn't know whose it was."

"So you wanted to shine the light in the truck driver's eyes?"

"Yeah," he said. "I told your dad I'd ride through the development occasionally and keep an eye out for anything that didn't look right. Sometimes kids have been known to go in houses under construction and do some damage. I thought somebody might be in here doing something that shouldn't be done."

She put her face close to the door. "Like. . .using the bathroom?"

"C'mon, Laurel, quit playing games. My foot hurts. I need to sit down."

"There's a floor," she teased.

He moaned, but she unlocked the door.

As soon as she opened it a few feet, his arms came around her waist. "Gotcha." He laughed. "Don't you know better than to open a door to someone you hardly know?"

She looked up into his face. His expression was not at all ominous. But she did feel threatened. A man that good-looking, holding her close, his eyes moving to her lips and then locking with hers, the beating of two hearts together, and his quickness of breath as he stared at her all mingled to make him very dangerous to her—emotionally.

She gave a small nervous laugh and tried to step back. He moved away. She said the only thing—well, not the only thing—but the best thing that came to mind. "Did I really hurt you?"

"That was quite a whack right on the top of my foot."

"Okay, where's the flashlight?"

"In my hand."

She took it and laid it on the cabinet top, where it could shine across the commode and bathtub. "Now sit here."

He gave a short laugh. "I didn't come in here to use the bathroom."

"Keep the lid down. Now sit."

While he sat on the lid, Marc wondered if he should run to protect himself or give in to her whims. He decided to see it through. She lifted his right foot, untied the bow, and loosened the shoelaces.

He helped remove the shoe, then the sock, and propped his foot on the edge of the tub. Leaning across his leg she turned on the faucet in the tub, tested it, and then had him move his foot under the cool running water.

She sat on the side of the tub and rubbed the top of his foot and then the bottom as gently as if stroking a newborn kitten.

"Someone told me once," she said quietly, "to let water wash away the hurt and take it down the drain."

"That's what my mom used to say to me when I was little."

"I know," she said. "You told me."

"When?"

"About ten years ago at a house you were helping build. I fell and hurt my hands."

"I'd forgotten that." She'd remembered. . .all these years? "I was a college student then."

Laurel nodded. "I thought you were a man."

He smiled. "So did I. But in the past I've known a lot of good men—your dad included—and I've come to realize I'm not half the man he or some others are."

Laurel smiled. "I'm beginning to think being what we ought to be takes a lifetime."

He gazed at her for a long time, wondering if she might be

having the same thought as he—a thought he hadn't expected to have—that maybe they might consider that lifetime. . . together?

Someday, he was thinking, *I will tell you that you caressed the right foot, ministered to it. But it was the left foot you struck with your fists.* It hadn't really been hurt. Her fists coming down on his tennis shoes had done no damage whatsoever, even though a bone in that foot had only recently healed.

But he wouldn't tell her for a long, long time. He hoped there might come a day when the two of them would be so close they could almost take each other for granted, when they could say anything to each other.

For now, he wanted to cherish this moment. He'd had many thoughts and emotions concerning this beautiful young woman. He'd wanted to be near her, to know her better, to earn her respect and trust. He'd wanted to hold her, much like he'd held her earlier. When she raised her face to his, he'd wanted to kiss her lips.

But all that, as wonderful as it might be, faded in comparison to what she'd done. She'd loved his foot. She'd caressed his foot. She had a servant's heart. She had a loving nature.

"Does it feel better?" she asked.

"Yes," he whispered and closed his eyes while she turned off the water and gently wiped his foot with a paper towel.

He'd just told himself that a kiss couldn't compare with her so gently touching his foot. However. . .

He stood, and so did she. He leaned toward her, and already her face, lovely in the soft moonlight, was lifting toward his. Somehow, it seemed, his lips had been waiting for this moment all his life.

The kiss did compare. . .quite favorably.

The words Charlie had spoken to him flooded his mind: "Someday you'll get caught."

Marc swallowed hard as he sat and began to pull on his sock, then the shoe. He'd asked, "Who would want to get caught?"

Charlie had said, "Anyone who falls in love."

Marc thought his heart might beat from his chest. Fish got caught, too. And sometimes the fisherman threw the catch back into the river.

Please don't throw me back, Laurel.

Chapter 10

Charlie asked Laurel to come into his office after she arrived at work on Tuesday. "I hope you've decided to take the day job," he said. "I'm impressed with your knowledge of plants and the way you connect with customers."

Laurel was sorry things hadn't worked out better with Mindy. She'd had the thought that after she started her landscaping business, Mindy might want to work with her. That wouldn't happen now. And the store did need someone. "Yes, I'll take the day job."

Working with plants and people always lifted her spirits. She loved talking to people about their plants and helping them decide what might be best for landscaping.

She knew her dad had come in to talk with Marc and to thank Charlie and others who had helped with the plan to catch those who had been stealing from houses. Late in the afternoon, her dad stopped in.

"Laurel, you won't believe who I ran into here at H&H." He didn't give her time to ask. "Martha Billings. You know, from church."

"Yes, I know her. What do you mean, Dad? Did your cart run into hers?"

He gave her a warning look. "Nothing like that. At Sunday school we were laughing about what's going on at H&H and that everybody would think the shoppers were looking for a mate. But she said she really needed to replace a bathroom medicine cabinet and asked my opinion. Most women don't know about things like that." He held up a hand. "I know you're not most women. I taught you about carpentry early in your life."

Laurel nodded and tried not to show any expression. But she was thinking that even she could pretend not to know anything about carpentry if it meant getting help from a man in whom she was interested. "So you planned to meet here?"

"No, no. She called and asked if I could today, but I told her I had business to attend to here at H&H and didn't know how long that would take, so I couldn't promise. I told her to go ahead and be looking for a cabinet. I was walking down the aisle, and there she was." His small laugh sounded like a nervous one to Laurel.

"So how'd it go?"

"No problem. We looked at cabinets. She liked my suggestion. I can go over there and whip that cabinet out of the wall and put in the new one. Won't take long." He paused. "You know what she asked me?"

Another rhetorical question?

"She asked if I ever go to the Asheville Bravo Concerts. I told her that I hadn't been since Carolyn died, but I used to enjoy them. She said I should go."

Laurel didn't think this was a time to joke. "Are you going?"

He nodded. "I. . .think I'll help her out. She doesn't like to go to a lot of places alone at night. She's a fairly young widow, and her few single friends don't care for a lot of the concerts. You know. . .opera, symphonies, and such."

Laurel smiled. "Well, Dad, that's nice of you to help her out." Knowing he was staring at her, she tried not to show any emotion that might make him change his mind.

"Um, Laurel. . ." He paused. "Do you suppose you and Marc might like to go with us?"

She smiled then, knowing her dad was ill at ease about going on what looked like a date. "I like that idea."

Laurel's dad invited her, Marc, and Martha out to lunch after church on Sunday to "discuss the issue of the Bravo Concerts," as he put it. "I think it's nice to go out with friends," he said while they ate.

Martha smiled sweetly. "It's always nice to have friends."

Laurel glanced at her and saw the little gleam in the woman's eyes. The two of them shared a secretive smile before Martha picked up her iced tea glass. Friendship was wonderful, but sometimes a friendly relationship could turn into something even more special.

Thinking of that, Laurel addressed Marc. "By the way, that was some article in the paper about you. Let's see. . ." With her elbow on the table, and her fist under her chin, she looked at the ceiling as if trying to remember. Then she looked around at her dad and Martha. "The reporter called him 'a real man' and 'a hunk.' "

"Now you're embarrassing me," Marc said.

"Oh, don't be embarrassed," Martha said. "If I were young enough to talk that way, I'd call you a hunk, too. And I'll admit I've seen some very nice-looking men at that store."

Laurel watched the pink color begin to come into her dad's face. She looked back at Marc. "I was surprised at how positive you were in that newspaper interview."

"Surprised?"

"Yes, you didn't make men and women seem desperate or ugly."

"Right," her dad said. "Marc, I don't necessarily agree with one of your statements, but it caught my attention. You said a woman who knows her way around tools and hardware is irresistible to a man."

Martha spoke up. "I prefer a man who knows those things."

Her dad's face had that pink hue again. "Like I said, I don't necessarily agree."

"Oh," Martha said, "but I was most impressed, Marc, with your saying that all people would like to have someone to love."

"Marc," Laurel said, "were you speaking about the opinion of the store as a whole, or were those your personal opinions?"

"Definitely personal." He gave her a long look.

"When you talked about this before, you didn't seem to approve of couples meeting that way."

"I didn't approve—until recently," he said. "But after reading the negative remarks one newspaper reporter made, I thought he shouldn't have gone that far. Then, after the paper printed a retraction, I found myself nodding and agreeing. And it wouldn't be good business for H&H if I came off negative."

"Oh, so that's your reason."

"No," he said immediately. "If that were my attitude, I simply wouldn't have allowed the interview. I've come to feel that H&H just might be the best place in the world for couples to meet."

She didn't want to take for granted that he was referring to her. He might be referring to her dad and Martha Billings, so she didn't say, "Me, too."

Laurel was glad she had accepted the day job, which meant she and Marc could see each other in the evenings and on weekends. She'd asked if he'd like to come to the singles' class at her church.

He'd hedged, then given her a quizzical look. "I don't know. Lately I've been thinking about trying out a few couples' classes. I mean, we are a couple, aren't we, Laurel?"

She nodded. "I believe we are."

"I know I'm falling in love with you."

"I've loved you since I was thirteen years old." Seeing his eyebrows lift, she added, "But I forgot about it for several years. Now it's coming back."

He laughed. "Was that puppy love?"

She shook her head. "If so, would that make what I feel now a mature dog love?"

Although she knew she was in love with Marc, she liked their playful way of talking about it. She had a tendency to be impulsive, which allowed her to appreciate Marc's more cautious characteristics. Her dad said they complemented each other well.

Also, she knew that Marc's allowing himself to become

344

serious about a woman was something new for him.

They visited his grandmother one evening on what the nurse said was "a good day." Although Mrs. Goodson seemed slow in processing things, she knew Marc. He had taken pictures of the flower beds, and his grandmother was delighted to see them.

She loved the begonia. She gave Laurel a long, studied look. "You have a lovely girl here, Marc."

Laurel saw the look of love in his eyes for his grandmother. "I know. I'm glad you approve."

"Oh, I do."

To Laurel, the statement felt like some kind of blessing, coming from Marc's grandmother, who meant so much to him.

The next few weeks were full of activity. Laurel was delighted to learn that the couple who wanted to get married at H&H was an older man and woman. Both had lost their spouses years ago and never expected to marry again until they met in the Garden Shop. Laurel volunteered to arrange plants and trees in a way that would make the event even more special.

"Great idea," Charlie told her. "You fix it up right and I'll call the newspaper reporters. This is going to be great publicity. Oh, and I'll make sure there's cake and punch for all our staff and customers after the ceremony."

She loved talking with Lola, the bride-to-be, about the plans. Lola was as excited as any young bride Laurel had ever seen. "I know this is unconventional," Lola said, "but I feel young and adventurous again and wanted to do this. And we're going to Hawaii for our honeymoon. Ricardo said I could do whatever I want." She tapped Laurel on the shoulder. "Now that's the kind of man every woman should have."

Laurel fell in love with the couple. And on the wedding day in mid-July, the couple stood inside an arbor laced with white flowers on a green vine. Tall trees had been placed on each side of the arbor, and lovely colorful plants enhanced the décor.

Only a few family members were present. Lola said a huge reception was planned, but they'd wanted the wedding to be small. Laurel thought they looked wonderful. Lola wore a light blue dress, and Ricardo wore a dark blue suit.

The staff in the Garden Shop had worn dressier clothes than usual. They took off their smocks in honor of the wedding and stood back from the wedding party as the vows were exchanged.

Laurel stayed near the glass doors between the Garden Shop and main building in case a customer entered and insisted on buying something or wasn't aware of the wedding taking place.

She felt hands on her shoulders, and a voice whispered, "This isn't too bad. Maybe getting married at H&H is all right."

She looked around and up at Marc. "It's very meaningful to them. This is where they met."

He nodded and stepped up beside her. His brow furrowed. "Would you consider getting married in the parking lot. . .by the trees. . .in the rain?"

She stifled a laugh. "I prefer a church."

He nodded and caught her off guard by saying quite seriously, "Have I told you that I love you?"

Her head slowly came around, and she looked up into his

blue, blue, loving eyes. He meant it. He'd come right out and said it. "Not exactly that way," she said.

"I want to find a romantic place and tell you that I love you."

"I'll look forward to that."

When the pastor said, "You may kiss the bride," Marc leaned close. "Later," he promised.

She looked over her shoulder at him as he walked back into the store. He glanced back, too, and winked at her.

Her heart beat fast at the anticipation of. . .later.

YVONNE LEHMAN lives in the mountains of western North Carolina, which provides the setting for many of her novels. She is a best-selling author of more than forty books, including mainstream, inspirational romance, mystery, the White Dove series for young adults, and the widely acclaimed *In Shady Groves*, reprinted by Guideposts as *Gomer* in their Women of the Bible series. Yvonne was founder and director of the Blue Ridge Christian Writers Conference for seventeen years until 1993. She now plans and directs the Blue Ridge Mountains Christian Writers Conference for Lifeway/Ridgecrest Conference Center. She is the recipient of numerous awards including the Dwight L. Moody Award for Excellence in Christian Literature, Romantic Times Inspirational Award (first in nation), the National Reader's Choice Award (twice), and first place in the inspirational category of Booksellers' Best Award (judged by booksellers across the nation). She is a member of several groups including ChiLibris; American Christian Fiction Writers; the Faith, Hope, and Love chapter of Romance Writers of America; Mystery Writers of America; and the Writer's View. Yvonne has a master's degree in English (literature) and has taught English, creative writing, and professional and adult studies at Montreat College in Montreat, North Carolina. Visit her Web site at www.yvonnelehman.com.

A Letter to Our Readers

Dear Readers:

In order that we might better contribute to your reading enjoyment, we would appreciate your taking a few minutes to respond to the following questions. When completed, please return to the following: Fiction Editor, Barbour Publishing, Inc., P.O. Box 719, Uhrichsville, OH 44683.

1. Did you enjoy reading *Carolina Carpenter Brides*?
   ❑ Very much—I would like to see more books like this.
   ❑ Moderately—I would have enjoyed it more if _____
   _____
   _____

2. What influenced your decision to purchase this book?
   (Check those that apply.)
   ❑ Cover   ❑ Back cover copy   ❑ Title   ❑ Price
   ❑ Friends   ❑ Publicity   ❑ Other

3. Which story was your favorite?
   ❑ *How to Refurbish an Old Romance*   ❑ *Can You Help Me?*
   ❑ *Once upon a Shopping Cart*   ❑ *Caught Red-Handed*

4. Please check your age range:
   ❑ Under 18   ❑ 18–24   ❑ 25–34
   ❑ 35–45   ❑ 46–55   ❑ Over 55

5. How many hours per week do you read? _____

Name _____

Occupation _____

Address _____

City_____ State _____ Zip _____

E-mail_____

If you enjoyed
CAROLINA
CARPENTER
Brides
then read
The
Spinster Brides
OF CACTUS CORNER

*Four Women Make Orphans a Priority
and Finally Open Doors to Romance*

The Spinster and the Cowboy by Lena Nelson Dooley
The Spinster and the Lawyer by Jeri Odell
The Spinster and the Doctor by Frances Devine
The Spinster and the Tycoon by Vickie McDonough